# UN-HOLY GRAIL

# Un-Holy Grail

## by
## Keith Holmes Jr.

eBooks2go

Published in the United States
by eBooks2go, Inc.
1827 Walden Office Square, Suite 260, Schaumburg, IL 60173

ISBN-10: 1-5457-0447-3
ISBN-13: 978-1-5457-0447-9

Library of Congress Cataloging in Publication

# TABLE OF CONTENTS

# INTRODUCTION

This is where it begins. I got close to immortality, but the grail was not mine to hold. The grail has returned, like it does every ten years, and I *will* have it this time. Although, it doesn't appear that it will be near even my fifth priority—at least not while fighting demons, Hunters (whose goal is to destroy powerful members of humanity), and my good ol' daddy issues.

# CHAPTER 1

## Go

I woke up or at least I thought I was awake. I couldn't really tell anymore. This whole thing seemed like a big dream, with all the superpowers, magical findings, and the golden Holy Grail tower that could be seen from hundreds of miles away.

"Good morning, Arcadia!" the TV blasted.

"Today is November 27, and as you should know, the year is 2068."

Yeah, it was real this time. Though the oddly precise mention of the date did leave me with my doubts. I grabbed the golden Desert Falcon, a plasma charged version of the old-fashioned Desert Eagle, that I kept under my pillow (don't ask) and checked the remaining charge only to be pleasantly surprised to find a full plasma battery. I flipped my legs over the side of my bed. I always slept fully-clothed—no telling what could happen these days. I holstered my favorite gun and stood beside my bed.

"Another grail sighting in Soltania today, just off the coast of Florida," the news anchor said.

I'd been to Soltania before, but not to hunt for the grail. It did help that the North American continent, newly known as "Arcadia," was only about a three-hour boat ride from Soltania. This was, of course, assuming you still owned a conventional speed boat. Like every other thief or upper-class member, I had a spacial cycle. And for the sake of my image, don't ask which one I am. The apartment should speak for itself, though. Besides, this baby could break the sound barrier with ease, making it worth acquiring.

"There are already grail hunters there as we speak," the TV chimed in.

Well, that was exactly what I'd expected. I had hoped I could beat them there. I collected my gear—the usual gamma blades and energy cartridges—and jumped out of the small apartment building's window. I landed on my spacial cycle and cranked the handles. The black and purple cycle was labeled with my name: Jonathan Cain. It had cost a small fortune for that paint job so of course I had to show it off. After all, this was my prize possession and most valuable item I owned. Though I wish I could've gotten it in blue, considering purple wasn't really my thing.

"All right, let's go!" I shouted at the top of my lungs.

I drove at full speed toward the water. The cycle glided swiftly over the sea, escorting me on my way to Soltania.

# CHAPTER 2

# HER

I arrived at Soltania ahead of schedule. When I touched land, I could see the giant gold tower the grail brought to every location it traveled. I stepped onto land and was greeted by the blistering heat. The second I arrived, I could hear gunfire. It was close, but not aimed at me. I then saw a young girl—she couldn't be older than fifteen—running, bullets hitting the sand all around her. I quickly reevaluated my previous age estimation. I watched as she shot back at her attacker—or attackers, I couldn't tell—with a gun that was larger than her arm. I heard a cry of pain, and the bullet storm stopped for a moment. The girl, however, didn't stop running. She was kicking up sand as she sprinted before a singular bullet caught her in the shoulder. She cried out and rolled a couple feet before she came to a halt. She lay motionless in the sand. The figure that presumably pulled the trigger walked over to her hardly twitching body. The man kicked her in the abdomen with such immense power that she flew back into a nearby boulder. She gasped for air, her lungs almost collapsing, before sliding down the boulder. She crumpled into the sand face-first before attempting to lift herself up.

"You've caused me a lot of trouble, girl," the man said, gripping his bleeding side.

He put the barrel of the gun to her forehead as she had managed to sit herself up against the boulder. When she realized she was probably going to die, her eyes widened. Her light brown eyes welled with tears, but she wouldn't let them fall. I could tell she was trying to maintain some kind of pride; she didn't beg for her life or make any real sound.

"Should I make your death slow and painful?" the man asked, even though it wasn't a question.

He yanked her long red hair and pulled her to her feet. She cried out in pain and grabbed his arm. She wasn't nearly strong enough to pry herself loose and simply dangled from his arm as if begging to live. He kneed her in the stomach causing her to cough blood onto the dark sand. She fell to her knees, spitting blood to the ground. She raised her wounded body and made an attempt to crawl for her gun, which was about fifteen feet away.

"I can't let you do that," the man said.

He had some pretty strong legs because he once again hit her so hard she landed in the sand almost right in front of me. Blood oozed from her shoulder into the sand. The girl's eyes were glazed over, and she clutched her side with her good left arm. I kneeled down and lifted her head up so she wouldn't choke on the blood filling her mouth. As soon as I did, she spat blood to the side. She looked up at me, struggling to speak.

"Help me, please." She mouthed the words slowly before passing out in my arms.

"This isn't your problem, sir." The man didn't move from where he was as he spoke. "I suggest you stay out of this."

I considered his words, but this girl couldn't be over eighteen years old. She had a life to live, and I made up my mind that I couldn't let this man take that from her. I laid her down gently on the sand before standing to my feet. I slowly drew my golden Desert Falcon and pointed it at him.

"I can't watch a young girl die," I told him flatly.

"This heroic ideal of yours will get you killed," he responded.

Without a word I fired a blast. It was aimed for his right leg—I didn't need to kill him—but he dodged to his left quicker than I had anticipated. He drew his own gun, an AK-47 with a laser attachment, and let bullets rain toward me.

*Speed multiplication, times ten.*

My ability to alter my body's limits at the cost of my magical reserves was unique to me. I had consumed one of the false grail's contents and instead of eternal life I was granted this ability. I dodged the bullets ten times faster than humanly possible. A multiplication by ten was, however, my limit. I got closer and closer to him before he was even done emptying the gun's magazine. Before he knew it, I was behind him.

"How did you—" he began before I broke all the bones in his body.

*Strength multiplication, times six.*

With a kick to the kidney, I sent the man flying. He crashed into the ground and comically bounced three or four times. When he finally stopped, he crashed into the side of an abandoned building, which collapsed on him on impact. I took a deep breath before swiftly walking back to the young girl I'd left in the sand. I tried to shake her awake, but there was no response.

"What to do now?" I asked myself out loud.

I knew exactly what to do. I reached in the compartment of my spacial cycle and took out a healing gel designed to stop wounds from bleeding. The only downside was it hurt a lot. I applied the gel on her shoulder after removing the bullet with some tongs I had in the same compartment. She whimpered when I did that, but she outright screamed when I applied the gel. She shook and kicked during the procedure, but calmed down after a couple minutes.

Night was falling and the temperature of the desert dropped to around nineteen degrees Fahrenheit. The girl had clearly dressed for the desert during the day and was wearing some dress-code worthy short-shorts and a crop top. I gave her the cloak I wore to hide my face from the normal sand storms. I got back on my cycle and sat her between the handlebars and my body. I knew of a nearby city and figured I would take her to a hospital before resuming my quest for the grail. Unfortunately that was not at all how it went down.

# CHAPTER 3

# GOLD

By the time we made it to the hospital she had awoken and was already making a speedy recovery.

"Thanks for saving me ..." the girl said from her hospital bed, eyes cast downward.

The fact that she needed saving seemed to bother her. In fact, it appeared to be tearing her apart. I came out of my thoughts to ask her about herself.

"Sorry. Under the circumstances, I never caught your name." I said, making an effort not to shame her by accepting her thank you.

She paused for a long time, maybe trying to find a way to hide her identity, but she couldn't think of a way around it.

"It's Mia, Mia Alves," Mia said.

"Well, I'm Jonathan Cain, if you wanna do the full name thing," I told her.

There was an odd sort of muffled laugh from her before she went quiet once more. She looked at me, studying my face. I couldn't tell what she was thinking but up close, Mia must have been around twenty years old.

"I'm nineteen," she said, answering my puzzled expression. "How old are you?"

"Twenty-one," I replied without much thought.

Her eyes widened in surprise. Mia opened her mouth as if to say something but no words came out. She awkwardly looked down at the floor and appeared to trace the lines of the tiles with her eyes.

"I thought you were a lot older than me," she muttered.

"I thought you were a lot younger when I first saw you," I replied.

There was a long silence before Mia giggled. I raised an eyebrow before brushing my white strands of hair from my eyes. Now able to see my eyes, she was looking intently at their golden glow.

"Are you interested in how this happened?" I asked as I gestured to my white hair and gold eyes.

She nodded and stood up to lean against one of the white walls. Before I began my story, I took a good look at her. She might have been nineteen, but her body was that of a fifteen year old girl. Not like I cared, but her figure was rather undeveloped. She was around five foot three, about nine inches shorter than me. After a swift analysis of her frame, I took a seat in a medium-sized metal hover chair. Taking a deep breath, I began to tell my tale.

# CHAPTER 4

# FALSE

"I went to find the grail with one of my brothers and father during its last run ten years ago," I began. "My brother, Jacob, is four years older than me. He knew more about the world then since I was eleven and he was fifteen. My father was a strong man, so strong that he took us to the top of the grail tower unscathed."

"What's the grail tower?" Mia interrupted.

"You went hunting for the Holy Grail without knowing what the tower was even called?" I questioned.

"I'm not a grail hunter. I'm looking for someone who went hunting for the grail," Mia said. "My older sister left me alone ten years ago when she entered that tower."

As Mia spoke, she tightened her grip on the bedframe. Talking about her sister must have made Mia angry because she soon burned through the metal frame. The melted metal didn't seem to hurt her either. She shook the burning liquid off her hand and onto the floor.

"You have false grail powers?" I asked, surprised.

"My sister brought me what she thought was the actual Holy Grail," Mia recalled grimly. "It just gave me the ability to control fire through my emotions. It also kept me up at night. My insides were constantly on fire because of it."

"Why didn't you use that in the desert?" I asked Mia.

"I had already taken care of ten guys with my ability before I ran out of magic," she replied.

With the ability to burn through steel, the amount of magic it would take to exterminate ten grail hunters didn't surprise me. Most false grail users had a small well of magic power because said well was newly opened. The magic well can only grow through constant use. I've used my ability since I was eleven. Mia must have used hers since she was nine.

"Anyway, the grail tower is a traveling fortress that comes and goes as it pleases," I continued. "Since the grail room has billions of different grails, but the same water, it's hard to tell which grail is the true one. The grail room is at the 99th floor of the grail tower. My father took my brother and me all the way to the top."

I recollected the memories as I spoke.

"We each picked a grail that we each believed was the real one. My brother picked a silver and black chalice, but I picked a gold one."

I smiled as I said the next piece.

"My father, he was a simple man, picked what looked like a dented tin can. We all dipped our cups into the water and then with a shout of cheers we drank."

I looked at Mia, who was now completely absorbed by my words. I finished my tale with a smile on my face.

"I gained the ability to adjust my body's powers however I want. My brother lost his emotions but gained double the smartest human's intelligence and a hitman's mindset. My father, I believe, drank the actual Holy Grail. Before he drank my father was an older man, in his late fifties. After, he looked younger than a man in his twenties. After our round of drinks, the tower collapsed around us, but when we should have been crushed, my brother and I woke up completely unharmed at home. My father was nowhere to be found."

That last sentence of my story hit home with Mia. I wanted to ask her what was wrong, but she had completely composed herself after a few quick blinks. I decided to avoid prying at Mia's past.

"What do you plan to do now?" Mia asked me.

I paused briefly. I wanted to tell her a lie so she wouldn't want to tag along. I also decided against that idea.

"I'm headed for the grail tower," I replied after a long silence.

She had a mischievous grin on her face before she walked over and pushed me back. I didn't exactly like being pushed too much, but I found her attitude humorous. Mia's smile widened, which made me smile too.

"Take me with you," she commanded with four short words.

I grinned right back at her. Mia was being incredibly aggressive, but some part of me enjoyed every second of it. That part of me also took over for a moment.

"With pleasure," I responded, despite better judgment.

# CHAPTER 5

# KNIGHT

Together, Mia and I made our way back into the desert. She rode on the back of my spacial cycle, wrapping her arms around my waist like a biker's girlfriend. I can't say I didn't enjoy her clinginess a little. To my pleasant surprise, we weren't confronted by any grail hunters when we arrived at the tower. The tower was stationed in the middle of the desert and its height made it easy to find. I parked my spacial cycle in some bushes about two miles away. I opened the compartment of my spacial cycle and handed Mia her Galil rifle. I also grabbed a duffel bag with all the things we would need.

"Why did you park so far away!" Mia whined as she took the gun.

"I don't want anyone to steal my bike."

"Doesn't it have a hand print lock?"

"It does, but I feel safer like this."

Mia muttered something, but I made no effort to hear it. We trekked over the remaining desert and arrived at the front of the tower. The giant golden tower had a large door that was at least ten feet tall.

"In we go," I said.

Mia gulped, attempting to swallow her inner fears. I sympathized with her uneasiness but said nothing to comfort her. I pushed the surprisingly light door open slowly. I didn't enjoy the sight that awaited before us. I knew the grail tower had a dungeon boss on every floor. If you defeated said boss, you could advance to the next floor. I, however, didn't expect the boss to be the first thing you see. I thought about regrouping, but the tower sucked Mia and I in so fast we couldn't retreat. We tumbled inside the large round room. In the center of the room stood a tall, six foot nine knight. He had on a suit of armor that looked so dark it was darker than black.

"Look at the size of his sword!" Mia exclaimed.

I did and I didn't enjoy what I saw. It was a long, silver great sword. When I say long I mean around six feet long. Oh and did I mention he was lunging at us? I rolled to the left while dropping my bag, but Mia stood her ground. She fired a blanket of fire laced bullets from her Galil. They bounced off the knight without stunning him at all. The knight slashed at Mia, but all he caught was air. Mia ducked underneath the attack and rolled behind him. She made a small wall of flames as she backed away. It didn't seem to hurt the knight, and neither did the bullets she continued to fire at him.

"This isn't getting as anywhere!" I shouted to Mia.

"Yeah, let's try something else," Mia responded calmly.

I drew two plasma blades and tossed one to Mia. I then raised my Desert Falcon and pointed it at the knight. He charged at me. I stood still and waited for him. He was incredibly fast, but Mia was fast enough to block his sword swing with her plasma blade. Thanks to our synchronization, her block left the dark knight wide open for attack. I fired a charged shot from my Desert Falcon, hitting the knight directly in the chest. It blew off a chunk of armor and sent him flying. I thought the knight was dead and so did Mia.

"Is the whole tower going to be like this?" Mia asked me.

"Unfortunately, it gets harder," I replied.

We were sadly mistaken, but not about the tower's degree of difficulty. The knight, now at least seven times faster than a normal human, got up and swung at Mia. I reacted just in time.

*Speed multiplication times eight*

*Strength multiplication times four*

I stopped what would have been Mia's decapitation by an inch with my plasma blade. Mia jumped back as the knight began relentlessly slashing at me. I blocked and dodged the attacks as I was slowly being backed into a corner. As soon as my back hit the far wall, I kicked off it. My strength and speed multiplication helped me crash into the knight with my shoulder. It sent him back, but he recovered immediately. He charged again, but was stopped by a wall of flames created by Mia.

"Cook him!" I shouted to her.

The knight turned to face her only to be consumed by a flaming shell. The fire only burned the dark knight for a couple of seconds before Mia relented. To my dismay, the knight stood, only slightly injured. His armor had melted off and his face was exposed. The burning metal didn't appear to damage him at all.

"Just my luck," Mia spat.

The man's eyes were black like coal and his hair was the same. He lifted his long sword and pointed the tip at me.

"Prepare yourself!" the knight shouted as he switched to a fighting stance.

I gripped tighter on my sword with both hands after putting my gun away. He charged quickly, but my multiplications allowed me to keep up. I blocked his strikes while dancing around him to avoid his long swings. I waited for an opening and it came in the form of a straight thrust. I drove in close after using my blade to redirect his. When I was in close, I decided to gloat a little.

"You're wide open," I said with a smirk.

I kneed him in the stomach, causing him to fly back while the oxygen would hopefully leave his lungs. He rolled a couple of feet, landing directly in front Mia, who unloaded her Galil into his chest. He lay still, but something didn't seem right. There was no blood spray or cry of pain.

His arm twitched, and I immediately shouted, "Mia, get back!"

She tried but as she was moving, the knight caught her arm with blinding speed. Mia didn't react fast enough, and he tossed her over toward me. I caught her easily in my arms and she steadied herself on the floor. The knight's normal clothing was bullet proof. This was getting tiresome. I was about to order Mia to barbecue him, but the knight spoke before I could.

"You have bested me," the knight said as he took a knee. "This fight is no longer necessary."

"Wait, hold on, are you not the boss of this floor?" I asked him, in confusion.

"I am not," the knight explained. "I am Sir Aron. I am a knight with no affiliation."

"Okay, so why are you giving up?" Mia asked.

"I wield my sword against those I find evil," Aron continued. "You are the first to best me since I entered this place. In addition to that, you are both kindhearted."

What made him assume that? Deep down I'm …

"At least on the surface," Aron added, reading my mind.

His comment somehow put me at ease.

"Makes sense. Glad to have you on board," I replied without giving it any thought.

"Wait, we're going through with this?" Mia asked me.

"Sure, the more the merrier!"

Mia didn't say anything more on the topic. She looked disgruntled, but not to the point I thought she might have been. That must mean she expects Aron to actually be useful, regardless of whether or not she trusts him.

"Wait, what about your armor? Can you make do without it?" I asked Aron.

"My armor is merely an extension of myself," Aron said.

He flexed his hand and a black mist seemed to consume him. The mist soon faded and Aron's armor appeared on his body.

"Cool," was all Mia managed after a short silence.

"That settles it then. Let's go!" I commanded excitedly as I grabbed my duffle bag.

Mia trotted to my side and spoke under her breath.

"Are you sure we can trust him?"

"I brought you along," I replied shortly.

Mia frowned and said nothing more about me placing trust in Aron. She still remained rather annoyed. Her face said it all, especially with all the eye twitching. We walked through a straight hallway with no monsters and no boss as of yet.

"Hey, Aron, where are all the monsters and the floor boss?"

"Dead," he replied simply.

"Well that's reassuring." Mia muttered.

We walked with an oddly calming silence until we reached a grand staircase. There was a sign that showed an upward arrow and "floor two."

"And up we go," I said and began to sprint up the stairs.

What we saw at the top made me want to go back down.

# CHAPTER 6

# BLOOD

We stepped into a room that was filled with a crimson liquid. At first it didn't look like blood, but the smell quickly identified it as such. The hundreds of dead bodies also helped confirm my suspicions. Mia squeezed her nose with a look of disgust.

"Ugh, this is gross!" Mia exclaimed, shaking the blood off her sneakers.

"Did you do this?" I asked Aron.

He shook his head. He appeared to gaze toward the far side of the room, couldn't really tell with that helmet on. I followed his vision and saw a very frightening sight. A humanoid figure stood in a pool of blood. It didn't have a face but what looked more like a crater where the eyes and a mouth should be. It turned our way with a frightening and quick snap. Mia took a step back, but the staircase had been blocked off. It shook the blood off of its claws as it turned.

"Oh no, oh no, oh no, oh no!" Mia shrieked.

She was absolutely terrified, but I couldn't blame her. The figure just glared at us. Its body was red like the blood that was now up to our ankles. Instead of a hand with fingers it had six or seven claws. Then, suddenly, it opened its mouth—which I had thought didn't exist—to reveal a row of very sharp, bloody teeth.

"This doesn't look good." I grimaced.

"I … want … to … eat …" The demonic being snarled.

"Prepare yourselves," Aron calmly commanded as he drew his sword.

"Aye, aye cap'n," I joked.

"Not the time for that!" Mia snapped.

"Just trying to have some fun," I countered spinning my Desert Falcon on my finger.

The creature charged. Blood sprayed into the air as the demon tore through the filth. We moved away from the door in response. Aron charged straight ahead while Mia and I flanked him. Mia unloaded her Galil while I fired my Desert Falcon. We didn't do any visible damage, however. In fact, we only succeed in angering the creature. It snarled and dashed at Mia first. She raised her Galil in time to block the attack and the creature seemed to give up on her after one failed attempt. It landed on all fours and sank into the filth. The blood stilled and the creature was nowhere to be found.

"Where is it?" I asked, surveying the calm blood.

"Don't lower your guard," Aron replied, also unsure.

It was stressful to remain in this room, considering the creature could be anywhere and we had no way to know where. The blood remained still with the occasional ripple from one of us trudging through. Suddenly, the corpses that littered the room began to stand and grab their weapons.

"Why are they moving?" Mia asked in terror.

I had no answer for her as the undead men began to drag their bloody swords, axes, and spears as they sloshed toward us.

"Take care of them. I'll attempt to slay the monster." Aron delegated jobs to us.

"Alright," I agreed, seeing no reason to object.

Almost immediately the creature, unexpectedly, shot out of the blood pool and slashed at Aron. Aron blocked the attack with his gauntlet. He then countered by striking the demon in the chest. More blood sprayed from the creature and got on Aron's armor. The armor began to sizzle like the blood was melting it. It was probably acidic. Even though the creature was hurt, its attack didn't let up. It sunk its claws into Aron's now exposed shoulder. It didn't seem to bother him, however. He impaled the creature on his sword causing it to cry out in pain. It continued to claw at Aron, but his armor was too strong for the creature to cut through. Aron drove his sword into the ground so that the creature was pinned down. At least, it was until it appeared to sink back into the deep filth we stood in. I had no time to watch the battle, however, because the undead grail hunters were upon us. One of them got close to me, and I dodged his wide swings with ease. I raised my Desert Falcon and shoved the barrel into his throat. He had no time to react because I vaporized his head immediately. I looked over at Mia, who was having no issues as she gunned down the abominations. She, however, was going wild and wasn't bothering to aim properly to conserve ammo.

"Don't waste all your bullets!" I shouted over her gunfire.

Mia looked at me for a moment. Her eyes were glazed over with some kind of savagery I'd never seen in a person. She was unfazed, despite the blood and fire surrounding her. There was even some blood on her face, but she hadn't bothered to wipe it off. She suddenly blinked and it was gone.

"Ah, yeah, of course," she halfheartedly agreed.

I didn't even think she'd realized what transfixed state she had entered. She went right back to shooting at the zombie mob. A couple of them, however, got past her bullet hail.

*Strength multiplication times three*

To save plasma energy, I didn't use my Desert Falcon. I threw out my elbow and shattered the jaw of my new assailant. The dead man didn't let up and slashed again with his blood covered blade. I caught him by the wrist, snatching the blade from his grotesque hand. I took the jagged sword and jabbed it through his chest, but that wasn't enough. He moaned in rage and agony, but continued to claw at me though he'd been disarmed. I ripped out his blade and shoved it through his head. The zombie ceased all movement and grew limp on the end of the blade. I immediately dropped the weapon as the blood from the already dead man splashed onto my hand. Another undead grail hunter stumbled toward me but before I could react, a barrel of a gun was pressed to his head. He made no motion to avoid the attack. It was almost as if he welcomed the sweet release of death. Mia pulled the trigger and his head exploded in a ball of flame. The dead man collapsed into the filth below with a shallow splash.

"Good job," I commended Mia.

She didn't seem to have heard me, but she had stopped looking insane at the very best. Her eyes looked rather sad, but it was only for a moment.

"Sure," Mia muttered.

There was nothing more for the two of us to say, but the sound of splashing alerted us. I turned as Aron had the creature from before pinned with his sword again. I ran over to where the thing was flailing and stomped the creature's head into oblivion. My boot was covered in blood afterward. After the creature's death the room seemed to reset. The blood and bodies all vanished along with the creature's bloody corpse.

"Oh thank goodness that awful smell is gone." Mia breathed.

She was right. It felt normal in the room again. The blood that had gotten on our clothes also vanished. I readjusted my bag on my shoulder. After making it more comfortable, I turned to Aron. I was a little curious about something he had said earlier.

"Hey, Aron?"

"Yes, Sir John?"

"I never told you my name," I stated.

Aron's face was hidden by his helmet so I couldn't tell if he was fazed by me pointing this out. He gazed away from me and just stared. I followed his line of vision. If he was looking at something it must have been Mia. Although, she had a similar confused look on her face. Aron suddenly sheathed his sword and began to walk away.

"Hey, I—"

"I knew your father." Aron interjected.

That shut me up good. Aron's armor faded off of him, leaving only his sword behind. He had a somewhat sobering look on his face.

"Your father won't be the same when you see him," Aron almost whispered.

I was almost sure I heard him wrong. I knew better to just assume things, though.

"What do you mean?"

He pointed upward, gesturing to the tower.

"Once we ascend, he shall be there," Aron said. "The power of the Holy Grail has changed him; be ready to fight him if necessary."

I didn't quite understand what Aron was talking about, but I didn't ask any more questions. We walked in silence, but suddenly Aron veered left of the staircase to floor two.

"Where are you going?" Mia asked him.

"Shortcut," Aron simply stated.

"Shortcut? What shortcut?" Mia asked, looking at me.

I shrugged. I didn't know much more about the grail tower than Mia. I hardly remembered anything specific from ten years ago. Soon we reached what looked like an elevator. Aron clicked the only button which said "return to previous floor."

"This will carry us to floor number ninety-seven," Aron said. "That's the highest anyone has made it thus far."

"That's oddly convenient," I replied.

Aron looked back at me and his face displayed his skepticism. Mia and I both shared the uneasy feeling since Aron had also mentioned that no one had gotten past him. There was the possibility he hadn't been in the tower for all the time it had been present, though. At the same time, someone could've set us up for failure.

"Let's just go up." Mia gave in to the temptation of taking the shortcut.

Aron nodded in agreement, so I sighed and followed along. The elevator doors finally slid open to reveal a small child sitting on a stool.

"Going up?" the little girl asked.

# CHAPTER 7

# SWITCH

Mia and I stared at the kid. The little girl had long green hair and green eyes. She was wearing a black shirt and a skirt. Even Aron was confused by her existence.

"Don't just stand there, get in!" the little girl exclaimed.

We all slowly walked onto the elevator. As soon as the doors closed and the elevator began moving up, she just smiled at us, kicking her legs while sitting on the stool.

"What's your name and how old are you?" Mia asked the girl.

"I'm Sara and I'm nine hundred years old!" she shouted.

"Nine hundred!?" Mia asked surprised.

"That's not right, Sara," a voice emitting from what appeared to be nowhere said.

Suddenly Sara was gone. In her place sat an older looking version of the girl. Sara's black shirt and skirt were replaced with a dress. Her green eyes were now red.

"I'm nine hundred, but Sara is only nine," the older looking Sara said.

"So who are you, exactly?" I asked her.

"I'm Sara's ... split personality," the woman said. "Sara calls me Serena."

"Okay, Serena, are you a result of false grail powers?" Mia asked the easy question.

"No, I possessed Sara when she was born," Serena said. "She was born with the gift of element forming so I saw potential in her."

"Possessed her? Like a ghost?" I asked, surprised and confused.

"Not exactly. It's more like we're sharing her body."

That felt sort of wrong, but I didn't want to ask any more questions. I wasn't very interested and all that mattered was getting to the top anyway.

"Is element forming similar to my power?" Mia suddenly chimed as she let her hand catch fire.

Serena stared at the flame in surprise and suddenly there was a bright flash. Sara was back on her stool again. She was grinning and then seemed to remember something. Placing her hands out in front of her, she formed a small ball of fire. It didn't flare out and remained a perfect sphere of flame.

"I can do this, but I can't control elements that aren't mine," Sara said, still grinning.

Just then, the elevator arrived at floor ninety-seven.

"Take care, I guess," I said.

Aron stepped off and I followed, but Sara wouldn't let Mia leave. Sara held her in place with a strong shield of telekinesis.

"Sara, let me go!" Mia commanded. She tried to light her fire, but for some reason couldn't.

"That won't work. My wind will eat it all up!" Sara giggled, shouting over the high-powered wind.

There was another flash of light, and Sara turned back into Serena. Serena spun Mia around so that she was directly in front of her. She smiled at Mia, who gulped, swallowing her fear.

"You've got an especially delicious soul," Serena said, her eyes glowing red.

Serena then proceeded to jab her fingers into Mia's mouth. Mia didn't offer any vocal objection because her body just went slack. Whatever she was doing lasted for less than a second. When Serena withdrew, a red ball was pulled from Mia's mouth. There was a sort of tail on the ball that Serena held on her fingers.

"What did you—" I began to ask, but Serena cut me off.

"Pulled her soul out through her mouth," Serena said.

"So is she—" I tried to say, but I got cut off again.

It was starting to get annoying.

"Dead?" Serena assumed.

"Yes," I replied, huffing.

"Not exactly. I just took her soul." Serena laughed as she spoke.

The little red ball, which I assumed was Mia's soul, started spinning like a basketball on Serena's finger.

"What do you desire?" Aron asked Serena.

"I want you to take care of little Sara," Serena replied. "By take care of her I mean do it for as long as you live and with your lives."

"As long as you give Mia her soul back, you've got a deal," I said without hesitation.

"It's a little more complicated than that." Serena smiled. "After all, your word doesn't mean too much in today's society. You can't trust anyone. So I've made a certain magical contract."

I raised an eyebrow before narrowing my eyes, skeptical but also intrigued.

"Once you agree to these terms, you are bound by life to Sara," Serena explained. "Therefore, if you let Sara die you will too. The reverse, however, is not true. If you die, Sara will not."

"Alright, just give Mia her soul back and do the stupid pact," I responded.

I was confident that I could guard a little girl well enough for all of my life. I watched Serena give Mia her soul back. Mia fell to the floor, coughing like crazy.

"Please don't do that again." Mia wheezed between breaths.

"I, most likely, won't need to," Serena responded.

"Somehow that's not reassuring ..." Mia muttered.

I sighed. We really needed to get moving. I looked up at Aron, who hadn't spoken in a while. His face was completely expressionless.

"Well, do the pact so we can move on," I said, brushing the white hair from my eyes.

Serena walked out of the elevator, dragging a dazed Mia by her shirt. She came over to me and looked up into my eyes. Serena only stood to about the height of my chest. She put her hand over my heart and hers over her head. There was a short, burning sensation for a moment.

"That's it," Serena said as she transformed back into Sara.

When Sara appeared, on her pearly white skin was a blue crescent moon. I pulled my shirt out to see if I had one too, but my mark was that of a red sun.

"Serena says we should move on!" Sara cheered.

"Yes, let us advance," Aron spoke, having remained solid for very long.

"Let's never do that ever again," Mia said, struggling to her feet.

We began to walk, but something tugged on my arm. It was Sara, but she was using the wind.

"Hey, Jonathan, can you carry me?" Sara asked.

"Climb aboard the Cain train!" I smiled as I dropped to a knee.

Sara giggled, but Mia just scoffed.

"That's so lame," Mia said as Sara climbed onto my back.

"You're just jealous," I joked.

Mia stuck her tongue out at me but said nothing more. We then continued walking until we came upon a set of golden doors. There were four each leading a different way. Pausing, we surveyed the doors.

"Maybe each of us should take a door," I suggested. "If you don't find anything, then come back to the other doors?"

"Sounds like a plan," Mia said.

"I agree with the girl," Aron said.

"Do I get to kill things?" Sara asked.

The smile on her face was somewhat sadistic and really creeped me out. I did, however, need her to kill things.

"Yep, you sure do!" I cheered.

Maybe I shouldn't reinforce her sadistic tendencies, not that they were any different from my own. If you couldn't bash a couple heads in every so often, your life would be pretty rough in this day and age.

"Awesome!" Sara replied.

She stood by the door I assigned her to, jumping up and down with excitement.

"Alright, let's move," Mia said.

We all entered our doors and got to it.

# CHAPTER 8

# ℒANCER

When I opened the door and stepped in, it quickly shut behind me. The room was large but barren, like a medieval battlefield. Weapons, ranging from swords to spears, were stuck into the ground all around me. In the middle of the carnage, a warrior—who I assumed was male even though assuming is against my better judgment—sat in a gold suit of armor. He had a lance and a shield on his back. I took a step toward him, but his eyes flicked in my direction underneath the helmet.

"Don't come any closer," the warrior spoke.

His voice wasn't very deep and not high enough to be an older man's. He sounded like a child or maybe a woman.

"What happens if I do?" I said as I span my Desert Falcon on my finger.

I assumed that the knight was this room's boss. His imposing figure stood, but I exhaled in relief when I saw he wasn't taller than me.

"I'll kill you if you try it." He or she—I was second guessing—said.

The knight raised his lance above his head and swiftly brought the long weapon down to his side. The shield slid off his back and onto his forearm. It was larger than my chest and the lance was about as

31

tall as me. I fired a blast from my Desert Falcon, hitting his head. The shot made a dinging sound as it bounced of the armor. The golden gun made a loud beep indicating how little plasma energy it had left. I dropped it and my duffle bag onto the sand. I'd realized this was going to be harder than I had initially thought.

"Okay, that was a waste," I said.

"My turn," the warrior replied.

He hoisted the lance up in a javelin-like position. The lance started to glow a light blue color as he prepared to throw it. I pulled out my plasma blade, ready to slice the lance in half. The knight threw the lance at me, and I slashed down to destroy it. The lance, surprisingly, destroyed the plasma blade. Even the hilt of the blade crumbled in my hand. The worst part was that the lance didn't continue to fly. The warrior drew it back to him like a boomerang that only followed one path.

"Well, this isn't good." I grunted.

"Correct," the knight answered bluntly.

A good distance to my left, I noticed two short katanas lying in the sand. I exchanged a glance with the knight before dashing toward the weapons. He threw his lance, but I slid underneath it. I rolled and picked up the blades during the same action. I then jumped up and slashed them to each side to remove the sand.

*Intelligence multiplication times two*

I added to my intelligence so I would know how to wield the two short, one silver and one black, katanas. Raising my intelligence allowed me to infer how they were supposed to be used; it didn't actually tell me anything. It didn't help that I didn't know how strong this lance was, but I assumed I didn't need a strength or speed multiplication.

"Prepare yourself," I told the warrior.

"Ready when you are."

I charged, holding the blades at my sides. The blue aura rose off the lance and engulfed the warrior. My first strike hit the warrior's lance, but the short katana didn't break like my plasma blade. The warrior smacked the katana away with his lance. He then thrust the lance foreword, attempting to impale me. I slashed downward, driving his lance into the ground. I then stepped on it and jumped into the air. Before the warrior could do anything, I slashed down, cutting the shield in half. I then sliced sideways, managing to barely land a blow. The warrior, however, jumped back before I could cut deep enough to draw blood. The warrior staggered back, giving me an opening. I didn't feel like my swing produced enough power before, so I decided to up the ante a little.

*Strength multiplication times five*

I rushed the warrior but when I swung with the right blade, he dodged and caught my hand. I tried to pull back, but he was strong enough to keep me in place.

"I've caught you," the warrior spoke bluntly.

"Guess again!" I spat, attempting to run the warrior through with the short blade.

He smacked my hand down, causing me to drop the katana, and then caught my wrist. I twisted and pulled, but I couldn't get free.

The warrior's grip kept up. "It seems we've reached a stalemate."

"Not quite yet!" I shouted.

*Strength multiplication times seven*

I drew my head back and then drove it forward at full speed, head-butting the warrior. His helmet cracked, but he stood in the same place. A little blood trickled down my face, but I'd expected that. Then, suddenly, the warrior's helmet fell off. I was a little surprised it completely broke. The warrior was too because he gasped—no, wait, she gasped. Her flowing black hair rolled down her back from inside the helmet. Her sky blue eyes managed to look both confused and surprised.

"You're so strong," she said in awe.

"Why thank you," I responded. "Could … uh … you let go? You're hurting my wrists."

I'd expected to continue fighting, but I was left dumbfounded when she actually let go. I rubbed my wrists, which looked as if I'd been in shackles for days. Whether it was the armor or her, but this girl was really strong.

"No, I mean like really strong," she urged.

Did she mean herself or me? I was so lost in thought that I picked a sort of neutral response.

"Yeah, I know."

She groaned. "You can only destroy soul-bound armor with something of equal or stronger power."

"Okay, so?" I still didn't get it.

"Why are you so stupid?" the girl shouted at me.

"Who's being stupid? I just tried to kill you and now we're having a normal conversation!" I shouted back.

"Never mind that. You destroyed the helmet of soul-bound armor with your head!"

"When you say it like that, it does sound insane."

She sighed. "Ugh, finally you understand!"

The girl flicked her wrist back and her lance flew into her hand. She rotated the lance on her fingertips before it vanished into a blue cloud. Her armor also dissipated in this way. She was wearing a blue and black tracksuit with black boots. Crossing her arms, she stared at me. She was about five-eleven so she was looking up at me.

"So are we fighting or not?" I asked.

The girl shook her head. Good, this was getting tiresome. I began to leave heading back out of the door I came in, but suddenly she was in front of me.

# CHAPTER 9

# YIN

She held out her hand. "I'm Yin. Pleasure doing business with you!"

I grabbed her hand and shook it. "I'm Jonathan. What do you mean business?"

"Well, John … can I call you John?" Yin asked.

Suddenly her personality seemed super bubbly.

"Whatever floats your boat."

"Okay then, John…" Yin giggled "…I've been looking for someone strong enough to help me clear this tower, but I haven't run into anyone that powerful yet until I met you," Yin said with a mischievous grin.

"What's that supposed to mean?"

"I'm tagging along." Yin grinned.

I pondered the idea for a moment. We already had Aron and Mia, and now Sara. Was it wise to add another person who I was barely acquainted with? I reconsidered the pros of having someone with her strength, and it was decided.

"All right, come along then," I told her.

"Great, you won't regret this!" Yin cheered.

I grabbed my duffle bag and brushed the sand off it. I also tucked my Desert Falcon inside. I was about to sling it over my shoulder, but Yin held my arm down.

"Give it here," Yin said.

I obliged and as soon as the bag touched her hand, it disappeared into a blue cloud.

My eyebrows raised in question. "What did you do?"

"Ever heard of magic storage?" Yin began.

I tried to say I hadn't, but she continued despite me. "I'm assuming you haven't. You can put items inside of a pocket dimension created by a person's aura."

I was worried about my stuff for a second but since she was coming with us, there couldn't possibly be a problem.

"That's pretty awesome," I replied, impressed.

"I aim to please!" Yin giggled.

We left the warped room through the door I originally entered through. Aron and Mia were sitting in the hallway, both with minor wounds and blood splatters on their clothing. Mia was wrapping her arm in some medical tape when we approached her.

"Two things: where have you been and who is this?" Mia asked me.

"This is Mia Alves. Mia, meet Yin."

They shook hands. Yin cocked her head to the side and smiled sweetly. Mia just stared blankly ahead. She then frowned and continued to tie the bandage around her arm. She must have gotten it from Aron because she hadn't come into the tower with a bag. That, or she knew about magic storage which I had previously not.

"This knight in not so shiny armor is—"

Yin cut me off by finishing my sentence. "Aron, is it really you?"

She took a hesitant step toward Aron before quickly moving and kneeling down next to him. She removed his helmet and started to tear up when she saw his face.

"I-I never thought I'd see you again," Yin said.

Aron smiled warmly and stood bringing Yin up with him. Yin was at least a foot shorter than Aron, so she was left staring up at him.

"I've missed you, Yin." Aron stroked her hair.

This sent Yin over the edge. She sobbed into Aron's armor plate while Aron continued to stroke her black hair gently.

"So what's the story here?" Mia asked.

"This is my niece," Aron replied simply.

"It's not very becoming of me," Yin said between sobs. "I'm twenty years old now, and yet I break down like this."

"Nonsense, Yin. You're still a little girl to me."

Yin stopped crying and started wiping away her tears. She nodded over and over in response to Aron.

"Good girl." Aron smiled at Yin.

Suddenly I felt a small hand on my shoulder. I glanced to the side as Mia moved her mouth to my ear and whispered, "That's so sweet."

"I think so too," I whispered back.

After their meeting, Mia and I let Yin and Aron catch up a little. We sat around listening to the stories Aron told Yin about his adventures while trying to find her. The story got pretty sad very quickly. In short, Aron and Yin's small town was attacked and Yin was kidnapped six years ago and was only freed last year.

"I was cold and lonely," Yin began. "I wasn't the only person captured by those awful people. They abused us and had us do slave work day and night for years." Yin looked off into nowhere with a sad expression. "One day those people took us to a grail tower. Essentially we were decoys and cannon fodder. They gave us small knives to defend ourselves, but they weren't even strong enough to pierce their armor, much less kill any kind of monster we encountered. When we got to the top, there were only two slaves left. Me and a boy named Jacob, who had just become a slave the day before."

My eyes light up at the mention of my older brother's name.

"Did he tell you his last name or anything else about him?" I asked.

"He told me he planned to get me out. He said that I was some kind of exception. His last name was Cain, I believe."

"What was he really trying to do?" I said this out loud, but the idea was more for myself.

Yin didn't answer. It looked like she was searching my face for some resemblance to Jacob's.

"Are you brothers?"

I nodded.

"He saved my life, you know?" Yin started. "He distracted the people, my captors, while instructing me to drink from one of the grails. The ability I got was to freely control my magic circuit. I just need a base material for every act I perform. With that power, Jacob and I slaughtered them. We killed every last person, but I couldn't kill one man named Kent. He didn't beg for his life or fight back. He just said that the acts he committed were awful and to end him. Jacob said to kill him if I wanted and left. I couldn't do it. Killing an unarmed man seemed wrong so I just left him there."

"Sounds like him," I said while subsequently ignoring Yin's personal strife.

I knew Jacob didn't have a conscious or any emotions, but he never did something if it wasn't in his best interest. Just then the door swung open. The corridor we were in suddenly transformed into a ballroom. We were on the edge of the room when we stood up. Sara was standing in the middle of the room, holding a sign that read "go up to floor ninety-eight."

"I'm back!" Sara exclaimed. "I defeated the floor boss!"

Mia, Aron, and I weren't very surprised, but Yin didn't know about Sara.

"How did this little girl kill such a high-level floor boss?" Yin asked, completely confused.

"Let's just say she's a goddess named Serena inside the body of a little girl named Sara," I explained.

"At this point I'll believe even that," Yin responded.

We all walked toward the other side of the ballroom where the staircase was. When we reached it, we realized it wasn't a staircase but an escalator. A really long escalator at that. We hopped on and sat down. We were in for a long ride.

# CHAPTER 10

# GODDESS

After a long, awkward, and silent ride, we reached a large room that was shaped like a dome. In the center sat a ten-foot tall cyclops. When it stood, four bars appeared above its head.

"That's a large health bar," Yin said, equipping her armor and her lance in a misty blue flash.

"I didn't know floor bosses had health bars," I said, gazing up at the blue floating bars above the cyclops.

"How have you not noticed before?" Yin asked me.

I just shrugged, getting my Desert Falcon from Yin and drawing one of the short swords. The cyclops reached onto its back and drew an axe that was double the size of Aron.

"This might be a problem." Mia loaded her Galil.

Unexpectedly, the cyclops charged while roaring like a lion. It dragged the axe behind it, making sparks on the metal floor. Then it raised the weapon high above its head to strike. When it did most of us bolted to the right or left running out of the way. Sara stayed and waited for the cyclops's attack.

"Sara, move!" Yin shouted.

"Don't worry about her," Mia began. "She's a goddess, remember?"

The axe stopped just short of Sara's head. Strong winds blew against the axe pushing it back. The crescent moon on her forehead glowing brightly as ice suddenly started to appear around the cyclops. The pieces were all jagged with sharp points. Her green eyes were now blue, and I could see the ice reflecting off them. The ice shards impaled the cyclops from all angles. It roared loudly, still trying slice Sara in half. Then, suddenly, Sara winced. She jumped back before the axe fell, completely obliterating the spot where she once was. The attack had only cost the cyclops half its first health bar.

"He's too strong. I can't hold him." Sara winced in pain.

"Are you okay!" I called to her.

"I'm fine. He broke my concentration, so I have a pretty bad headache right now." Sara—no, Serena responded.

The cyclops attacked again, horizontally this time. Serena jumped preemptively and landed on the cyclops's axe. He continued through the swing, and Serena hopped off, landing in front of where the rest of us had gathered.

"We need to get more creative here. The cyclops is too strong for me to contain," Serena said.

"Indeed, perhaps a group attack?" Aron suggested.

I paused for a moment, thinking of a plan. I wasn't really paying attention to the position of the cyclops until Mia shouted, "Move!"

Everyone scattered this time, avoiding the overpowering strength of the beast. The attack demolished the ground where we once were. We all skidded to a stop when we gained some distance.

"I've got a plan," I began. "First, Yin will throw her lance into the cyclops's eye. While it's blind, the rest of us will hack away at its legs so it can't move. Then Sara, or Serena, and Mia will melt the metal around the cyclops, making it fall into a pool of molten metal, killing it. Any objections?" I finished.

"No, let's do it," Yin replied.

"Speak for yourself! Although, I think the plans fine," Mia said with strange hostility.

Yin launched the lance from her hand, flying it toward the cyclops's eye. It was on target, but the cyclops batted the lance away with its open hand.

"The plan is going to have to be more complex than that!" Aron chimed in.

The cyclops closed in on us, but I didn't run this time.

"We need to stop its axe," I said.

Aron drove his sword into the ground, awaiting the incoming horizontal attack. I placed my hand on his back.

*Strength multiplication times ten*

The plan was to reinforce Aron so we could stop the strike. Serena's—no, Sara's head was too scrambled to help us stop it. I felt Yin's armored gauntlet on my back. Hopefully this would be enough. Mia placed her hands on Yin's back for a little extra enforcement. As she did, the strike landed. We stopped the initial hit from the cyclops's axe but when it collided with Aron's sword, there was an explosion. Aron's armor blocked the flames, but the force from the explosion blew Mia and Yin back.

"Yin now!" I shouted.

She flung her spear, but the cyclops deflected it again. This time, however, I was ready. In the small opening, I threw one of the short katana at the cyclops's eye—except I hit just above the eye, stabbing it in the head.

"I missed!" I shouted.

Mia was on top of it. She propelled herself into the air with fire and grabbed onto the blade. She then pointed her Galil at the cyclops's eye.

"Look at this!" Mia unloaded the whole clip in its eye.

A full health bar and a half another disappeared from the cyclops's health. The cyclops roared and grabbed Mia, who yelped in surprise. Even blind, the cyclops was still powerful. It flung her across the room, causing her to roll and slide around thirty feet away.

"Mia, are you alright!" I shouted to her.

She sat up and blood trickled down her head. She placed her hand on her head then drew it away covered in blood.

"No, not really …" Mia managed before falling on her side.

Great, that was a problem for later. The cyclops swung its arms and its axe wildly.

"It has less power behind its swings," Aron began. "This is the most opportune time for attack."

Apparently Sara agreed because she resorted to our original plan. She raised her hand above her head. The crescent moon shone on her forehead as a large ball of flames continued to grow above Sara. Suddenly, I felt the sun on my chest burn slightly.

"Sorry, Jonathan, but I'm going to borrow some of your magic," Sara explained.

I felt a small chunk of my magic disappear from my magic circuit. The fireball grew larger than I thought it could. Sara threw the ball so it engulfed the cyclops and also melted the floor below it. Both of the cyclops's remaining health bars evaporated. The cyclops roared one last time as it melted away.

The room transformed into a similar ballroom, except instead of an escalator there was a canal. With a boat and an oar to boot. I just then remembered that Mia was down. I turned to see if she was still unconscious, but Yin was stitching up her head.

"I feel sick …" Mia groaned.

"You'll get over it," Yin replied.

She placed her hand on Mia's forehead and another on top of her head. A blue light radiated from Yin's body and onto Mia. When Yin drew her hands away, Mia had a scab over the wound. This, however, took about ten minutes.

"Now I just feel … tingly," Mia said with wonder.

"Yeah that'll last for a while," Yin responded.

"Good, she's alright." I breathed.

"We need to move," Aron chimed in. "More people will take the elevator up to this floor soon."

Sara was sitting on the boat, which was more like a raft, kicking her feet in the water.

"Let's go!" Sara cheered.

We all walked toward the boat while I looked down the tunnel the canal went through. You couldn't see the end of it, making it look pretty foreboding.

"Just what is that kid?" Yin sighed, snapping me out of my thoughts.

"Some kind of goddess," Mia and I replied simultaneously.

# CHAPTER 11

# KING

"Row, row, row your boat, gently down the stream. Merrily, merrily, merrily, merrily, life is but a dream," Sara sang with a strangely nice singing voice.

I'd been "rowing the boat, gently down the stream" for around twenty minutes now. Our small talk consisted of, mostly, what might await us in the next room.

"I think it'll be a giant golden falcon!" Yin wondered.

"It'll probably be a bunch of flaming hell hounds," Mia chimed in.

"Neigh, it will be a warrior with a sword forged by the gods," Aron added.

Just then I saw something at the end of the tunnel. It looked like silver thread. Inside of the thread was some woman, but she had extra appendages sticking out of her body. The limbs, however, looked like those of a spider. She noticed me as well and smiled creepily.

"No, you're all wrong," I began. "It's a spider woman."

The boat rolled into the room until it bumped into land. We got out, completely surrounded by giant spiders. They were about three feet tall, five feet wide, and six feet long. The spiders just stared at us with their glowing red eyes.

"Can I burn them?" Mia asked quietly.

I looked around the room before making eye contact with a woman who had spider legs growing out of her back.

"Not quite yet," I responded.

The spider woman crawled down to where she was before standing on her human legs in front of us. One of her spider legs reached over and caressed my cheek. It felt disgusting.

"So you're the one of the homunculi?" the spider woman asked.

"What do you mean?" I asked.

"It's quite simple, really. I've been told to give you some … insight," the spider woman said as he moved her spider leg behind me.

She pulled me to her with ease. I was lifted off my feet and forced a good distance into the air.

"John!" Yin called, but when she tried to follow the spiders blocked her path.

She slashed at one of the giant spiders, cutting it in two. The rest of the spiders screeched and began to attack. The spider woman forced me to look at her, so I wasn't able to see what was going on. I, however, felt the heat of flames and the spray of insect blood on my back.

"We're coming, Jonathan," someone shouted over the sounds of combat.

I couldn't tell who it was, but my attention was quickly taken away from them. The spider woman licked her lips and caressed my cheek again, but with her real hand. Somehow it actually felt the same. Maybe even a little worse.

"Hands off, lady!" I commanded, trying to push her, but she didn't even flinch.

She continued to appear to examine me before speaking.

"Jonathan Cain," the spider woman began. "Your father didn't birth you, at least not the traditional way. You and your various siblings were created by the scientific cloning process of the C.R.P."

That caught me off guard. If she was telling the truth, then what exactly was I? I wasn't going to believe her words so easily, though. I didn't have anything to say so the Spider woman continued.

"C.R.P. stands for cloning research project. The main three of you were created at ages eleven, fifteen, and seventeen. The rest I don't have any information about. Before you ask, I'll prove it; not only do you not have a mother, but you also have no memories of what would have been eleven years with your family. Before you freak out, you're not a clone. You were produced asexually using your father's cells."

I still didn't understand how she'd gotten this information or why her delivery of it seemed so automated. Why did she think not being a clone was any better than being a test tube baby?

"S-so what exactly is my purpose then?" I quickly asked the spider queen while I had begun to freak out.

"You, specifically, keep the real Jonathan in check. His job is to destroy his father," she replied.

"I don't follow," I lied.

"The people traveling with you all have no idea that you're just a shell created by this tower. They, also, never need to know. Your only exist to keep *him* from being free. The real question is can you outlast him?" the spider queen asked.

I didn't need to be told my job. Keeping the original owner of this body from being free was my whole existence. I did, however, have something else to say and one more thing to ask.

"I know what I'm supposed to do, but what about the actual Jonathan?" I asked the spider queen.

"Forget him for now. Because, you see, your father awaits above." The queen was finished.

Right after that I felt a sharp pain in my neck. I saw the spider queen's large teeth jabbing into my neck, but my body had gone limp. I started to see colors and felt myself began to fall.

# CHAPTER 12

## FATHER

I was pretty out of it. I must have passed out after that. The news shouldn't have shocked me that much. Even if that was something about the real Jonathan and not directly me, neither of us had known about it. I blinked a couple times. I still couldn't see, but I could hear singing. It sounded like David Bowie's "Life on Mars." I was sure Sara was singing it now. I felt a hand stroke my hair a couple times and another hand holding onto mine. My sight was coming back, but it was still hazy. I groaned, feeling around the soft surface I was lying on. When I did I heard a yelping sound. I sat up and looked right. When I did, my vision returned and I was looking at Yin's pale face. We were also way too close to one another.

"Oh thank God you're still alive!" Yin exclaimed as she shook me into clearer consciousness.

Even though I found the way Yin was acting strangely odd, I still didn't know where I was. I scratched my head and yawned before groaning.

"What happened?"

I surveyed the room since Yin was seeming to be searching for words to explain. Mia was sleeping next to me on the ground, using my duffel bag as a pillow. I'd forgotten I'd even had the thing. Yin must have let it out of her magic storage. I pulled the black bag into my magic storage on the fourth try. I hadn't mastered that ability, but I was a fast learner. After I put the bag away, I began to survey the room. Aron was sitting and playing a white piano that had red keys. Sara was singing along with the rhythm of the sound. The two together made the room seem more relaxing than it probably should have been with all the blood-stained, white walls. Aron didn't have his armor on, only his normal clothes. Without armor he looked a lot older that I expected. I was surprised I hadn't noticed before. They were playing a song I didn't recognized, but still liked. After appreciating the music and waiting for Yin to say something, I decided to flick Mia in the forehead to wake her up. She sat up, shook the hair out of her eyes, and looked at me. Her face lit up and became flushed with color at the same time.

"Jonathan, you're okay!" Mia exclaimed, hugging me.

"What did I miss?" I managed to ask, even though I was surprised by the warm hug.

I hadn't notice it before, but her body seemed to be on fire. It was hard to touch her skin without pulling away. I had to multiply my flame resistance so I could sustain the hug.

"First we had to kill all the spiders and that spider woman," Mia said after pulling away. "Then Yin had to suck the poison out of your neck!"

I looked at Yin who looked a little angry.

"I ... it was no big deal." Yin smiled at me but proceeded to glare at Mia.

What was up with her? It was like she was trying to hide her act of healing. It wasn't really a big deal.

"So are you guys ready to move on?" I asked.

The music stopped. Sara stopped singing and Yin's face hardened.

"Did I say something wrong?" I asked no one in particular.

"We heard a bit of what the spider lady said. Jonathan, what will you do when you see your father?" Yin asked.

I didn't know and couldn't look at her. I'd already been asking myself this same question. I was going to speak, but something deep inside of me seemed to begin to tick.

*"Tell the truth, you phony!"* a voice commanded from deep inside of me.

The poison must have broken the barrier I'd built between us because I could hear him now. I didn't want to listen to *him*, but the voice was right. No point in hiding anything.

"It's not very kind of me, but I'm probably going to kill him," I began. "I'm afraid that I could hurt people without wanting to. I'm afraid I'm not supposed to exist, so I want to ask him if that's the case. Once I know why I'm here, then I can kill him to keep him from controlling me," I finished.

I didn't get a response from anyone, so I began to walk away toward the giant door that led to the 100th floor. I was almost there, and I wasn't planning on looking back. Then I felt a tug on my sleeve. I turned and looked down at Sara.

"Don't leave me. I'm going with you," Sara stated bluntly.

"Same goes for the rest of us," Mia said.

"Aye, we won't let you meet the man that decides your fate alone, young lad," Aron said.

I looked around the room at my loyal friends. If I were a weaker person I would have cried.

"Let's go meet my dad," I said.

I began to walk toward the door again, but this time they followed. When we reached the large gold door, I didn't open it.

*Strength multiplication times ... nah*

I didn't need a multiplication for this one. I kicked it in. When we entered the room, it looked more like the entangle way of a palace. There was a large staircase with quartz pillars on either side. At the top sat a man wearing a lab coat. His gold hair matched his gold eyes. He was holding a crystal chalice, but he was also swirling it so the wine inside would spin. When we entered the room, he simply stared.

"Ah yes, you're Jonathan, correct? Although, you're the lesser version, I see," the man, who was mostly my father, asked in an oddly British accent.

"That's right, meaning you're my dad, right?" I asked, ignoring his insulting comment.

"Since you were asexually produced, I'm more of a sperm donor than a father. Also you specifically are not even remotely my son," Dad said.

"So what do I call you?" I asked, continuing to ignore his knowledge of the real Jonathan.

He paused to think. His thinking didn't take long.

"Ah, I've got it! You'll call me Gene!" Gene cheered.

"What, why?" I asked.

"So many questions," he responded. "It's because you have my genes, get it?"

"Got it, Gene." I smirked.

"When you say it like that it sounds stupid." Gene frowned.

"I hope I didn't upset you." I smiled at Gene.

"Shut up," Gene halfheartedly commanded with a sigh.

I shrugged. He wasn't as intimidating as I thought he would be. I couldn't even feel any killing intent.

"So how come the spider queen on the previous floor knew about me?" I asked Gene.

He beamed at the mention of the spider queen, like it was something he was proud of.

"When I drank from the Holy Grail, I became able to control the tower. Not your false grails either. I drank the real one. So, I figured I'd give you some insight on your existence since it would take little to no effort for me to do so," Gene responded.

"That's why the bosses were so easy," I joked.

"Shut up!" Gene growled this time.

Gene then looked everyone over for some reason. He stopped and gazed at Aron before frowning.

"So, even you're here. I hope you're still not mad about the disposal of your niece-*in-law*. Her family did adopt you after all."

"I'm not mad. Although, that's only because she's standing over here," Aron replied as he gestured to Yin.

"What do you mean you disposed of me?" Yin asked.

Gene looked confused, but his face quickly changed to one of sudden realization.

"When you were twelve, I believe, your father gave you to my colleagues and I to perform some … experiments. Of course we found you to be below what our standards were and, against Aron and your father's judgment, we sold you to some slave drivers. All your memories form eight years ago till when the slave drives took you were fabricated so you wouldn't remember. But don't fret. We didn't do much of anything to you. Just tore some pieces into that lion soul of yours," Gene causally explained something so horrible.

He, in fact, seemed to relish in the memory of his experiments.

"You … experimented on me for at least two years. Not only that, but you're the reason I was stuck with those horrible people …"

Yin's eyes were downcast and her fists were clenched. She looked really mad. I would be too. In fact, I should be. I am literally just an escaped lab project.

"Yes, precisely," Gene replied before taking a drink.

How cold. Although, it wasn't surprising.

"I'll kill you!" Yin growled.

Gene paid her no mind. He then looked to the hourglass which had suddenly appeared between us. I was almost positive it wasn't there before, but I had no way to verify that claim. The last of the sand spilled to the bottom of the time keeper. Gene got up and began to walk down the steps beneath his throne.

"Sorry to inform you, Jonathan, but I'll have to kill your friends now," Gene said between sips of his wine.

"Ah, there's the killing intent," I said aloud.

"What?" Gene asked.

"Just something I was thinking about," I replied. "Also, does killing all my friends include killing me too?" I asked.

"I'm only going to harvest your organs for my research, but don't fret, you wouldn't be alive without me anyway." Gene smirked, casually looking at the swirling red wine.

"Before you go all Wolverine on me, I have a question. What did you make us, my brothers and me for?" I questioned.

"For the sake of research! Heart-pounding, blood-chilling, and life-ending science! I want nothing more than to rule the world! I had three of the most powerful homunculi under my control! Of course, the three of you ruined it by drinking those cursed false holy grails, and I lost my control over you! I am already producing another homunculi that will be stronger than all three of you, though! I do need human bodies to complete it, however. You three would be the easiest to obtain!" Gene ranted, cackling like the madman he was.

"Did he just call me a homunculus?" was all I could manage to say.

That was the second time today I'd been referred to as such.

"That seems insulting," Yin chimed in.

I silently agreed with her. Also he was creating another one? That couldn't be good, and I didn't even know if I could beat him anyway. Just what kind of power did Gene have? I looked to my left at Aron and Sara. They looked prepared. I looked to my right at Yin and Mia. Yin had her armor on and lance ready. Mia was loading her Galil while lighting small fires around the room.

"Oh, so you plan to attack?" Gene asked.

Nobody responded.

"Alright, but first let me show you how truly powerful I am." Gene grinned viciously.

Then suddenly he was gone.

"Where did he go?" I looked up and down the room.

"Behind you!" Yin shouted.

I turned only to be hit with what felt like a mace or some other blunt object. I rolled back, blood trickling down my face. I looked and saw Gene standing where I stood. He was holding out his fist to show he had simply punched me.

"Eat this!" Mia jumped back while shooting her Galil at Gene.

Gene raised his other hand and the bullets stopped dead on contact. Mia then surrounded Gene with fire, but with a wave of his hand the fire dissipated.

"You're just too weak," Gene said as he appeared in front of Mia.

He punched her in the stomach, causing her to suddenly go slack. He tossed her body over toward me. I turned Mia over and checked her pulse. She was just unconscious.

Aron lifted his sword without a word, and Gene looked back at him. His gold eyes shone bright, just like mine. Then he was behind Aron, holding Aron's sword. He drove the sword through Aron's back until he reached the hilt in one quick motion. Aron cried out, but managed to turn and punch Gene with enough force to punch through steel. Gene, however, reacted as if he'd only been slapped. Gene then backhanded Aron, smashing his helmet.

"Aron!" Yin cried out.

She charged Gene with Sara and me in tow.

*Strength multiplication times ten*

I attempted to punch Gene, but he simply glided behind me and met me halfway. He kneed me in the stomach, sending me flying back. I sat up, wiping the blood from my mouth, to see Gene choking Yin, who now had little to no armor left on her body. It had mostly been ripped off. Sara, now Serena, shifted the ground below Gene, making him fall and drop Yin. She then froze him, along with a large distance around him.

"That should slow him down." Serena huffed, already exhausted.

"First time in combat?" I asked jokingly.

"Forth actually." Serena gasped.

They'd never fought anything before meeting me? I only pondered for a moment longer before realizing Aron was mortally wounded. Aron sat, his own sword driven through him, against the wall. Yin ran to his side, tossing her cracked helmet off along with dispelling her broken armor.

"Don't die Aron!" Yin cried.

"Sorry, Yin, but this old knight is about to lay down his sword," Aron responded between bloody coughs.

He then placed his hand on Yin's head and his armor vanished. Yin's tossed helmet also vanished and so did her lance.

"Don't go," Yin sobbed, holding onto Aron's now limp hand.

Aron was already gone. His body even vanished like he just faded out of existence. Only his sword remained behind. It was the only thing that could prove the swordsman even existed in the first place. Yin summoned her armor back, but now it was red with pointy edges. Her lance was now a katana in a color that could only be described as darker than black. It had a golden lion insignia on the side. The lion somehow seemed to be alive. I got chills all of the sudden. The whole tower seemed to shake with evil energy oozing from Yin's body.

"I'm going to kill you." Yin walked toward Gene, who had somehow thawed himself out.

"Haven't you already said that? Don't make promises you can't keep," Gene taunted.

"Die …" Yin said with no emotion in her voice.

"Oh dear." Gene seemed to realize something and backed away.

She swung the sword at Gene, who dodged it. He continued to dodge Yin, doing his best to avoid contact with her. Yin slashed through the floor, which was completely vaporized on contact. One of her swings came close enough to slice through Sara, but Sara dodged what would have been a deadly strike. Gene was bobbing and weaving, but Yin wasn't really aiming for him. She was just destroying everything. The room's ceiling began to collapse and one of the chunks came dangerously close to crushing an unconscious Mia.

"Yin, stop!" Sara shouted.

She attempted to hold Yin back with a powerful wall of wind. Yin, however, continued to move toward Sara at a really slow pace. The sword dragged behind Yin, creating a large crater as it ate away at the ground. Yin reached Sara, who couldn't move due to the loss of energy she suffered from trying to hold back Yin. Yin raised the katana high above her head. She was prepared to slice Sara in two.

"Yin, you've got to stop!" I called to her.

Yin looked over at me. Her eyes, in the helmet, were soulless and dark. I ran to her, realizing she wasn't listening. She swung the katana in a diagonal path which Sara managed to throw herself out of the way of. Yin raised the weapon high above her head, ready to execute Sara. I intervened. Without thought, I grabbed the katana and pulled it back so Yin was pulled toward me. The sword burned my hand, but I chucked it before it could do a lot of damage.

"Sorry about this," I said.

*Strength multiplication times two*

I tore of Yin's helmet and put my hand over her mouth and nose. She bucked and screamed, but I wouldn't let her get any air. The spikes on her armor drove into my shoulder and lower chest, but they didn't cut deep enough to be fatal. Eventually Yin stopped struggling and passed out. Her armor and the demonic katana dissipated. I let Yin's unconscious body fall. She immediately began coughing. I looked at Gene, who had been standing idle this whole time.

"Is your little drama, or romantic drama I suppose, over?" Gene asked, somehow still sipping from the same chalice.

"You really make me mad," I replied.

"Ditto." Gene laughed.

He pulled out two mini-guns from literally nowhere. They had just blinked into existence.

"I suggest you run," Gene said, raising the weapons.

I hightailed it. The bullets tore through the wall making it look like Swiss cheese. I felt the air being cut through as Gene continued to spray bullets. I picked up Mia's unconscious body in stride. As I continued to move, I saw Aron's great sword.

"This better work," I said to myself.

I pointed my hand toward the weapon and focused on putting it in my magic storage. I ran over toward Serena who was holding Yin. She blew a hole into the wall revealing the outside.

"Jump!" Serena shouted as she dove through the hole.

I hesitated. I looked over my shoulder quickly to glance at Gene. For some reason he had stopped firing. He just smiled oddly at me.

"I thought you would've jumped by now," Gene said, breaking the silence.

"What, you expect me to die in the fall?" I asked.

"No, Mr. Cain, I expect you to die if you stay here," Gene replied, lifting the heavy weaponry he held.

"Wait was that a James Bond refr—" I began, but he started to fire at me.

I jumped, somehow, without getting hit.

# CHAPTER 13

# FALL

The fall was long, like, very long. Imagine jumping out of a one-hundred story building. That's around 1,000 feet of just falling. I was descending fast, but air resistance helped lengthen the free fall. During all this I began to consider my options. I could harden my body and survive the fall, but if my body was hard I couldn't break Mia's fall. I was still trying to figure out how to break our fall, but suddenly I started to fall slower. Strong gusts of wind strategically pushed into me from below. The ground was very close now, but I landed like I had a parachute on. I switched my hold on Mia from under my arm to bridal style. I looked around and saw Yin covered in cuts and bruises. She was being supported by Serena who had most likely stopped my fall.

"Don't thank me or anything," Serena smiled at me.

She sounded like she was joking, but her face said otherwise. She looked completely out of gas. She was huffing and wheezing like she had just run a race. Sweat was dripping off the ends of her hair, moistening the sand below her. The moon on her forehead glowed brightly then dimmed quickly over and over.

"Thanks," I said before turning toward where my spacial cycle was.

I laid Mia down in the sand before looking behind myself at Yin and Serena.

"Wait here. I'll be right back," I said.

I started running before they could ask questions or object. It wasn't a long run to where the cycle was hidden. At most it took a couple minutes. I pulled the bushes and twigs off the cycle before hoping on it. I grabbed the handle bars and twisted. There wasn't a roar like a normal motorcycle. More like a light humming sound. I zoomed over to where the girls were. That took no more than a few seconds.

"Let's get going," I said, swinging my legs over and off one side of the cycle.

I scooped up Mia and placed her unconscious body on the handle bars. I sat behind her and gripped the handle bars. I felt Yin wrap her arms around my waistline.

"I'm going to borrow you," a drowsy sounding Yin said.

I rolled my eyes, not exactly thrilled with having to pay attention to three passengers. The cycle was barely long enough to accommodate four people. I looked back and saw Serena sitting on the far edge of the cycle.

"I'll make sure they don't fall off," Serena said before transforming into Sara.

All three of them were dipping in and out of consciousness. I couldn't exactly take three unconscious girls to a hospital without a real explanation so I decided on the next best thing: my apartment. The drive was pretty boring. Mia never woke up completely, and Yin sounded and acted drunk when she did. Sara remained dormant the whole time. She was likely regaining her energy. It took about twenty minutes to get to our destination. It didn't take long to carry the three of them up the stairs to my humble abode. At least it was late so I didn't have to worry about being seen and reported. I let Mia and Yin sleep in my bed and Sara sleep on the couch. Then I showered and changed, despite feeling awful. My new outfit was a black shirt and black pants with boots, the color of which I'm sure you could guess. There was a black cloak with a hood as well. I also took the time to wrap all our wounds, though they weren't horrible by any means. My apartment wasn't very spacious, and I didn't have any extra blankets or pillows besides the one I left over Sara. I leaned my head back against the side of the couch and drew the cloak over me to shield myself from the cold. I drifted off into sleep for maybe five minutes. I was awoken by Sara tugging on my sleeve. I looked at her, but I didn't say or do anything.

"Tell me a bedtime story!" Sara laughed.

I smiled at her, but then I frowned. I didn't know any kids' stories.

"Alright, let me think of one."

She didn't say anything and it was too dark for me to see her reaction. I just assumed she was happy. I had a lamp on the other side of the couch. It was a touch lamp so all I had to do was get my hand on it to power it on. I got up and felt around until I felt the cool metal, but the sudden burst of light hurt my eyes. I blinked a couple times before my eyes adjusted. I turned to look at Sara, who was sitting on the couch in her blanket. I sat on the edge of the couch and glanced over at Mia and Yin. They were fast asleep with Mia's arm draped over Yin awkwardly.

"So you want to hear a story?" I asked Sara.

"Yeah, but make it long so I can fall asleep to it," Sara responded.

I thought for a moment until I decided to tell her a slightly altered version of my life. I was doing it on the fly, though, so I hoped she wouldn't notice. I also hoped she liked it enough to not request something else.

"Alright, there once was a boy named Zack," I began. "Zack lived with a king who was older than him. Zack and the king were partners in crime."

Sara's eyes were beginning to close but then they opened suddenly. I frowned for a second, hoping this would go quickly, but continued.

"One day, while Zack and the king were sitting in their castle, there was a knock on the door," I said. "A beautiful princess entered their humble little castle. Soon the three of them were the best of friends. Zack and the princess got married and helped the king manage his castle."

I noticed that Sara had fallen asleep and cut the story off there. That was good because I was running out of material anyway. I sighed and went back to my spot leaning against the couch. I, however, had to get up again when I realized I'd neglected to turn off the lamp. As I got up, Mia and Yin giggled behind me. I looked over my shoulder at them.

"Nice story, Shakespeare." Mia laughed quietly.

"How does it end?" Yin asked.

"Do you really wanna know?" I replied, ignoring Mia's comment.

"Yeah tell us." Mia spoke for both of them.

I sighed. The story didn't have a happy ending. Didn't really have a happy beginning either.

"Zack and his wife Ana used to live with me here," I began. "They shared the bed and I slept on the couch. They died when a bunch of angry grail hunters we had thwarted the day before attacked my apartment two years ago," I finished.

Yin and Mia looked at each other then back to me. I pulled the hood over my head without a word.

"Hey, Jonathan?" Yin questioned sadly.

"Yeah," I replied sort of monotone.

"You should come sleep in the bed with us," Mia suggested.

I didn't expect that and I wasn't interested. So many levels of awkward to sleep in the same bed as two girls.

"I'm alright here, but thanks for the offer," I replied, looking back at the both of them.

Yin didn't seem bothered by my refusal, but Mia grinned mischievously.

"If you don't, I'll call the police and tell them you kidnapped us."

No way. Mia wouldn't, would she? It wasn't a risk I was willing to take since I had other things to do besides being incarcerated.

"Alright, I'll come sleep with you two," I responded.

"Great!" Mia cheered, but Yin remained quiet.

I stood up and walked over to the bed. I tossed my boots off along with the cloak. It was barely big enough to compensate three people. I squeezed in between the two of them and did my best to fall asleep while avoiding unnecessary contact. I think I succeeded.

# CHAPTER 14

# PARIS

I woke up the next morning with my face near Yin's and Mia was wrapped around my arm. I moved slightly but didn't want to wake the girls. I somehow managed to escape the bed without waking either of them. I glanced toward the couch at Sara who was fast asleep but was now Serena. The time was about 10:00 a.m. I wasn't surprised we hadn't slept that long. I walked into the kitchen and the phone began to ring. I picked it up quickly so my guests wouldn't be roused.

"Hello?" I said.

"I need you on the Eiffel Tower in Paris, France. Leave in an hour," a voice almost whispered.

"Who is this?" I asked.

"You know who it is. I'll meet you at the top of the Eiffel Tower," the voice persisted.

The line went silent after that. I listened to the dial tone for a second.

"Hello, hello!?" I repeated until I realized I'd been hung up on.

My best guess would be Jacob as the mystery caller. Since the phone was old, I couldn't see the person who was calling like one could with a holo-phone. The caller ID on this digital phone was blocked. The holo-phone was just a glove or some other object base, but it displayed a hologram of the other person in your palm or another object. I didn't own one and I had never used one either. I also didn't need it since I never questioned random calls from my most mysterious brother. He had called me from France before, but that was less vague. Zack had been a weapons dealing tycoon which was also how I'd gotten my spacial cycle. I looked into the fridge and saw some bacon and eggs. Both were a couple days from their expiration date. Then I looked into the pantry and saw some pancake mix. I had an hour.

## *Mia*

I woke up with Yin sleeping on my left. I was sort of upset that Jonathan had left. I heard the sound of plates clattering coming from the kitchen. I flicked Yin in the forehead to wake her up.

"Who do you think's cooking?" I asked.

"I don't care." Yin sounded rather upset.

"Okay ... rude. What about you, Sara?" I asked as I looked to the couch.

Sara was sleeping and drooling onto her pillow.

I got out of the bed, crawling over Yin who groaned in annoyance. I continued to creep toward the kitchen area. I tiptoed so I wouldn't alert anyone. I glanced around the corner to see a stack of pancakes on the table. It smelled like bacon as well. Jonathan turned around while holding a large plate of bacon and a big bowl of eggs. I pulled back around the corner to avoid being seen.

"Mia, what are you doing?" Jonathan asked.

I sighed, expressing my annoyance with the fact that I'd been seen. I walked slowly around the corner, twiddling my thumbs and feeling guilty for not thinking he could cook. It was 2068; the stereotype for at-home cooks should've been dead by now.

"So, what's up?" Jonathan asked after I didn't say anything.

"I wanted to cook," I responded shyly.

He looked puzzled for a moment. Then he put his hand on top of my head.

"You can cook next time," Jonathan said with a warm smile.

"Yes!" I shouted, waking up the rest of the apartment.

I waited for Yin and Sara to make their way into the kitchen. Sara did as I expected, but Yin went to the bathroom instead. When Sara arrived, the two of us awkwardly sat at the table waiting for Jonathan to be done and for Yin to join us. After what felt like an eternity, Yin finally sat down. I sipped the almost expired orange juice in my glass and kept waiting on Jonathan. I glanced at Yin, but she wasn't talking. She kept to herself and stared at her glass. She was swirling what was left of her water in a tall glass, but did so quietly. Sara seemed lost, just staring into her cup of day-old but still drinkable milk. Yin glanced at me, but only for a moment. I smiled at her, but she, however, looked away without acknowledging me.

"Hey, Yin, are you okay?"

She fumbled with her glass of water and almost dropped it. Jonathan didn't react at all. He was too busy setting the table and was probably also lost in thought. Sara didn't care either, but Yin's eyes narrowed. Her gaze was like getting stabbed, but with thousands of tiny needles. She looked really mad I'd asked about her well-being.

"Yeah, I'm fine." Yin grunted, but her words sounded like lies.

"I don't think you're telling me the truth," I said, sipping my orange juice.

Yin glared at me. She opened her mouth but didn't seem able to find the words she was looking for. She looked away again and seemed to think before turning back to me.

"Why are you okay?" Yin asked, quiet but angry.

I hadn't noticed before, but her eyes were really red. As if they'd been rubbed or she'd been ... crying.

"What do you mean?" I questioned, because I hadn't put the pieces together yet.

"It feels like I'm the only person here who cared about Aron!" Yin spat, finally getting Jonathan's attention.

"That's not fair, Yin," Jonathan calmly added to the conversation.

"What do you mean by fair? I just lost my uncle and no one has said anything until I brought it up!" Yin continued in a rage.

"You don't have to get angry. We can talk this through with our inside voices." I suggested.

"No, you don't get it. Aron was the only member of my family that made an effort to look after me. He was the only person that I could talk to! You two just seem to get happy whenever you talk to each other," Yin snapped.

I opened my mouth to ask her to calm down, but Yin cut me off before I could even begin.

"What's worse, my dad won't let me come home till I find a suitor! I'm not a romantic! What am I supposed to do?"

At this point Yin was just ranting about her life. It didn't sound good either. Was her father actually pressuring her so hard? It sure seemed like it.

"Yin," Jonathan forcefully uttered her name.

"What?" Yin asked after she caught her breath.

Jonathan pulled a silver great sword out of his magic storage. I'd never used it before myself, but I think it's how you summon weapons and armor to you. My sister had mentioned it once. Jonathan tossed the weapon to Yin. She, somehow, caught the hunk of metal with ease and immediately recognized it. She began to cry and hugged the blade even though its sharp edges dug into her hands.

"I heard once, from my... disappointing father, when you die with this sword your body disappears and your soul transcends. Fitting isn't it?" Jonathon asked.

I gave him a confused look. I wasn't sure why he would ever be told that. He looked at me and his eyes seemed to have been someone else's for a moment. He brought his finger to his lips and hushed me quickly.

"Yes, yes it is." Yin choked on her tears, snapping me out of the trance.

"All better?" Jonathan asked calmly.

Yin didn't give any indication of having heard Jonathan. She continued to cry until she seemed satisfied. After all the excitement died down, we went back to sitting awkwardly.

"Can we eat? I'm hungry," Sara demanded more than asked.

Despite what had just transpired, I laughed. At first I was just cackling like a hyena, but Yin and Jonathan joined in. Soon the table went from depressing to covered in laughter. Sara, however, had no idea why everyone was laughing.

"Let's eat! Let's eat!" she began to chant while banging on the table.

"Yeah, let's eat." Jonathan said as his laughter died down.

Everyone jabbed their forks into a piece of bacon, a ton of eggs, and a pancake then moved it to their plate. There wasn't much conversation during the meal. Jonathan didn't seem to like to talk and eat and neither did I. Yin, however, would randomly ask questions. She seemed to have perked up again. To be honest, it was kind of creepy how quickly she'd recovered.

"How much is the rent here?" Yin asked Jonathan.

Jonathan swallowed before replying. "About $700 a month."

"That's really low," Yin said in surprise.

"The prices are lower because so many Canadian people are still flooding into the various countries. It's a worldwide thing," Jonathan explained before going back to his meal.

"You think they would raise the prices because of that," Yin said after a pause.

"Some companies do. Though the better thing to do is to make sure they can get homes. Besides, the less vacant the more money the owners make," Jonathan replied.

I remembered about the attempted genocide of Canadians. It happened a year before I was born, but it was all people talked about until I was eleven. The entirety of Canada had become radioactive. At least most of the people had been evacuated beforehand.

"I'm surprised they haven't all found new homes yet," I threw in my two cents.

Nobody replied. Then suddenly Jonathan stopped eating.

"We're going to France," Jonathan announced.

This was totally unexpected, making me feel as though I'd missed something before.

"What for?" Yin was the first to ask.

"My brother called. He needs me in Paris," Jonathan replied while jabbing his fork into the last of the eggs.

I looked at Yin, who shrugged.

"It'll take six hours to get there, and Sara has to come, but you two don't." Jonathan said.

I wanted to go. Paris had been one of my dreams. I looked at Yin who looked determined to see if Jonathan and I hooked up, if nothing else.

"I'm coming too!" Yin and I said in unison.

Jonathan didn't look very surprised. In fact he just laughed and stood up.

"I knew you girls would come," Jonathan said. "Now then, let's get going."

"Yes!" Sara cheered.

I would say we all grabbed our things, but Jonathan was the only one with stuff to grab. He equipped the short katanas he had found while fighting Yin. The left blade had a sun like pattern on it. The sheath on the same blade was white. The right blade had a black crescent moon like pattern. The sheath for that blade was black. I'd never actually examined the katanas before.

"Jonathan, those katana are Sunrise and Nightfall." Yin sniffed, wiping away her tears.

"What do they do, exactly?" Jonathan asked curiously. "Also why are you suddenly telling me about them? Last but not least, how do you know?"

He seems to ask way too many questions at once. Then again, I was no better.

"It's the least I could do to repay you for giving Hope's End to me," Yin said. "Sunrise can use light energy to fire lasers and cut through things that aren't indestructible. Nightfall makes the user invisible when being held alone. My dad made swords like this back when he was a blacksmith and told me all about all kinds of strange weaponry," Yin finished, still wiping her eyes.

I'd thought Jonathan would be satisfied knowing how the blades work, but he still had one more question.

"How come the katana didn't activate when I fought you?" Jonathan questioned.

"You don't know how to channel your magic into objects. Although, I could teach you if you'd like?" Yin asked.

"That'd be nice," Jonathan said as he walked away. "Now let's go."

"Yes!" I said.

We were going to Paris, and I was really looking forward to it.

## *Jonathan*

After we all had hopped onto the spacial cycle, we began our journey to Paris, France. I packed food and drinks so we wouldn't get hungry or thirsty. Everything I brought was in bags and wasn't expired yet. Since driving across water was no problem from the cycle, everything was going smoothly. About three hours in and we were already halfway there. The spacial cycle had an auto drive, so Yin spent the time trying to teach me to manipulate the katana.

"Close your eyes and take deep breaths. Think of your power as a river," Yin told me. "Let it flow into the blades, costing you little to no energy."

I felt my magic begin to flow into the blades. I felt a slight heat from Sunrise and Nightfall. It tingled. I opened my eyes and both katanas were glowing different colors. Sunrise had a golden ray like that of sunshine, while Nightfall had a blue glow like that of moonlight. I looked up at Yin while I sheathed the katana. She was smiling happily at me.

"Well done." Yin grinned at me.

I took both her small hands in mine and shook them vigorously.

"It's all thanks to you," I said.

Yin blushed a little but didn't say anything. Meanwhile, Serena was teaching Mia how to not use so much of her energy so quickly.

"You should light one small, high consumption fire and let it feed off the oxygen in the air," Serena explained to Mia.

"What's a high consumption fire?" Mia asked.

"A flame that quickly eats off of oxygen and grows larger for you to command," Serena says, lighting a small blue flame in her hand.

The flame gradually began to grow. It grew to the point that it was bigger than Serena's head, but the crescent moon on her forehead wasn't glowing. To me that meant Serena wasn't using any magic to make it grow.

"That's so cool!" Mia exclaimed.

She placed her hand out in front of her. Mia closed her eyes and tried to mimic Serena. Her efforts didn't get her anywhere. A small blue flame appeared, but it sputtered and died quickly. Mia looked frustrated after she attempted it many more times. Then she suddenly looked upset instead of frustrated.

"Why can't I be as strong as you three?" Mia asked.

"Not everyone is as talented or genetically gifted like us," Yin explained, consoling Mia.

"You think so?" Mia asked hopefully.

"I'm sure of it," Yin responded confidently.

Mia smiled and continued to try the ability out under Serena's tutoring. I, on the other hand, got lost in thought. I wondered what my older brother was doing now. I also wanted to know what he wanted.

## Jacob

Of course it snows on the first of December. I wondered how close my youngest brother was to Paris. It was cold, but my jeans and sleeveless hoodie weren't appropriate for the weather. My scars burned and my heightened senses didn't help, especially the one over my eye. That bullet wound always hurt the most. I blew into my hands, attempting to warm them, but without any real effect. Snowflakes touched the ground lightly without making a sound. How I envied them. Just floating freely, without responsibility and without a care. Though I could only envy them in theory as I couldn't tell how it actually felt. I was standing atop the Eiffel Tower in an area blocked off from the normal public. Suddenly, my most powerful weapon began to glow red. Brimstone was the strongest fully-auto pistol in existence. It also glowed when a life force was approaching me with any type of idea or intent aimed toward me. I didn't need to glance over my shoulder or look at Brimstone to feel her. I could hear her black hair with a neon pink streak rustling from the wind. Behind me stood Marguerite. She was a French woman at the age of twenty-three. She was also my closest friend. Although, maybe I should say ally. I'd kinda of lost a grip on what friendship was. I couldn't even remember how to have a healthy relationship. The one I was in right now was anything but that.

"What's is it?" I asked.

"J-Jonathan and his fr-friends are forty-five minutes away," Marguerite said in her familiar stutter.

"Hey, Marguerite?" I began.

"Y-yes, boss?"

"What are friends? What do you define as friendship?" I asked.

I didn't truly get it. I couldn't seem to get what it meant. Azazel had convinced me to memorize the dictionary, but all that knowledge didn't give me anything concrete. I stared at Marguerite, waiting for a reply. Her eyes were wide and her mouth was agape, but I couldn't describe the emotions she was feeling. I couldn't describe the emotions I was feeling.

"F-friends are pe-people you can definitely tr-trust and re-rely on," Marguerite answered finally.

"I guess that makes us friends," I said while turning away.

The city of France looked so vast, wide, and bright. There was another word I was thinking off, but I couldn't seem to associate it properly. I looked back at Marguerite again. She was the same word, but I couldn't think of it.

"Ja-Jacob, I-" Marguerite began.

"What is it?" I asked her.

"P-Paris looks be-beautiful, right?" Marguerite stuttered.

That was the word I was looking for. Beautiful. I liked the sound of it at the very least. I knew it as a compliment, and I had seen movies where the protagonist used it on the heroine. So I decided to do the same.

"Just like you," I muttered, taking a metal cylinder out of my pocket.

I didn't understand the emotions behind calling Marguerite beautiful. She seemed stunned, but I just turned away. I powered on the electronic cigarette. I had smoked before, but this was safer and the effect was the same. It let me feel a little. Nicotine was a lower-level drug anyway. Nothing like Trinity, which was a problem my team had been combating all around France. I puffed a cloud of the vapor mix into the night sky. Marguerite should be aware of my issue with not being able to feel any emotions, not that I could worry strenuously about it anyway. I was only capable of *thinking* about caring. I heard Marguerite walk up next to me. My eyes were closed to savor the feeling of smoking. Calmness ...

"Th-they've to-touched gr-ground in Br-Brest," Marguerite stuttered.

"Good. Set up for them," I said, spinning around, opening my eyes as well.

The party was about to start.

## *Jonathan*

I eased onto land slowly before speeding up again. It was hard to control auto drive in crowded streets and public areas so I took over. Luckily you could cap out the bike at a low level of speed with the maximum being 90 miles per hour. It was late at night in France, and we were going to hit Paris in thirty minutes or so. I kept to the outskirts of the different cities and towns so I could avoid hitting anything or anyone while going max speed. The time passed quickly, and soon we were in Paris. I had to slow down to within the speed limit to get close to the tower easily. The Eiffel Tower looked like it did on TV. It also looked like whoever made it was compensating for something.

"You never did tell us where we were going," Yin more so stated than asked.

"Sorry. It didn't exactly seem important," I replied.

"We could be going to a drug ring or something!" Mia raved.

We shared a laugh as I parked the spacial cycle in a conveniently empty parking spot labeled for motorcycles. It was conveniently empty as well. I say conveniently because every parking spot was taken up to the point where people were parked on the road. I led us to the entrance for the tower. As I had suspected, it was closed. My brother was the type of person that planned.

"Hey! Look up, idiots!" a voice of a young girl said.

Despite the insult, we all looked up. There was a young girl sitting on a broomstick. She had a witch's hat, which helped her fit the bill.

"What!?" I shouted back.

"Hold on. I'll bring you up!" the girl responded.

Suddenly the four of us began to float.

"You must be doing this, right?" Yin shouted to the girl in surprise.

"No ish, Sherlock. Now then, up we go!" the witch responded.

Mia screamed in surprise as we suddenly shot upward.

"No, no, no, no, no, no, no, no, no," Mia repeated as we quickly zipped toward the top of the Eiffel Tower. I guess she had a fear of heights—that or being yanked up by an invisible force. The second one was truly more frightening.

"This is fun!" Sara shouted.

She, however, was flying all around using her own powers. The wind had become stronger than before and began to make Sara deviate from where we were headed. She was suddenly stopped and pulled back to where the rest of us were.

"Stop moving, runt!" the witch girl shouted.

Sara frowned as I opened my mouth to ask how high we were going, but I soon found out. We suddenly stopped ascending before we reached the top of the tower.

"In we go!" the witch said suddenly.

We were all moved swiftly toward the side of the tower. Instead of crashing into it, we merged inside. As soon as we got into the dark room, we stopped floating, which caused us all to hit the ground with a thud.

"Ow, that hurt," Yin scratched the back of her head.

"Let's not do that again." I dusted off my clothes.

"You idiots are going to have to get down the same way," the small, witch girl said as she hopped off her broomstick.

She looked at all of us disapprovingly. She almost seemed more annoyed and playful than actually angry. It was also evident she had adopted the use of more childish insults. Maybe this was her solution to a cursing problem.

"Jacob, I don't get it. Why do we need help from idiots like these guys?" she complained.

"Lia, just put up with it," Jacob responded.

I could tell it was my brother even though the darkness hid his face. Then there was suddenly light. The surprise about the light was its source. Lia had three small purple flames swirling around her body. They somehow seemed brighter than normal fire.

"Do you have fire grail powers too?" Mia asked as she lit her hand on fire.

"I don't have lame Holy Grail powers. I was born with this," Lia said, gesturing to the purple flames that started swirling around the room.

Mia frowned. Her eyebrows started to twitch slightly. She looked really mad, more than I'd ever seen her. In fact, her eyes literally began to blaze.

"Lia, grail powers aren't lame," Jacob stated.

"I'm sorry." Lia bowed her head repeatedly toward Jacob in apology.

Even though the apology was geared toward Jacob, Mia calmed down.

"Forget it," Jacob replied. "Regardless of your abilities, I'll take you to our hideout before I tell you what you're here for."

I wasn't worried about Jacob betraying me in some way. I had been to France with Zack and Ana before. I, however, didn't know if the hideout had changed at all.

"Lead the way," I responded.

# CHAPTER 15

# DOWN

After floating down from the Eiffel Tower, thanks to Lia, the six of us headed down toward Jacob's hideout.

"So where and what exactly is this place?" Yin asked curiously.

"It's a little something Outcast has been working on," Lia responded.

"Who's Outcast?" I asked.

"Me," Jacob replied.

"What'd you get that name for?" I asked.

It was odd for anyone to believe Jacob deserved any kind of nickname.

"They call him Outcast because he took all of us in. The unwanted, the good, the evil, and even the leaks," Lia explained.

"What's a leak?" Mia asked.

Lia opened her mouth to say something, probably insulting, but I spoke first.

"A leak is a being that was created from a grail tower, but is able to survive outside it. Any living thing created in a grail tower normally can't. Leaks are also self-aware, unlike most monsters in the grail tower, which usually have one purpose," I explained to Mia.

"Sadly there aren't many good leaks. I do, however, know a leak," Lia said while spinning her broomstick around her body.

"Really? What's he like?" Mia asked, suddenly excited about the idea of leaks.

"Calm down. You'll meet him soon enough," Lia replied.

At that moment Jacob randomly turned down an alleyway. We had been walking straight since we left the Eiffel Tower so it was kind of weird. Regardless of random left turns, we arrived at a rundown looking pub.

"Outcast Corner," the sign on top read.

Jacob walked in followed by Lia. The four of us, however, remained outside to look at the place.

"This is their hideout?" Mia asked Yin.

Yin shrugged and we went inside. The place was as rundown on the inside as it was on the outside. It was empty except for one man who had empty bottles of pilsner lagers scattered all around him. His head was down, and he was holding the bottle out in front of him as if he was thinking of taking a sip.

"Can I have another, please?" the man asked, completely coherent.

"F-finish th-the one you ha-have," the woman at the bar replied.

The man suddenly moved and downed the bottle immediately. He tossed the bottle to her which she caught.

"How about now?" he asked.

She made a funny face before throwing him another full bottle.

"Thanks, Marguerite," the man said before sipping from the bottle.

"No pr-problem," Marguerite replied.

Jacob walked over to Marguerite, who already had the swinging door open for him.

"A-are you sure abo-about th-this? Marguerite asked.

"I think this way has a higher chance of success," Jacob replied.

He walked past her and we followed. Jacob moved to the back room where the alcohol was held. There was a single green bottle sitting on top of the highest cabinet.

"Lia." Jacob said her name like a command.

"Yes," Lia replied.

She lifted the bottle from the top of the cabinet and shoved it into a round hole in one of the freezers. There was a clicking sound followed by the sound of gears turning. The door suddenly swung open revealing a dark down stairs area.

"Nice," I managed, stunned.

"It is pretty cool," Lia said as she followed Jacob inside.

Mia was the last person in our line. When she walked past the door, it slammed shut, leaving us in total darkness.

"What just happened?" Yin asked no one in particular.

"Give it time." Jacob replied.

After a couple seconds, the lights flicked on. The place we were in was completely white and just a tunnel. It went a little further down into a dark purple-colored room. We all headed down toward the room as it was the only place to go. We walked the distance in silence. Nobody knew what to say. When we reached the bottom floor, we were greeted by surprised looks from twenty or so people. They were all wearing full body suits that seemed to be made of kevlar. Their only colors were black with purple highlights. I noticed the sound of light piano playing in the background of the crowded room.

"Welcome back, boss," A deep voice said.

A large, milk chocolate-colored man walked over to where we were standing. He was wearing the same suit, but he had a purple lightning bolt on the front of it.

"Hey, Virgil. This is my brother Jonathan and his friends Sara, Mia, and Yin," Jacob said.

"Odd, it's like a female squad is escorting your brother," Virgil said then let out a hearty laugh. It was a booming sound akin to thunder. He slapped me on the back, and I chuckled awkwardly with him. "I'm just kidding around. Welcome to the family," Virgil said, holding out his hand.

"Thanks for having me help out your team." I took his hand in mine and we shook.

I immediately noticed his grip. It was not only strong, but I felt a slight shock upon touching him. I flinched, but played it off since I couldn't tell if he had felt it.

"Jonathan, Virgil is second in command of Amethyst Squad," Jacob suddenly interjected.

"So who's in charge then?" I asked.

Virgil jabbed his thumb back behind him toward the corner of the room. There was a shadowy figure wearing a composer's outfit. He was gently moving his long dark fingers across the keys of a grand piano.

"He's a leak named Zortam," Jacob said.

"He's more than a leak," Lia responded, a little overtaken by the sound of the music. "He's the strongest leak there is. He's more of a god."

"Let's go meet the captain," Virgil said, changing the subject.

We all walked toward Zortam, saying hello to other Amethyst members as we went. They mostly had masks on, but those without ranged from all colors and probably from all over the world. When we reached him he had already stopped playing.

"You're Zortam, right?" I asked.

He turned to look at me. His face gave me chills. He had no mouth and his head was oval in shape. His eyes were a color that could only be described as amethyst, which suited him perfectly. Zortam then stood, rising high above all of us. He must have been at least seven foot five.

"You are tall," was all I could utter as I looked up at him.

Lia ran up and gave Zortam a hug. He didn't react at all except for moving his long hand and patting her on the head. For some reason Sara gave him a hug too.

"Oddly, the Strains seem to love Zortam as well as young children," Virgil said.

"What are Strains?" I asked my brother.

"A Strain is a human born with special abilities," Jacob explained.

"They have a name?" I asked, never having heard of it before.

"Not exactly. It's something we had thought of because of Lia's last name," Jacob replied.

"Strain?" I asked.

"Yes," Jacob replied as monotone as ever. "The world doesn't know of their existence due to the introduction of normal false grail powers into everyday society. However, it's not like anyone or anything is trying to hide it."

"You said Strains plural. How many are there?" I asked.

"Seven in total. We're all sisters as well. It's kinda like a Virgin Mary thing. There's never a father involved in our births," Lia chimed in.

"I see," was all I could say.

"Thanks for the introduction, Virgil, but we're moving on to the next room. Both Strains can stay behind if they wish," Jacob said, suddenly walking toward a round door.

"I'm staying here," Sara said as she sat, swinging her legs on the piano.

"Alright, I'll come get you later," I told her.

Sara nodded in reply, and I turned to catch up with Jacob. Mia and Yin were staying a little behind Jacob, not wanting to walk with him. I couldn't blame them too much as he was frightening at times.

"He's kind of scary. Like a robot," Mia whispered to me.

"He's still my older brother," I replied casually.

"Are you sure? You're, like, six-two, but he's around five-six or something," Yin said.

"Yeah, he's kinda small," Mia agreed.

I looked down at her and the freckle-faced girl looked up at me.

"You're one to talk," I finally said.

Mia was about to reply, but her attention was taken away by a dinging noise. We entered the circular door which turned out to be an elevator. The conversation stopped, and we all stood awkwardly not wanting Jacob to hear us. When we stepped of the elevator into a sapphire-colored room. Yin, Mia, and I held back so the conversation could continue.

"So what does it mean? Extra speed?" Yin asked resuming the conversation.

"I mean, that's how we were created so …" I trailed off.

"You have no idea why they made him short then?" Yin asked.

"Yeah …" I scratched the back of my head.

"Why are you all walking so slow?" Jacob asked, still monotone.

We sped up to catch up with him. When we did he stopped.

"I'm not short. I'm average height," Jacob said before continuing to walk toward a revolving door.

"How did he hear us?" Mia asked no one in particular. "Also, why does he care?"

There was nothing to be said; I was the only one with an answer, but neglected to say anything for a moment.

"I think it's part of his ability. Although, I could be wrong. And I have no idea why he might care," I chimed in eventually.

"Why didn't you warn us?" Mia asked as we headed through the revolving door.

"I didn't think about it," I responded.

"You know you don't think about a lot of things. Also, these are things you're supposed to tell people," Yin said as we entered a room full of people.

They were wearing the same kind of suits as the Amethyst Squad, except their color was sapphire. Jacob stopped and swiveled his head, sweeping the room quickly. He stopped on a man with sapphire-colored hair and glasses. Those weren't his most defining features. Not only was he six-five, he also had a set of white wings growing out of his back. His jaw was also oddly perfect along with his nose. The combination made his face fully symmetrical through and through.

"Gabriel!" Jacob called to him.

The angelic man turned before gently floating to us.

"Meet my brother and his friends," Jacob introduced us calmly.

"A pleasure," Gabriel said, bowing his head.

"Likewise," I replied, bowing also.

Jacob opened his mouth to give introductions, but Gabriel spoke first.

"It's nice to meet you all, but I must be going," Gabriel said as he flew away, not waiting for a reply.

"What does he have to do?" I asked Jacob.

"Train his squadron," Jacob replied without giving it much thought.

He started moving swiftly forward toward another lift. I sped-walked to catch up and talk to Jacob.

"What do you mean by training?" I asked.

"It's simple, really. The members of each squadron fight their leader," Jacob said without a thought.

"Isn't that kind of unfair? For the leaders, I mean," Mia interjected.

"Not at all. They're squad leaders for a reason, you know," Jacob replied.

With that, Jacob walked away toward the next elevator. We followed after giving each other questioning glances. The next room down was a ruby red-colored one. When we reached the main room it was totally empty.

"Where is everyone?" Yin asked, looking around.

"The room on the left is a training room. Care to take a look?" Jacob asked.

"Sounds fun," I said.

Jacob turned to the left toward a round door. He stopped in front of the door and then just stared at it. Suddenly a light flashed toward Jacob's face. It seemed to travel all across his face like a scanner. Then the door suddenly opened.

"Follow me," he said before walking through.

We followed right behind him. The door led to a long hallway. On the side was a windowpane which went down the entire hall. Jacob walked over and glanced down through the window. I walked over next to him and looked down as well. There was a girl with sleek black hair standing in the center of twenty or so other men and women.

"Don't hold back! Try and kill me if you can!" the girl shouted with a creepy grin.

Suddenly black wings grew out of her back and from black flames a black rapier appeared in her hand. She swung the sword, slashing through the air with such force it caused a gust of wind. The soldiers took nervous steps back. There was an odd amount of pressure that seemed to be seeping from her body. The reinforced glasses was no match for the dark power and it began to crack. The cracks allowed the wind to force its way into the hall.

"Who, no, what is she?" I asked Jacob, surprised.

"The Archangel of Death, Azazeal," Jacob replied.

Down on the battle floor one of the soldiers charged at Azazeal.

"I guess one of you is brave!" Azazeal shouted.

The boy was attacking head-on, but suddenly he was behind her. He slashed from the back fast as light.

"Man, you're quick!" Azazeal said as she spun around.

She deflected the attack with ease, using her blade swiftly. Then she spin-kicked the boy in the back as he stumbled past her. He bounced once, rolled, and managed to end the motion on his feet. The boy's blond hair flopped down in front of his eyes. He then pulled it back, huffing. Azazeal looked down at him.

"Is that all you got?" Azazeal asked, brushing the black hair out of her eyes.

The boy seemed to smile, as if he was enjoying the punishment. A girl with long braids and dark skin gestured to him. She appeared to call him to her, and he vanished. As soon as he did, the other soldiers all charged at once. Azazeal dispatched them quickly, dodging, blocking, and countering every hit they attempted to land. Soon only the blond-haired boy, a brown-haired girl with pale skin, the girl with the braids, and a dark-skinned man wearing sunglasses were all that was left.

"W-wow. She's amazing," I stammered.

"Indeed, she is good," Jacob replied, seeming to need to substitute amazing for good for some reason.

"You four are all that's left? Same as last time, right?" Azazeal asked.

"Yes, and we'll get you this time," the brown-haired girl replied.

She lifted up her hands. Between her fingers were little black balls. The dark-skinned man adjusted his sunglasses before taking some sort of boxing stance. The blond-haired boy slashed his iron sword through the air. The dark-skinned girl's skin appeared to explode into flame. The fire, however, began to wrap around her body, making a cocoon. It appeared she was going to remain like that for a little while.

"Oh? It looks like you mean it," Azazeal said with a grin. "Then come," she beckoned to her squad members.

The brown-haired girl tossed the black balls toward Azazeal.

"Light, go now!" she shouted at the blond-haired boy.

Light only nodded in reply.

Suddenly he was gone in a bright flash only to appear behind Azazeal. He slashed at Azazeal, who jumped in the opposite direction. After she dodged, he moved once more and moved all the unconscious bodies away from Azazeal.

"Gotcha now," the girl said.

Then she was gone as well, but she appeared just below the ceiling. The black balls she had tossed were floating in the air around Azazeal. The balls exploded into a flashing light. Azazeal, however, jumped out of the explosion, away from where the blond was a second time. She did, however, drift back toward the dark-skinned man.

"Lock, now!" Light shouted.

"Yes!" Lock responded.

He threw a hard right, connecting with Azazeal's side. She gasped for breath before tumbling back.

"No fair ... I can't move ..." Azazeal complained.

"Amy, we've got her this time," Lock said.

"That ... is where you're wrong," Azazeal gasped.

Suddenly, she was gone. Completely. Amy landed from the air and looked around on the ground.

"Where did she go?" Light asked no one in particular.

"It is true. You really would be surprised how rarely people look up," Azazeal said as she floated in the air above them.

I couldn't comprehend how she did that. It wasn't teleportation, but she was so fast I barely saw her move.

"It's called Overdrive. She can't use it very much, but she can break the light barrier with it," Jacob explained, probably having seen my confused face.

The three attackers looked up in surprise, but the girl with braids continued with her odd ability.

"Come down here and face us!" Lock shouted up at Azazeal.

"You asked for it." Azazeal replied.

Then there was one quick motion and all three of them were down. Azazeal smirked, wiping blood from the corner of her mouth. She seemed to stumble while mouthing, "That's enough of that," to herself.

"You all did well. Until next time …" Azazeal said before floating up to where we were.

Except she stopped in the air. She turned back in time to dodge a blast of flame coming from the dark-skinned girl. It ignited her hair, but Azazeal quickly smothered it with her hand. The fire had come from the girl's mouth, and her body displayed an image that one would associate with a dragon. A scaly, red tail stemmed from her rear, and her skin was the same scaly red. She had wings that looked torn in some places, but functional. Her fingernails had been replaced with sharp, pearly white claws.

"Hey, Rylen, watch the hair!" Azazeal growled.

Rylen didn't reply and spat more fire toward Azazeal. The archangel batted her wings and caused the flames to dissipate. Rylen, however, charged in just as soon as it did. She slashed Azazeal across the abdomen, drawing a spray of blood. The archangel didn't make a sound, and she slashed Rylen across the chest. The girl began to fall down as her own blood shot out of her, but she managed to stay in the air with a mighty beat from her tattered wings. She shot up and thrust her claw forward toward Azazeal. The archangel blocked the attack with her rapier and brought her leg into Rylen's stomach. The girl doubled over but was able to deliver a gut punch of her own from that position. Azazeal reeled back, but immediately flew higher in the air and delivered a bone-shattering axe kick into Rylen's head. The dragon-girl wasn't prepared to take the blow and was sent crashing to the ground. As her body landed with a thud, her dragon-like features faded in a short burst of flame. The battle was over and Azazeal was victorious. At first she looked as if she'd been worn out. She was gasping for air and doubled over then landed on the ground and immediately dropped to a knee. Her wounds, however, already began to heal themselves. It was slow going, but I could tell from where I stood above that the bleeding had already stopped and the cuts were beginning to close. Azazeal suddenly exhaled before floating up to where we were watching.

"Hello!" she exclaimed.

She then slashed her blade through the glass, shattering it with ease. I jumped back in surprise, but Jacob just stood there. Azazeal's rapier dissipated as she floated into the corridor.

"You're back, my love," Azazeal said, wrapping her arms around Jacob's shoulders.

"Who says my love anymore?" I picked up on Mia whispering to Yin.

"Indeed," Jacob replied, probably not to Mia's comment.

Azazeal made a motion to kiss Jacob, but he stopped her by putting a finger to her lips. She didn't seem all too surprised by the rejection, but pulled back sadly despite that.

"There's no reason for us to make a fusion now," Jacob said.

"Why can't I kiss my husband?" Azazeal pouted.

Jacob didn't reply, but it was because he'd already given her a reason. That reason, however, was not one I was familiar with. She floated in the air upside down in front of Jacob. He just looked up at her as she grinned. Azazeal then glanced over toward me.

"Who's this hunk of man meat?" Azazeal asked, floating over to me.

She floated sideways toward me. I backed up a little, but she stroked her hand through my hair as I looked at her uncomfortably.

"My little brother," Jacob replied.

"I wonder if he's as big as you ... where it counts" Azazeal giggled.

I didn't want to know the answer to that.

"Hey, hands off!" Mia said, stepping in between me and Azazeal.

"Thank you," I whispered into Mia's ear.

"I don't like this little succubus one bit," Mia replied back.

"Aw, how weird. It appears you two haven't played house yet," Azazeal giggled.

"What's that supposed to mean?" I asked.

"Nothing. Nothing at all," Azazeal responded with a grin.

She was now leaning onto Jacob's back with her arms draped over his shoulders. She nuzzled her face into his neck, but my brother didn't react to her affection at all.

"Don't be bothersome, Azazeal," Jacob commanded.

"Aw, you're no fun," Azazeal whined as she floated off of his back and onto her feet.

As soon as she began to stand, her wings retracted into her back with a burst of black feathers. She sighed and stood, suddenly looking mature, behind Jacob.

"Follow me. You too, Azazeal." Jacob gestured back to the main room.

"Are you just going to leave them there?" Yin suddenly asked.

I hadn't thought about it until now.

"The combat rooms all double as healing stations. The magic in there will heal them quickly," Azazeal explained.

As if on cue groans and the sounds of movement could be heard in the combat room. I looked through the glassless window to watch as the soldiers began to stand. I looked at Rylen especially to see if her sword wound had already closed up. It hadn't completely, but similar to Azazeal's healing it had stopped bleeding, but was slowly reforming the missing skin.

"Are you all content with that?" Jacob asked, impatient.

He didn't seem like he cared whether or not we were. It looked as if he would leave us behind either way.

"Yeah, we can go," Yin replied.

"Stick behind me then." Jacob began to head back toward the room we had entered from.

"Right," I said, walking behind him.

After returning to the main room, we walked toward the next elevator.

"Just one more and we're there," Jacob said.

"Where exactly?" Mia asked.

"Your new base of operations," Jacob replied.

# CHAPTER 16

# CHANCE

The elevator went down further and faster than ever before. It was like that old ride at Disney World: the Tower of Terror. We all stumbled and grabbed onto the railings in the elevator. Everyone except for Azazeal and Jacob, unsurprisingly. The lights in the elevator flashed on and off before everything came to a sudden halt.

"Let's never … do that again …" Yin said, trying to gather herself.

"Agreed." Mia huffed.

"Too bad. You're going to have to get out of here somehow." Azazeal laughed.

"I think I'll just stay down here," Mia replied.

"Follow along," Jacob commanded.

We did as he said, just as we'd done this entire tour. The walls on this floor were dark. There was, however, light from magic flames through the long corridor.

"You're all rooming with someone. The names will be on the doors to either your left or right." Jacob gestured both ways.

"Are the rooms coed?" Mia asked.

"Only Jacob and I have a coed room," Azazeal said, brushing up against her one-dimensional lover.

"The cafe is at the end of the hall. Washers and dryers are in your rooms. I suggest you get some sleep we have a full day tomorrow," Jacob said, completely ignoring Azazeal.

"Hey, we never agreed to stay here!" Mia argued.

"Speak for yourself," Yin tried to say but was out shouted by Mia.

"I said good night," Jacob replied emotionlessly.

"What do you mean good night? We have no plans to stay here!" Mia continued arguing.

"I said good night!" Jacob suddenly snapped.

His eyes went red. The whole place seemed to shake. I could feel something cold but deadly coming from Jacob. I stumbled back. I was never scared of something so much in my life. Azazeal, however, wasn't fazed at all. In fact, she stood between Jacob and us. She put her hand over his eyes and the shaking stopped. The red faded from his eyes. He stumbled before Azazeal caught him.

"Sorry you had to see that ..." Azazeal trailed off.

She supported him toward a room a little further down the hall. They stumbled in, but Azazeal gave us a look as she passed through the door. She looked sad. The door closed quietly behind them. Mia collapsed to her knees in shock. Yin leaned on the wall. I couldn't move at all. I just stood trembling in fear.

"You guys must have seen a ghost," a voice said.

I snapped out of my fear-induced trance. I turned and looked back to see a smiling blond boy.

"I'm Light, you're Jonathan, right?" he asked, holding out his hand.

"Uh, yeah," I said, taking it.

He then turned and smiled at Yin and Mia. His grin literally lit up the room.

"You guys should catch some z's. I'm your roommate, Johnny Boy, so follow me," Light said.

I was still too dazed to argue with or question Light. Although Johnny Boy? What'd he call me that?

"Yeah," I managed, following behind him.

Yin and Mia had already gone into their shared room, so I wasn't worried about them. I thought of Sara for a moment, but she was safe with Lia, I hoped. Light was walking in front of me before he suddenly stopped next to one of the rooms. He looked back at me and smiled. Suddenly he vanished in a flash of gold light. I went over to the door. "Jonathan/Light," it read. I opened the door to reveal a pretty small room. There was only one other room that lead to a bathroom. A set bunk beds seemed to be where we would stay, and Light was fast asleep on the top bunk, like he had been sleeping for a long time. In fact, the room was completely pitch black. The only reason I could see was because I had multiplied my vision by two. I took off my cloak and shirt. I can't normally sleep in a bed with a shirt on. That incident at my apartment was a special case. Boots and socks were off next. I sat in the bed and closed my eyes. I forgot to turn off my vision so I could just barely see through my eyelids. I could also see Light, but not his body. Just the light itself floating in the bed above me.

*"Is he real?"* I asked myself.

Although the question fell on deaf ears. Of course it was asked in my own mind.

*"I'm not deaf ears, Johnny Boy,"* a voice said in the back of my head.

*"Shut it, you,"* I thought.

The voice didn't respond, making me feel less insane, though I knew the reason the voice had come on and who it belonged to.

"Good night, Light," I said, forgetting about that.

"Good night, Light, huh? Sounds like a bad joke," Light responded.

I didn't think to ask how he heard me or responded. He was sound asleep for sure. It didn't seem that important to me though. Drifting off to sleep was a lot easier than usual though.

# CHAPTER 17

# $\mathcal{L}$ONELY

## *Azazeal*

I woke up in his arms. Same as always. Regardless of how he believed he felt, I could tell what he was thinking. If I left now he'd start having nightmares. Jacob's greatest fear was nothing you could easily inflict on him. There was no creature of the night that could terrify my love. His only fear was being lonely. The cure for that fear was me, an immortal archangel that would never leave his side. I looked up at his face. Jacob looked so still. Then, suddenly, he frowned. He began to shake lightly and his bare chest began to tense as if he was flexing. He held me tighter, trying to ease his pain. I winced slightly. His strength was greater than that of a normal human. To help him rest, I planted a light kiss on his lips. His facial expression relaxed, and he stopped shaking. My only job for now was to put the man I loved at ease. And I was darn good at it. Excuse the usage of darn, hard cursing wasn't really my thing. It wasn't really anyone's in this day and age. Nobody wanted to be seen as vulgar anymore. The idea had lost its cool edge. I nestled my head back into his chest. I might as well catch some sleep. I'd need it if the plan continued as it should tomorrow. What time was it anyway? Never mind. As long as I'm with him it doesn't matter.

★ ★ ★

## *Light*

It was finally morning. I'd left my main body asleep so it could recover. My soul clone, however, was just waiting around for the sun to rise. Since we were underground, I had to leave another clone of my soul on the surface so I could see the sun rise. The time zones in France were different from Australia, so my watch was wrong and I had always been too lazy to change it. I recalled the soul clone I had waiting above. It merged with the version of me that was awake. I then merged this clone with my real body. After that, I woke up. For real this time. I could feel the life forces of my allies through the walls. The only people awake were Jacob and Azazeal. They were also doing unmentionable things. I was glad I couldn't see their bodies clearly, just their aura moving close to one another. I tapped Johnny Boy on the face. He wouldn't wake up immediately, though, and I'd be gone when he did. There were some people I had to see. I passed through the door to the next room. Mia and Yin were cuddled together sleeping. Why didn't they have a bunk bed? Except they did. The top bunk was destroyed and its pieces were scattered across the floor. Whatever, it wasn't important. In the next room over, Lock and some other guy were sleeping on bunk beds. I tapped him on head and he woke up.

"Not cool man, I'm sleepin'," Lock said, yawning.

"We're going to go train as always. Should I get Rylen and Carl?" I asked.

"Aight, dog, but could ya let me wake up for a sec? Also, don't bother with those two," Lock replied, rubbing his eyes under the sunglasses he always wore.

"If you say so," I said before going invisible.

While Rylen was by far the strongest of us, Carl was close to the weakest. He was so self-centered, though, that he wanted no part of our plans. Rylen just didn't need us to have a chance at winning. Despite that, I didn't want to be seen by Lock's roommate. I also had to get Amy after I got Lock. We had some work to do if we ever wanted to be promoted.

"Alright, let's hit it," Lock said, getting out of the bed.

"Stand still," I commanded.

I reached out my hand and teleported Lock to the front of Amy's room. I then went through some walls before I arrived in the room. Amy, however, was already up.

"I've been waiting." She yawned, spinning the black marbles in her hands. "You are thirty-seven seconds late. Again. At least you're consistent with that."

"Sorry. I'll send you there," I replied.

"Alright, but forget about Rylen and Carl," Amy said, still yawning.

"Lock said the same thing, but are you sure? The more the merrier, right?" I pushed the idea forward.

"If you care about them that much then go ahead. Just send me now." Amy gave in.

I teleported her and Lock, who was outside the door, to the training room.

I didn't follow, however. I looked all around Outcast Corner until I found Rylen. She was up eating as usual. She wasn't capable of going to sleep, but eating replenished her energy faster than sleep would. While the dragon-girl couldn't fall asleep, she could be knocked unconscious. Though, according to her, that just bred awful nightmares. Regardless, she was chowing down on some raw meat when I appeared at the table. Her eyes lit up in surprise, but said nothing and continued to tear into the giant steak. I watched her and waited to pick my moment to speak. When it didn't seem to come, I tapped my finger against the table, but not impatiently.

"What ... do you want?" Rylen burped within her question.

"Do you want to come train with us?" I asked.

Rylen seemed to consider the idea. This was a first; she shot me down every other time I tried to ask her. Instead of answering, Rylen took a giant gulp from a nearby milk bottle. I waited patiently for her to answer me. When Rylen realized I wasn't going to just leave, she wiped her mouth and spoke.

"Why do you care if I'm any good in combat? Wouldn't it make it harder for you to get promoted anyway? I don't want to make it any harder for any of you," Rylen asked with her usual compassion.

Despite appearances, Rylen displayed some sort of affection for every person at Outcast Corner. She knew something about everyone and everyone knew her. It was just how she was.

"You're always looking out for everyone, but never take the time to better yourself. I'm just offering you the opportunity to do so," I pressed on despite her.

Rylen wasn't surprised by my explanation. In fact, she probably knew more about me than anyone else. The dragon-girl laughed before standing and quickly walking toward my side of the table. She planted a kiss on my cheek but took a nervous step back before I could do anything to return her affection. I resisted the urge to say something to her, but the words faded away as soon as I thought about them. In fact, I always had trouble talking to her. Rylen fidgeted in place before returning to her seat.

"Go, uh, s-see if Carl will train with you. I bet that's ... uh ... that's where you'll go next anyways," Rylen kinda stammered with a warm smile.

I was going to say something, but the words went away again. I nodded and stood. I was about to go, but I decided to do something different. I walked over to Rylen and planted a kiss, but not on her cheek. Our lips touched and the warmth that radiated over her body at all times washed over me. I pulled away and stood awkwardly above her. Rylen opened her mouth to say something, but I teleported to where I knew Carl was before she could. I was afraid of what she might say, but happy I managed to express my feelings for her in some way. The tingle and warmth of the kiss were fresh on both my mind and lips. I probably would have just relished in the memory for longer if Carl wasn't staring at me.

"What do you want, pretty boy?" Carl growled in his German accent.

The moonlight made his brown hair and blue eyes gleam. He had been where he always was, sitting on top of Outcast Corner. His bowl-cut caused his hair to fall across his eyes but that added to his intimidating demeanor. Being frightening, however, was his ability. He could force people to fear him, and he could feed off their fear for strength and sustenance. He'd told me once, though, that the power had a terrible side effect. He said he always had nightmares even if he only closed his eyes for a second too long.

"I … uh … wanted to know if you would come train with me and the gang?" I asked.

Carl narrowed his eyes and allowed his fear-charged magic to seep out of him. I instinctively took a step back but didn't teleport away.

"Leave me alone, spirit, or I'll scare you so bad you'll piss yourself."

His threat wasn't as empty as it may have seemed. There was no way to describe the visuals that Carl showed people when he was forcing his fear onto them. That didn't mean there weren't any.

"Are … are you sure?" I managed, despite the mounting terror.

Carl stood, but visions of red and black began to sneak into my vision as he did. Suddenly, the German dashed forward and was standing in front of me. He was barely five-ten, but his body was incredibly muscular. He reached his hand out and grabbed my head, forcing me to look him in the eyes as he shouted at me.

"Leave! Now!"

A whimper escaped my mouth as Carl thrust me onto my back. I scrambled to my feet and did as he asked. I teleported to the training room to avoid fighting. The room was cold and dark as always. When

I arrived, Lock and Amy were having a conversation about kitchen supplies.

"Do you use metal knifes or the plasma blade?" Lock asked.

"Metal knifes. I feel like having plasma burn through my food could give me some radiation induced disease," Amy replied.

"Same, metal knifes seem to be less dangerous," I added while gasping for air.

"Just me then?" Lock asked no one in particular.

"Yep, just you," Amy replied.

She looked in my direction suddenly and frowned.

"You got messed up by Carl, didn't you?" she asked.

"Let's get to work." I ignored her while laughing nervously.

"Frak yeah." Lock pulled off his black sunglasses.

Frak was a more PG solution to cursing. Something we'd come up with since we hung around with kids more often than not. His soulless black eyes were still kind of creepy. My color changing eyes weren't any better, though. Between the three of us, Amy was the most normal. She wasn't a demon or a spirit. Just a girl with false grail powers.

"Let's brawl," Lock said, snapping me out of my thoughts.

He rushed Amy first. She tossed the black marbles, scattering them across the room. Lock threw a punch, which came close to hitting Amy before she teleported away. She kicked Lock in the small of his back but wasn't able to follow up the attack because I sped in between them. I knocked down her second attack before planting a soul punch in her midsection. Soul punches don't do much exterior damage, but they wear away at your soul. They also have incredible knock back. Amy fell back, but she teleported before she could fall. I had neglected to remember where Lock was and when I turned around, his fist landed squarely with my jaw. It didn't help that I had a glass jaw as well. I dropped to a knee and tried to move, but Lock's paralysis stopped me in my tracks. I took a second shot from Lock, which sent me careening back. The paralysis wore off in midair, and I teleported to a safe spot in the room.

"Why do you hit so hard?" I gasped.

"Demons are way stronger than humans, Light," Lock said.

"Yeah, I noticed," I said, gripping my face.

Now I'd lost track of Amy, though. Seeing souls did me no good against a girl who could teleport. In fact, she was right next to me now. She planted a kick which would have knocked me out, but I managed to phase through it. After my slick dodge, I threw an uppercut from my crouching position at Amy. She teleported away before I could land the blow. I, however, moved at light speed to where she was. I then landed a strong left into her midsection. She gasped for air, but I showed no mercy. I followed up with another punch to her jaw. Amy was shocked, but teleported before I could hit her again. She, however, teleported right in front of Lock without her knowledge.

"You're wide open," Lock said before connecting a hard punch with Amy's temple.

She was knocked unconscious because of Lock's paralysis hitting a vital area. Now it was just me and him.

"Jus' you and me, Light," Lock said, cracking his knuckles.

"I was gonna say that," I responded.

I moved back at light speed a couple feet. We both had ranged attacks, but mine were faster and extremely effective. I created a ball of light in my palm. Lock clenched his fist, generating a purple-ish glow.

"You can't stop this," I said, aiming the orb his way.

"Don't look down on me, punk," Lock replied, cocking his fist back.

Lock fired first and I countered. Lock's attack was like a giant purple fist while mine was a golden energy orb. The collision and feedback were so intense I had to shield myself. I didn't, however, except Lock to jump right through the explosion. His shirt was burned off and his leather pants were tattered, but he was too close for me to dodge as phasing and teleporting took a second of preparation. He grabbed my head with his hand and slammed me into the cold, metal floor. It hurt way more than I could describe. Lock stood while releasing my now bleeding head from his grasp. He pulled a pair of sunglasses out of his pocket, which were somehow unscathed, and put them on.

"You lose, lil' Light," Lock said.

I blacked out after that.

## Amy

I was just surprised Lock was able to knock Light out in one shot. Of course, I wasn't any better, but he'd always been stronger than me.

"Wasn't that a little … excessive?" I asked Lock.

He looked at me and smiled.

"He'll live fo' sho'," Lock replied. "He's a spirit after all."

"It still surprises me that my two best friends are a spirit and a demon," I said, shaking my head in disbelief.

"Comes with the gig, girl," Lock said in reply.

"Yeah, but you two are so amazing and I'm so … not," I said, feeling sorry for myself.

"You're strong for a human, fo' sho'," Lock said.

He came over and offered me his hand. I took it and climbed to my feet. His hand was huge, and he was basically grabbing my wrist.

"Thanks, Lock," I said.

"No prob," Lock replied.

Light's body shone for a second before it disappeared. He then reappeared, healed and standing.

"Don't you know any restraint, Lock? My head hurts now." Light grabbed his head.

"You were asking for it, fo' sho'," Lock replied with a smile.

"Yeah, whatever." Light grinned as well.

Their rivalry over who was stronger was something to behold. The score was now Light twenty wins to Lock's twenty-one. I only had a measly three wins. Sometimes, it seemed as if they were fighting over something more than their rivalry. Regardless of my win total, I always smiled after these training fights. This way we could see how much we've grown. Light noticed my smile, and grinned right back at me. I felt my cheeks warm a little. This was odd because I was sure I didn't care for Light that way. I was really only attracted to other women for the most part. Light might have been the exception, though.

"Hey, Amy, you ok?" Light asked.

"Uh, yeah I'm fine!" I exclaimed.

"Okay, we should go to the cafe before all of Marguerite's cooking gets eaten," Light said.

"Fo' sho'," Lock agreed.

I felt the warmth of Light's ... well ... light surrounding me. Then I felt myself begin to move. This mode of transportation is more effective than my teleportation, but it still felt weird. I arrived in the cafe with my teammates to see the newbies were already up and eating.

## *Jonathan*

We ate in silence. It was awkward because I'd never met any of Jacob's allies. Jacob sat across from me and to his left Azazeal and his right some guy wearing a tuxedo and a plague doctor mask. He wasn't even eating either. Mia and Yin sat on my right and left around the round table. They still seemed in shock about last night. The man who I recognized as the drunk guy from the bar also sat at the table. He was, of course, wasted.

"Yin," Jacob began suddenly.

Yin was cutting a piece of sausage on her plate before Jacob said her name. When he did she cut right through the sausage, the plate, and stabbed the table.

"Oh … uh … yes?" Yin asked sounding nervous.

"Can you pass the salt?" Jacob asked.

"Oh, of course," Yin said, flustered.

She used her aura to float the salt across the table. Jacob grabbed it out of the air and handed it to the masked man. He pushed up the front of his Medico della Peste mask. I only caught a glimpse, but it looked like he had no facial features other than a grotesque mouth and incredibly shriveled skin. He then proceed to uncap the salt and eat, more like drink, the salt. His long tongue slid inside the bottle emptying its salty contents. After devouring it, the mask went back to hiding his freakish mouth and face.

"What's your name?" I asked without thinking.

"My name?" He began his eye holes glowed a bright white. "I have never had a name that can be spoken by mere mortals. I go by similes and metaphors. A name would perhaps be helpful, but I'm known best for my feats. I am the man who knows no death. The shadow that follows you down the alley. The monster that watches you sleep. The darkness that drags across the moon at night. The hound of death. I am the plague itself. You, however, can call me … Grim," Grim finished.

"That's not scary at all," Mia said sarcastically.

She was visibly shaking. This guy was on a whole other level of fright, even if everything he was saying was rather cliché. It still didn't scare me as much as Jacob.

"Did you have to monologue it?" Azazeal asked.

Grim didn't even as much as glance at her.

"It's, uh, nice to meet you, Grim," I managed.

"Likewise," he replied.

I needed something to distract me from the situation so I looked around. I glanced over at the motionless body of the drunk man. I noticed his bottle wasn't labeled, so I reached for it to see what kind of alcohol it was. That turned out to be a mistake. I didn't even see him move or feel myself fall. Suddenly I was on the floor with a knife to my throat, except the blade was coming out the tip of the man's boot.

"You try that again and I slit your throat, boy," the drunkard casually slurred.

"Yes, sir. Mister ... uh ..." I didn't know his name.

"It's Flyx to you, boy," Flyx said before retracting the blade and removing his brown boot form over me.

I climbed to my feet and back into my chair. Breakfast quickly escalated to a more frightening activity.

"I wouldn't mess with Flyx if I were you, Jonathan. Guy is so drunk the whole world moves in slow motion for him." The brown-haired girl I had seen before advised.

"Do we know you?" Yin asked.

Even though it sounded condescending, Yin's gaze seemed to show her interest in the girl. She kept looking at her up and down. The other girl noticed, but continued unmoved.

"Ow, my pride," the girl laughed, but seemed uneasy. "I'm Amy and this tough guy is Lock."

She gestured to the taller, dark-skinned man standing behind her. Lock only grunted in greeting.

"Lock has an inferiority complex. He has to assert his dominance at all times." Light, who I didn't notice due to his lack of presence, giggled uncontrollably.

"I don't have no sort of complex or nuttin' like that," Lock said, but he was smiling when he did.

The three of them seemed to mesh well together. They were so happy. Must be fun not being alone as often as I was. These past couple of days had been my first with other people in a while. Since I was trapped in my own thoughts the three of them just kinda stood there.

"We're just gonna go now," Amy said while smiling and backing away slowly.

"Uh, yeah, bye," I managed while snapping out of my thoughts.

My little group sat in silence while Jacob chatted about some kind of contract with Azazeal.

"We go tonight. Simple. It's that simple," Jacob said, getting fed up with Azazeal.

"But you won't tell me what we're doing! Is it an assassination contract? Are we taking down a demon portal? I'm dying to know!" Azazeal asked, continuing to pester Jacob.

"I'll tell you after breakfast." Jacob waved his hand dismissively.

That did remind of something Jacob said before.

"What exactly do you want us to do?" I asked.

"I'll tell you after I eat." Jacob scooped a spoon of oatmeal into his mouth.

"My turn." Azazeal opened her mouth.

Jacob casually shoved a spoonful into her mouth. Azazeal swallowed it but shuddered afterward.

"I hate oatmeal." Azazeal pouted.

Jacob shoved another spoonful into her mouth to spite her.

"You have to eat it," Jacob said bluntly.

"Yeah, I know," Azazeal replied through her stuffed mouth.

"If you don't mind me asking," Mia began, "what kind of relationship are you in?"

"We're obviously lovers." Azazeal giggled, snuggling up against Jacob.

Jacob allowed her to do so as if he was either used to it or didn't mind.

"It's a little more complex than that," Jacob responded.

"How so?" Yin asked.

"To do our fusion it requires us to be as in sync with each other and as close to each other as possible," Jacob explained.

"Fusion?" I asked, intrigued. "What like combining into one person?"

"Precisely," Jacob replied.

The conversation continued as Mia, Yin, and I asked Jacob and Azazeal about their fusion. Grim had already left and the lunch room was emptying out quickly as well. The fusion technique really left no room for slacking. One little mistake and the fusion could fail when you needed it most. Not to mention one really odd rule.

"You have to have sex?" Mia asked in disbelief.

"Once a week," Jacob replied.

"It's really not that big a deal," Azazeal said, confused due to Mia's surprise.

"Well, like … What's the reason for it?" Mia asked.

"It promotes two people temporarily becoming one," Jacob explained.

"Even still …" Yin said, muttering something behind it.

"What was that, Yin? I didn't hear what you said," I asked.

"Ah … uh … it's nothing." Yin said, dodging my question.

We sat awkwardly for a couple more seconds.

"Hey, it's Sara!" Yin exclaimed, attempting to avert everyone's attention.

"It's been awhile," Sara said, smiling.

It was Sara and she was returning with Grim and Lia. There was something different about her, though. She was taller and less childlike. She still looked like a child, but not like a six year old.

"What happened to you?" I asked, confused.

"…aged me," Sara replied with alarming clarity.

Who did what? Did she mean to say Grim? I couldn't understand what she had said before.

"Aged you?" I questioned, ignoring the strange words I'd heard.

"…power is decay. He can make anything age as much as he wants," Lia explained.

There it was again. The sounds were the same, but I couldn't even sound them out.

"There are negative repercussions, however," Jacob suddenly said. "For every six years aged, a human soul must be sacrificed. So tell me … whose soul did you use?" Jacob finished.

Where he'd planned to say Grim's name some other language I couldn't understand came out. I tried to repeat it, but I just wasn't capable of making those sounds.

"One of the souls I keep on me," Grim said without much explanation.

"Then it's fine," Jacob said, going back to sharing his cold oatmeal with Azazeal.

"Why do you keep souls with you?" Yin asked, reasonably shocked.

"So I can use them for things such as this," Grim replied bluntly.

Though I could hardly see his eyes, it looked as if he seemed annoyed by Yin's question. As if the answer should've been obvious.

"How do you acquire souls, exactly?" I asked, though I didn't really want to know the answer.

"I tear them from the lifeless corpses of beings I have slain. The souls call out to me when they lose their body," Grim explained.

It was more so frightening that his voice did not change or waver during that. It made me think he'd already told someone this before. In the same way as well.

"That's a happy thought," I replied, chilled.

"It shouldn't be. There's nothing good or happy about what I do," Grim replied.

"Sarcasm," I replied quickly, hoping I didn't upset him.

"Ah, I see." Grim said as he turned and walked off.

"I can't figure that guy out," Yin said, seeming emotionally drained by the conversation.

She put her head down on the table in her arms.

"I think he's nice deep down," Sara said with a smile.

"Don't kid yourself, kid," Lia replied.

She immediately began to laugh, fully aware of her little joke. Azazeal waited for her to calm down before speaking through spoonfuls of cold oatmeal.

"Yeah, don't bother. He's a nobody like the rest of us."

"What do you mean us?" Sara asked.

"Our little organization. You know? The Black King's Outcasts," Azazeal replied, playfully stressing the last part.

"Who's the Black King?" Mia asked.

"That would be me, again," Jacob began, finally done eating his oatmeal. "The King's Court is a newly established world army force. I have no idea how none of you have heard of it, but maybe news has managed to travel slower despite new technology."

Jacob stopped and glared at all of us. He was insinuating our stupidity, but didn't mention it. He then continued as if he'd never stopped.

"Regardless, we specialize in exterminating magical enemies that threaten humanity's survival. There's a king for the original five colors of the rainbow and the colors white and black. The color aligns with their strongest elemental ability," Jacob finished.

"I thought you didn't have an ability?" I chimed in.

"You would be correct in thinking that," Jacob answered.

"So what's your element then?" I asked.

"Void magic."

"Never heard of it," Mia said.

"This is the most effective way to display it," Jacob said.

He aimed his hand in a claw like position at the empty bowl of oatmeal. A black aura surrounded Jacob's hand and then transferred to the bowl. The black aura swallowed the bowl and it vanished. Jacob then pointed his hand toward the sink. The bowl reappeared from a black cloud to the sink.

"That is so cool!" Mia said in glee.

"Wait, didn't you only gain double your normal human ability from the Holy Grail?" I asked in surprise.

"It's holder magic," Jacob said, gesturing to one of the two rings on his finger.

"What's holder magic?" Mia asked, confused.

"How are you so clueless?" Lia sighed, shaking her head.

"Even I know this one," Sara said, giggling.

"Sh-shut up!" Mia yelled, but the two witches just laughed.

"Some people don't have natural magic ability, so they use items to work as an amplifier for their magic power," Jacob explained.

"So what's the other ring for?" Yin said, referring to the shiny ruby ring.

"It's our wedding ring," Azazeal interjected, pointing to the similar ring on her finger.

"Does that mean you have to be married for the fusion to work?" Sara asked.

"It's not necessary, but the closer the bond between us the better," Azazeal said with an odd smile.

"I don't quite understand it myself, but Azazeal said it would help," Jacob added.

I had almost forgotten. Jacob, even with his binding relationship, didn't really feel much of anything. What a sad situation to be in, especially for Azazeal.

"Enough about us. I have a job for all of you," Jacob said, snapping me out of my thoughts.

"You mentioned a job earlier ... what is it?" I asked.

"It's an assassination," Jacob said while standing up.

Assassination? It better not be an innocent person.

"You're going after the previous Blue King. A man named Xavier Vaughn. Although you might know him as the Yeti," Jacob explained.

"Do you mean the walking tank that captured China all by himself for Russia during World War Three?" I asked, recognizing the nickname.

"That's the same man, indeed," Jacob replied.

"So, if he's the previous Blue King why are we after him?" Sara asked.

"The king's order was established thirty years ago. New kings were only appointed a couple months ago. It used to be a shadow organization, but we've recently gone public. Though everyone on the original King's court was forced to leave due to age. The Yeti, however, didn't leave without wanting something. Xavier is after the new Blue King's head. She is the one who replaced him, after all," Jacob explained.

"So we're tasked with defending the new Blue King and killing the old one? Also the new Blue King is a she?" Mia asked.

"It's more complicated than that, and yes she is. The title remains king regardless of gender," Jacob replied.

He waved his hand and the room became consumed in darkness. I couldn't see anyone else at all. I held my hand in front of my face, but I couldn't even see its outline.

"What's going on?" Yin asked, but not to anyone particular.

There was no answer for a moment, instilling a small sort of fear in my throat. I swallowed and took a deep breath as Jacob began to answer her.

"I'm moving us."

"Where?" I asked in the darkness.

The darkness began to fade as I asked my question. When it did, Mia, Yin, Sara, Azazeal, Lia, and I were all standing behind Jacob who was sitting. Jacob was resting his chin on his fist, in front of a round table with six people other than himself.

"Welcome to Kings Court," Jacob said.

# CHAPTER 18

# WEAK

"I can't believe you brought all these people here," one of the members of the court sighed.

His voice was booming with a rough American accent. He shook his head disapprovingly. I looked at him, but his face was hidden by a violet domino mask that covered all of his face excluding his mouth. His violet hair was the only thing I could distinguish from the others. The other kings had similar masks, but with their respective color. Even Jacob wore a black mask.

"Don't fret, Viper. We need them to solve our … problem," the man in a red mask said.

"I know, but don't you think we could kill him ourselves?" Viper sounded bothered by our presence. "What do you think, Guardian?"

"Both my brothers are a necessity if this job is to succeed," the king with the green mask spoke.

Guardian waved an arm that looked like it was made of vines and tree branches dismissively before averting his gaze toward some far corner of the room. What did he mean by brothers? I thought for a moment before realizing Guardian's identity. I tried to speak, but the words were blocked and the sound was sucked from the air. Trying harder to speak burned my throat.

"Those who aren't kings cannot speak," Light, who was wearing the yellow domino mask, said.

Even though he spoke to me, Light made a shushing motion with his index finger. His smile and voice alerted me to who was behind the mask. Not to mention his bright yellow hair. Why did I know so many of the kings? Three out of the seven kings were people I had met before.

"I ... don't need to be a king," I managed despite my throat burning from the effort.

The kings, however, didn't seem surprised.

"Your youngest brother has some skill, Guardian. Still, overpowering a speaking barrier spell isn't an amazing feat. Although, might be at a run for your spot, Dust," Viper grumbled, looking at the white domino mask wearing king.

Dust glanced at me and cocked his head slightly. I looked him over as well. He looked almost like a child. His gray eyes were visible through the mask, but he was also very small, just over five feet tall. We both analyzed each other before Dust looked back at Viper and grinned.

"If he works for it, he can have it." Dust crossed his arms in defiance.

He didn't really seemed bothered with the idea of me threatening his position. I didn't know if I wanted his position. I didn't even know if I could fill the requirement for being the white king. That domino mask did look cool, though.

"Speak if you wish," the man in the red mask said.

Talking still burned my throat. I opened my mouth, but the burning intensified. I, however, fought through it.

"What, exactly, do you want us to do?" I managed.

I wanted to ask if Guardian was Jackson, but the mission was a more pressing matter. Especially since it shouldn't be too hard to ask later.

"Kill my father. That is your mission," the female king in the blue mask said.

Her father? So Xavier was her dad, huh? More importantly, was she okay with her father's death being on her hands?

"Can you easily cast away your father like that?" I asked aggressively.

I would have enjoyed the luxury of having a father who loved me. Not a father who wanted to use me in his experiments. Even though I essentially was an experiment... Whatever, that's besides the point.

"Outcast, make your brother hold his tongue," the Blue King said.

"I have no power over him," Jacob replied.

"Then I'll cut out his tongue," the Blue King said.

A large spike made of water began to form above her. Then it suddenly began to bubble before evaporating into the air.

"Calm yourself, Aqua. Your hostility is unwarranted," the red king said.

"Don't get in my way, Nova. I'll crush you if I have to," Aqua raged, throwing multiple water spikes at him.

"Don't get mad," Nova replied as the water evaporated before it could hit him.

Even through the domino mask you could tell Nova's eyes were ablaze. He was clearly strong, but also scary—mostly because I couldn't figure out his ability. It looked like something akin to spontaneous combustion, but he was able to melt water so easily it couldn't have been that.

"Regardless of family matters, you'll be sent on your mission in the next three hours," a clearly irritated Aqua said, snapping me out of my thoughts.

"Take care of this, Outcast. Don't make me have to clean up your mess," Viper said.

"Of course," Jacob responded.

He stood and the room began to get dark. Suddenly we were back in the cafeteria at the bottom of Outcast Corner. The jump seemed faster this time.

"Get your gear. We leave in twenty minutes," Jacob said.

"Don't we have three hours before we need to go?" Sara asked.

"Won't be necessary," Jacob replied bluntly.

"How many people are going?"

"Yin, Jonathan, Mia, Sara, Azazeal, me, and three combat elites that I recruited," Jacob replied.

"Isn't that overkill?" Mia asked.

"Not for Xavier. He's seven feet of muscle. His magic is stronger than all of ours combined. The only weakness he has is his slow movement speed," Jacob responded.

The Yeti was a terrifyingly powerful man.

"If that's the case, shouldn't we bring more people?" Yin asked.

"I would if I could, but there are more important things that they have to do," Jacob replied.

"Everyone has been talking about other things or more important things even. What exactly is going on?" I asked, getting frustrated.

"A gate to Hell is open and we can't close it," Azazeal replied.

"Every one of my resources are tied up holding the demons back and finding a way to close the gate. Although, some people have been calling them rifts as an easier way to identify them," Jacob said.

I was too stunned to speak. A demonic gate to Hell? Nothing surprises me anymore, but this was a little much. I mean, I've fought sand surfers with laser guns and that was still more believable than this.

"Where is it?" Sara asked, completely unfazed.

"The catacombs," Azazeal replied.

"That series of tunnels underneath Paris or something else which has the same name?" I asked.

"The former, but that's all the time I have to spend on the matter," Jacob replied.

He walked off with Azazeal hovering behind him.

"Get ready to leave," I said, turning toward the hallway where our rooms were.

We walked in an awkward silence. Trying to push the idea of other-worldly demons out of our heads wasn't easy. We did, however, have a job to do. I pushed into my room, which was closer than the others. I closed the door behind me and turned on the light. When I did I saw Light napping in the top bunk. For some reason he didn't look peaceful. It was like he seemed very agitated about something. I had other things to worry about. I grabbed my Desert Falcon from the bag I had under my bunk and sheathed the katanas, Sunrise and Nightfall, into my utility belt. The golden gun went in my leg holster. That was all I needed. On my way out I heard Light move. I turned to see him sitting up on the bed.

"Don't die. I'd miss having a roomie," Light said before fading into a flash of bright light.

"I'll try not to," I said to the now empty room.

I opened the door quickly, but closed it slowly. Even though Light wasn't sleeping anymore it seemed like the right thing to do. When I looked down the hall, Jacob was standing by the elevator with Azazeal and three others. I didn't approach them yet. I wanted to wait for my group. Then I heard the sound of tiny feet behind me. Even though she was twelve now, she was still small. I turned to her. The green shirt and skirt were the same, but longer to fit her older body.

"I'm ready to go," Sara said, bursting with energy.

Mia and Yin came out of the room they shared. Yin had tied her hair into a ponytail and was wearing a black and white jogging suit. Mia hadn't changed except her shirt color was now black.

"That's everyone," Yin said.

"Let's go." I led the way down the hall.

The first of the three men greeted me when we made our way down the hall.

"Bonjour, I am Pierre." Pierre held out his hand.

I shook the French man's hand, which was rough and scabbed over. He was clearly older than me but at least three inches shorter.

"This is Roméo and Violette." Pierre gestured to his companions.

Roméo stepped forward and held out his hand. I shook it and said, "Hello." He, however, didn't say anything. The way he moved was kind of creepy as well. It was sort of a hunched, heavy stepping-walking, as if his back was injured. What made it stranger was he made no noise while doing so. His face was wrapped in bandages that only allowed me to see one of his eyes.

"Don't mind him," Pierre said while combing his hair.

"It's a pleasure to meet you, Monsieur Cain," Violette spoke.

"Likewise," I replied simply.

I reached out my hand, but she took a step back, afraid.

"Sorry, hands have about 352,000 distinct bacteria on them. I'd rather not chance getting sick," she said with a friendly smile.

"That's fair, I guess," I said, taken aback by the number she listed so eloquently.

"Let me introduce you to myself and—"

"We know who you and your friends are, Monsieur Cain," Pierre interrupted. "To us this is just another mission."

I blinked once, feeling sort of neglected as Jacob walked between us.

"Okay then, let's move," Jacob said.

We didn't take the elevator up. The room grew dark like the last time Jacob used void magic. It was not an all-encompassing darkness and took far longer than before.

"Where is Mr. Vaughn hiding?" Sara asked Jacob.

"Plain sight," Jacob replied.

It took around ten minutes for us to arrive at our destination. We appeared in the snow about half a mile from a giant mansion. "Vaughn Estate," a sign near us read. I immediately felt the chill of wind. We seemed to have arrived in the middle of a blizzard.

"It's so cold." Yin gripped her arms.

"I don't feel it," Mia responded.

"Nor do I," Azazeal added.

"It's because you guys aren't normal!" Yin complained loudly.

"Quiet," Jacob interjected.

"He'll be ready for us whether we flank around or not," Pierre explained, combing his hair again.

"Sometimes the front entrance is the best," I offered.

"I say front entrance. The front door is cleaned more so than the back or side entrances," Violette agreed.

"Frontal assault? Really?" Yin asked, sounding skeptical.

"Why not?" Mia seemed annoyed with the delay.

"Fine, let's do this." Yin sighed, finally getting behind the idea.

*Strength multiplication times two*

*Speed multiplication times three*

"I'll bust through the front door and we'll flood in," I said.

"I'll follow your lead if you think that'll work." Jacob grabbed his gun.

The weapon almost looked demonic, but I knew nothing about it. I ignored it for the time being and started charging the door at a full sprint. The snow made it hard to gain speed, but my multiplications gave me enough strength to get through it. Right when I reached the door, it opened before I could hit it. I couldn't stop running and I was clotheslined by a large, powerful arm. It hurt. A lot. I flipped through the air, moving deeper into the house before I crashed into the stairs. I was dazed and upside down, but I saw a large, pale, bearded man. He had so much hair on his head and face I understood why he was called the Yeti. I groaned, my mouth full of blood. I spit it to the side and righted myself. He hit harder than Gene, though that could've just been because of my own momentum. My ears were ringing and my head pounded, but I could see our group come through the front door.

"Jonathan!" I heard someone shout.

I managed to prop myself up using the handrail for the stairs. My jaw was definitely dislocated. I first put my thumbs inside my mouth on my lower back teeth then placed my other fingers around the bottom of the lower jaw. Despite the pain, I pressed down on my back teeth and pushed my chin up until I felt and heard my jaw pop back into place.

*Pain resistance times three*

The pain from fixing my jaw and my bleeding wounds diminished. Though I couldn't use this one too much, losing the feeling of pain entirely wouldn't be very good.

"I'm fine," I managed.

Xavier raised an eyebrow at me. He didn't look surprised but more so intrigued.

"I admire your will to fight. You would have made a great king in my court," the Yeti spoke with a booming voice.

I didn't respond. The others were trying to find a way around him, but Xavier was standing in front of me. His shirtless body made me wonder how he wasn't cold. Then I noticed his many scars and the stream of icy mist coming from them. It looked sort of like he was a piece of dry ice himself. I would have gazed more at his rippling muscles—it's impressive, don't judge me—but Pierre suddenly formed a bow and arrow out of thin air.

"Prepare to die, Yeti," Pierre spat.

He fired some arrows, which Xavier deflected with an ice wall. Pierre rolled to the side and shot around the wall, but Xavier caught the arrow in his icy grasp. It froze in his palm and he crushed it.

"I see, you're here to kill me" Xavier said.

The rest of our group scattered to the sides of the room, surrounding Xavier. He looked to the left and the right, but did not look bothered.

"Come try and kill me then." Xavier laughed.

Xavier threw the pieces of arrow in his hand at Pierre. He easily sidestepped them, but a spike made of ice jutted up from the ground where they had landed and broke apart. Pierre didn't move in time and the sharp ice impaled him. Pierre gasped and gripped at the block before slumping lifelessly on the spike. His bow fell to the ground and snapped in half on impact. His blood seeped out of his body causing the ice spike to sparkle red.

"Pierre, no!" Violette muttered quietly.

"Come, meet your fate," Xavier said, cracking his knuckles.

This was bad. Pierre was dead before we could even scratch Xavier. My legs still shook which kept me from moving at the moment. Is this the power of a king?

"We need to get to a room that isn't covered in ice!" Jacob commanded. "Go up the stairs!"

He was right. There was ice all over the place. I struggled to move further up the stairs, but I started to fall forward. Then I felt someone's arm around my chest. I glanced behind my shoulder to see an armored figure.

"Don't show weakness now," Yin said, pulling me with her up the stairs.

Mia, Azazeal, and Jacob came running behind us.

"We'll hold him off here," Violette said, standing at the foot of the stairs.

Mia stopped and turned but didn't say anything.

"Let's go, Mia!" Sara yelled, running past her.

Mia clenched her fist before running with us toward another room in the mansion. I'd recovered enough to not need Yin's support, though walking did shock my legs every so often. The hallway we entered had a singular door at the end of it. We raced to it, occasionally slipping or losing traction on the icy floors.

"Hey, Mia, they know what they're doing," Sara said suddenly.

"Yeah, but we …" Mia trailed off.

"You can't save everyone," Azazeal interjected.

When we finally reached the door, the conversation had died. I opened the door with extreme caution. I didn't want to get ragdolled again. The room we entered was like a ballroom, except it was also covered in ice.

"This will do," Jacob said.

"But it's covered in ice," Mia pointed out.

"Then let's melt it," Sara responded.

Mia smiled and cracked her knuckles. "Sounds like fun."

Those of us without fire sat outside of the room while it thawed.

"This is less fun than I thought," Mia complained as she stood holding out her hand.

It wasn't taking much to melt the ice and the two girls' fire was easily strong enough to evaporate the water. Sara seemed to be able to sustain a steady flame easily. At least, easier than when she was six years old. Jacob was crouched, staring down the hall. Suddenly, the whole mansion shook. The shaking was followed by multiple loud booming sounds.

"How long do you think they'll last?" I asked Jacob.

Right when I asked, the explosion sounds and shaking stopped.

"It's already over," Jacob replied standing from his crouched position.

"So ... what?" I asked.

"Violette is probably dead. Roméo will make his way here in, maybe fifteen seconds, give or take," Jacob replied.

"Does nothing faze you?" Jacob's disregard for human life upset me.

"What did you expect?" Azazeal answered my question with a question.

"I just think—"

Jacob cut me off. "Grow up." There was no emotion behind his words. "People die and life goes on."

"Speaking of dead people ..." Azazeal pointed out.

Roméo came down the hall with Violette on his shoulder. There was a trail of blood behind him as he walked, but it didn't seem like his. Violette had a hole in her stomach lower than the wound that had killed Pierre.

"You were right ..." I managed, frustrated.

"Rarely am I wrong," Jacob replied.

When Roméo reached us I could see the wounds on his body. His bandages were in shreds and blood seeped from the cuts on his battered chest, though it didn't spread very far.

"She's dead, right?" Jacob asked.

Roméo walked past Jacob and leaned Violette's corpse against the wall. Her brown hair fell in front of her dilated eyes.

"Indeed," Roméo spoke quietly.

"The room's thawed …" Mia started but trailed off when she saw Violette's body.

Sara appeared beside Mia. "Is she …"

"Dead? Yes," Azazeal answered.

"Let's get in the room and close the door. Xavier will be here soon," Jacob commanded.

"We can't leave her out here!" Mia suddenly shouted.

The hallway was set ablaze. The ice on the floor melted into water and quickly put the flames out.

"What do you want to do, Mia?" Yin asked. "She's already dead."

"Fine. Just forget about it," Mia muttered.

She walked past the rest of us, leaving a trail of flames behind her.

"I worry if this is something she should be doing," I said to no one in particular.

"What's that mean?" Yin asked confused.

"You know, killing people. Watching people die. At first I thought she was perfectly capable, but I've never seen her kill a human before," I replied.

"I'll be sure to talk to her when we make it back." Azazeal made sure to emphasize *when*.

With that everyone moved into the ballroom, the door was shut behind us. I got Sunrise out and aimed the blade at the door. It shined brightly, prepared to fire. We heard a loud crash from another part of the mansion.

"He's free," Roméo spoke quietly once again.

"Free of what?" I asked while shifting my footing nervously.

"The nightmare I trapped him in," Roméo replied.

"What kind of magic is that?" Mia asked.

"Fear magic," Roméo explained.

"Projections that trap people inside their own mind. It only works once per day, though," Jacob cut in.

Then there was a bang on the door. After that … silence.

"What now?" Sara asked.

"Duck!" Jacob shouted.

We all complied and for good reason. Several ice spikes broke through the big door. Nobody was hit, but everyone was near a spike.

"Move away!" Azazeal yelled.

Out from the big spikes came smaller spikes shooting out of them. I heard a cry of pain from someone, but I couldn't tell who it was. An ice spike sunk into my arm, but I didn't feel it. My pain resistance was still activated. I turned and looked for Sunrise which was a couple feet away. I scooped it up and turned around.

"Is everyone alright?" I shouted.

No reply. Everyone couldn't be dead so I waited for a response.

"Somebody help! Please!" I heard Mia cry out.

*Strength multiplication times five*

I ripped the bloody ice spike from my arm and stood. There was ice all over the room. I looked in the direction I'd heard Mia, but of course it was covered with ice. Well, not for long.

"Hang on!" I shouted.

I bashed through the ice spikes toward the sound of Mia's cries. I kicked through the last block to find Yin crouched over Mia, who was pinned to the floor. I looked over Yin's shoulder at Mia. Her arm was frozen up to the shoulder and there was a large spike stabbing in her hand. Mia turned and struggled but couldn't move.

"This is bad," Yin said.

"Can't we just melt her arm out?" I asked.

"This magic ice seems to merge with the affected person's body. If we melt it, her arm will melt too," Yin explained grimly.

"Wha-what sh-should we do?" Mia managed, distressed.

"We have to kill Xavier before frostbite kicks in and Mia loses her arm." Yin explained.

"How long until then?" I asked.

"Five minutes. Give or take. That ice is way colder than normal ice." Jacob cocked his gun, though it seemed unnecessary since the gun had no magazine. I also hadn't noticed until then that he wasn't anywhere near us.

"Sounds manageable," Sara chimed in, appearing out of nowhere.

"Get ready, he's coming." Jacob was standing in the rafters with Azazeal.

"Where are you?" Xavier asked.

I could see Xavier from where we were, but he couldn't see us. Yin stood and her gold armor flashed in the light. She summoned her lance and drew her arm back. A familiar blue aura consumed her body.

"I'll get him with this," Yin said confidently.

Just as she flung the lance, Xavier turned our way. The glowing weapon cut through the ice toward Xavier. When it reached him he caught it.

"How did he ..." Yin trailed off in shock.

Xavier smirked before tightening his grip. The lance was turned into a block of ice and shattered.

"You'll have to do better than that," Xavier said.

"Here's better," Jacob responded, firing his demon gun at the Yeti.

Xavier threw up an ice shield in time, but it didn't cover his entire body. A couple of the bullets made contact with non-vital spots on his body, causing him to grunt in pain. The rest were deflected by the shield.

"Congrats, you damaged me." Xavier cracked his neck in annoyance.

Xavier raised his hand and fired an ice blast at Jacob. They weren't spikes this time, but large, brick-like blocks of ice. He calmly shot them out of the air without flinching. The tiny shards of ice flew past us and hit the wall.

"Next please," Jacob said, aiming his demon pistol.

"You fool," Xavier replied.

The tiny shards of ice shot out and surrounded Jacob, covering his body just below his shoulders in ice.

"Miscalculation ..." was all Jacob said.

I aimed Sunrise at Xavier, who looked my way at the same time. I noticed Azazeal flying stealthy above with her black rapier. I nodded to her and she winked at me. I'd attack directly and Azazeal would attack from above. Hopefully the Yeti couldn't defend against both of our attacks.

"Eat this!" I shouted, firing the light beam at Xavier.

Xavier created a block of ice that doubled as a mirror. I knew what was going to happen, but it was too late for me to stop my attack. The light beam was reflected upward and caught Azazeal, going into and through her shoulder. She cried out in pain and fell to the ground in a bundle of scorched feathers. Xavier, in his moment of triumph, failed to notice Yin and Roméo approaching from his side. Yin jumped in the air and slashed down at Xavier. The blade connected with his shoulder and drew blood, but it didn't appear to faze him. Xavier grabbed Yin by the head and slammed her down into the ground. Roméo, however, capitalized on Xavier's half-crouched position and brought his knee to the Yeti's head. Xavier stumbled back into a wall. Roméo threw a punch, which Xavier batted away. Xavier hooked Roméo in the stomach, but didn't stop there. Ice shot from his hand impaling Roméo. Roméo cried out in pain, but his assault didn't let up. He broke the shard protruding from his back in half and stabbed Xavier in the shoulder with the sharp end. Xavier cried out in pain before Roméo kicked him deep into the wall and began to wail on him. The blows came in an endless stream. Roméo's body emitted a red aura. I wondered if that was what was identified as fear magic. Suddenly I heard a groaning sound and realized Yin was lying close to the epic fight. I ran over and dragged her body back to the safety of the ice wall. Her helmet had cracked open and the back plate of her armor was shattered.

"Did we get him?" Yin asked, slurring her words.

"Not yet," I replied.

Yin and I watched as Roméo continued to lay into Xavier. Then, seemingly effortlessly, Xavier caught one of Roméo's punches. Blood spilled from his mouth as he climbed out of his hole slowly.

"Die, you disgrace of a king's guard," Xavier spat.

He froze Roméo's arm up to the shoulder. Then he chopped down ward and cut it off. Roméo watched as his arm was removed from his body but didn't react at all. Xavier then kicked Roméo back, sending him crashing through the ice wall. Those of us who weren't injured or frozen watched his body roll behind us. For some reason I didn't want to run to him. I felt it. Just a little. I felt scared of Xavier.

"Roméo! Are you alright?" I called instead.

He didn't reply but pushed himself up with his remaining arm. The red aura surrounding his body was waning, but still there. Xavier stepped through the hole of ice shards. His face and body were bloody, but he seemed to have already recovered. Without hesitation, Sara launched a fireball at the Yeti. The flame ball was meet with an ice shard, turning it into steam. This process repeated, but it was clear this was a losing battle.

"A little help!" Sara called, struggling.

I aimed and fired Sunrise at Xavier, who immediately reflected it back at me.

*Skin durability times ten*

I was running low on magic, but I had enough to do a large multiplication. The blast from Sunrise hit me in the center of my chest. It burned like crazy, but it didn't break a layer of skin.

"Darn it, that hurt." I rolled around in pain.

"This isn't good." I heard a still disoriented Yin say.

I looked around to see Sara who was now an ice statue. She looked surprised as if when she got hit it was completely unexpected. With that and Roméo down we were in a pickle. This was getting too far out of hand. Xavier then turned toward Yin and me, who were both in no condition to move.

"Can't move," I heard Yin say lazily.

I saw Xavier raise his hand, and I moved my body to shield Yin. Then all I felt was cold.

# CHAPTER 19

# RAGE

## Mia

I watched in horror as all my friends were frozen. I felt too weak, so powerless. Roméo and I were the only people in fighting order now, it seemed. My arm wasn't more important to me than friends' lives, right? I stared at the frozen limb. It made me so angry.

"Ah, screw it." I said aloud to nobody.

I reached over and grabbed my arm just below the shoulder. I hesitated. Then I heard a groaning sound. I looked over, straining my neck, and saw Yin climbing out from under Jonathan's frozen body. She crawled over to me and turned herself over. She sat up as blood trickled down her face. She said nothing, simply gasping for air instead.

"Hey, Yin?" I began, wanting to be sure she was listening.

"What?" she asked, dazed.

"If I die, it's been fun."

Before she could answer I reached over and melted through my arm. It didn't hurt thanks to it being frozen and all. I shot up and bolted toward Xavier. I didn't have a plan. I just thought I'd hit him really hard. My right, dominant arm was gone, though. Hopefully I could throw a good punch with my left. I set my only arm on fire and punched.

Xavier made an ice shield to block my attack.

"Screw you!" I shouted when I made contact.

I punched right through the shield and connected with his jaw. I did damage for sure as he reeled back and looked at me angrily. The Yeti, however, didn't make a motion for retaliation. Suddenly, I felt a large hand on my head. I turned to look up and see a one-armed Roméo.

"It's up to you now," Roméo said.

The red aura around his body faded, but as it did, I felt power surge within me.

"What are you—"

Roméo rushed past me. He threw a punch, which Xavier batted downward. Xavier formed a sword out of ice and jabbed it into and through Roméo's midsection.

"See you in Hell," Roméo literally spat into Xavier's face.

He ripped the ice blade out of his stomach and smashed it into Xavier. The slash was at his throat and had a chance to kill the Yeti. The blade, however, snapped against Xavier's skin. The snapping sound was akin to that of a bone, which made me sick.

"You'll be going alone," Xavier said with a smirk.

He froze Roméo's entire body and then shattered it into pieces before I could move.

"Why do you heroes sit and watch your friends die. Like, move or something," Xavier said, wiping the blood from his face.

I wanted to kill him. I'd never wanted to kill someone so badly in my life. I let the fire that I had kept on my left side, so I wouldn't thaw out my shoulder, consume me.

"You'll bleed out if that ice melts," Xavier pointed out.

He was right. But even so ...

"I don't care!" I shouted in reply.

"Excuse me?" Xavier asked in surprise.

"Living means nothing if everyone you know and love dies!"

I used more magic and shot more fire than I ever had before. Xavier made a shield of ice to protect himself, but it didn't last long.

"Impossible ..." Xavier managed as I burned through his shield.

Then I stopped. The fire stopped shooting. I'd used all my magic at once. I dropped to a knee. I felt warmth that wasn't fire coming from the stump that was once my arm. I was bleeding.

"Did I fail?" I asked myself in shame and agony.

The pain was horrible. I managed to remain on one knee and looked at Xavier through blurry eyes.

"Well done," Xavier said, cutting into my self-pity.

I looked up to see his battered body. His skin was charred black. I couldn't believe he was still alive.

"How did it turn out like this? Where did everything change? Why be evil now if you were once so strong and just?" I asked, wincing, shaking from pain.

Where did it go wrong for this powerful man?

"I wanted nothing more than to be in charge again. To be my daughter's hero," Xavier spoke, adding to the room's pity party.

"Didn't you want to kill Aqua?" I managed through the pain.

"No. I just wanted my position back from her. I was refused and became enraged. Denial didn't sit well with me, so I tried to kill some of the kings."

"I still don't understand. Just ... why?"

"Listen, kid. Evil is something that … you can't describe to everyone or become willingly. It just … happens one day. A switch, a death, or some other trigger can cause that," Xavier said through coughs. "Remember that." Xavier fell, face-planting onto the ground.

I understood his words, his feelings, his ideals, but I couldn't seem to bring it all together. My mind was going blank. I fell on my good side, on purpose of course. I only saw feet rush toward me as I blacked out.

## Jonathan

Even in victory we felt defeated. While Xavier was dead and the battle was over, too many people had died and all of us were injured. Only Sara and Jacob were alright as they had only been frozen. Jacob's ring had broken in the conflict so we had to be manually transported, using helicopters, to Outcast Corner. They, of course, had a medical bay which is where I was now. Out of all of us, Mia had come out the most changed. She had the worst physical and mental injuries. As I looked at her now, peering into the medical area from the window, she looked so … broken. She wasn't sleeping and all she did was stare emptily at where her right arm would have been. It took a lot of convincing from the medical staff to get her to eat and drink, which she did slowly and passively. Maybe I shouldn't have let her come with me.

"Quit blaming yourself," I heard someone say.

I turned to see Light. He was smiling as usual, though it was a considerably less toothy grin. As if it was hard for him to keep up a smile.

"I can't help but think I could have done more." I turned away from him.

"From what I heard, the Yeti guy was a tough customer. Do you think you would have succeed if Mia hadn't been there?" Light asked.

"Well ... I ..." I didn't know what to say.

"It's not your fault. Just be happy she didn't die." Light patted me on the back, probably with a grin on his friendly face.

"Thanks for that, Light."

No response.

"Light?" I questioned, turning around.

He was gone. There wasn't any evidence he was even there in the first place. He was like some kind of ghost or something.

"He should really stop doing that," I said to myself.

I sat down on a bench in the hall. The whole medical area was one long hallway. I put my head between my knees and grabbed at my hair. I felt so frustrated. It had been two days and I had redone that fight over and over in my head. Even if it wasn't my fault that people were hurt or died all I could think was ...

"You think could've done more?" a voice cut into my thoughts.

I looked up to see Yin with bandages wrapped around her head. She'd been diagnosed with a concussion and was recovering. I guess she was allowed to walk the halls.

"If that's what you're thinking you need to get over it. It's been two days, Jonathan. You can't change the past," Yin lectured.

I noticed she didn't call me John this time. She didn't seem to be in the mood for it though, and neither was I.

"You're right, but it's still ..."

I couldn't even figure out why I was so upset with myself anymore.

"I've got news," a man's voice said.

I looked toward my left at a man who must have been the doctor. Doctor Royce Freeman to be exact; his full name was written on his name tag.

"What kind of news?" I asked.

"While Mia will make a full recovery, excluding the fact her arm won't grow back, there are some complications," Dr. Freeman explained, flipping through the sheets on his clipboard.

"What are the complications?" Yin asked, also worried.

"There's good news, bad news, and awful news," Dr. Freeman said.

"Awful news first, good news second, and then bad news last," I replied.

"Some people aren't good with death. Hearing about it is different, but seeing it ... they can't handle that. Mentally Miss. Alves may never be the same again," Dr. Freeman delivered the painful news.

I choked slightly. My fault. It was definitely my fault.

"Go on," Yin said.

"We do have a fully mechanical arm she can use. The bad side to that is the recovery and procedure is very painful," Dr. Freeman elaborated.

"I'll break all that news to her if that's okay with all of you," Azazeal said, coming from nowhere.

I looked at Azazeal. She seemed more serious than I'd ever seen her.

"I said I'd talk to her." Azazeal winked at me.

"Go ahead," I managed, still wallowing in self-pity.

"Don't be hard on her," Yin stressed.

"Not planning on it," Azazeal said as the door slid open with the wave of her hand.

The doctor walked away as did Yin. I was left alone in an empty hall. I watched Azazeal pull up a chair next to Mia. She was facing toward Mia and the wall so I couldn't see what she was saying. Whatever it was surprised, upset, and uplifted Mia all at once. In fact, I even saw her laugh. I couldn't tell how, but Azazeal brought the life back to her eyes. Suddenly, Azazeal got up and left. To make it even stranger, Mia smiled. Azazeal waved her hand again. The door automatically shut behind her.

"What did you say?" I asked, surprised.

"I just told her what the doctor said and that you were worried about her. That seemed to the trick." Azazeal replied.

I motioned to give her a hug, but she held me out of arm's reach.

"Go hug her," Azazeal said, gesturing to Mia. "And stop blaming yourself. You didn't make her come with you, did you?"

Azazeal turned away before I could answer. She walked down the hallway and turned a corner. When she did I began walking toward the door. I waved my hand and it slid open. Mia looked at me as I entered. I froze for a second before moving forward. I sat in the hovering chair that Azazeal had pushed over to Mia.

"So ... uh ... how are you feeling?" I asked.

"I feel like I lost an arm," Mia replied, but with a smile.

"Uh ... yeah, that happened," I said, not knowing how to reply.

"Sure did," Mia replied soberly.

Without any words to say, I stood and gave her a hug. Mia wrapped her arm around me the same way.

"Sorry about all this. It's all my fault," I explained to her.

She pushed me off and I met her rage-filled gaze.

"What makes you think you can blame yourself for a decision I made?" Mia said with a fiery passion.

Quite literally as the tips of her hair seemed to have caught fire.

"Sorry, but it's because if I hadn't asked you to come—"

Mia cut me off. "You never asked me to come with you. You even said Yin and I should leave and go someplace without you," Mia snapped.

"Yeah, you're right about that," I said, recollecting myself.

"So just let it go." Mia huffed.

"Alright," I managed after a long pause.

"I'm getting the arm by the way," Mia added suddenly.

"What arm are you talking about again?" I was so consumed with guilt I didn't know what she meant.

"The robotic one, idiot." Mia laughed playfully.

Now I remembered. I also remembered something else.

"Isn't that supposed to be extremely painful?" I asked, concerned.

"You're like the father I never had," Mia replied, smiling. "Don't worry. Temporary pain is better than not having an arm."

I sighed. She was tough. I didn't need to worry so much. If I started slacking, she could probably surpass me in overall ability.

"Alright. I think you can handle it," I said, smiling back.

She opened her mouth to speak, but stopped and looked past me as the door slid open. I turned around to see the woman from the bar.

"J-Jonathan, I ne-need yo-you for a se-second," she said.

I had planned to ask her what she needed, but her eyes looked wide and filled with fear. Whatever it was must have been important. I stood and turned away from Mia.

"I'll be back," I said without turning around.

I began to walk toward the woman as Mia spoke.

"Take your time. I'll still be here."

She sounded disappointed and more than a little sad. I felt bad, but I also didn't want to worry Mia any more than I had to. The door slid closed as soon as we exited the room.

"What's wrong?" I asked, looking down at her.

"I'll explain," someone said to my left.

I turned around and saw the angel from before. He hovered lightly but would have surpassed my height anyway. I believe his name was Gabriel.

"Gabriel, right?" I asked.

"Indeed. In the general matter of importance, however, my name isn't necessary. Regardless, we have a large problem and seventy percent of the people who can stop it are out of commission."

"Alright, who do we have to use and what the frak is going on?"

"The former yellow king, Julian Stinson, is preparing a weapon more powerful than what we're ready for."

"What kind of weapon? What for?" I had way too many questions that weren't being answered.

"I'd describe it as a giant cannon on an airship," Azazeal vaguely explained from my right.

"What kind of cannon?"

"Apparently it's a light cannon. One strong enough to obliterate Australia," Light chimed in, appearing from nowhere.

I knew what a light cannon was, but this was new. Light cannons' strength correlated directly to their size. It took an insane amount of magic power to fire just once. So a giant one would be as catastrophic as Light had explained. It didn't help that all four of the people around me looked either irritated or scared.

"How big are we talking?" I was still trying to piece things together.

"You've seen the full height of the Eiffel Tower, right?" Light asked.

"Of course. I couldn't exactly miss it."

"It's about that big." Light sounded bothered.

I was stunned. A light cannon the size of a person's arm could destroy a small building. Something as big as the Eiffel Tower was ... catastrophic.

"The worst part is yet to come," Azazeal chimed in. "We can only afford to send you, Amy, Lock, Light, and Theo."

"Why so few people? And who is Theo?"

"That's everyone who is capable of helping and isn't occupied already," Azazeal responded.

"I still don't know who Theo is."

I wanted to ask Azazeal why she couldn't help, but then I realized something. Not only was her shoulder completely wrapped up, she hadn't moved that arm at all. That's my fault too ...

"We don't have much time so let's move now," a voice said.

I looked past Gabriel to see a dark-skinned boy with blond hair. I looked him up and down quickly. He wasn't more than six feet tall. His body type, as much as I could see, was average. One of his eyes was blue and the other green.

"Quit undressing me with your eyes and let's move," he said, gesturing to Light and myself.

He began walking back the way we came and I followed.

"Where are you going, Light?" I heard a girl's voice suddenly ask.

I glanced over my shoulder and saw Light talking to the dragon-girl behind me. Everyone else had disappeared.

"To stop the ... uh ... light cannon ... of course."

"You better come back." The girl punched him childishly.

Light rubbed his arm as if the playful punch had injured him. They continued to look at one another awkwardly until Light finally spoke.

"I'll be back, I promise."

Rylen smiled brightly, but immediately stopped as if to hide her joy. She suddenly wrapped her arms around Light's waist and squeezed him to her. She was so strong that she appeared to lift him off the ground with ease. The strong hug didn't last very long as Rylen quickly set Light back down on his feet. She then smiled once more before running in the opposite direction from where we were headed.

"Hey, Light, we gotta go!" I called as the boy began to tug at my arm.

I began to follow him at a pace that was half fast-walk half jog. I glanced over my shoulder at Light, who was following closely behind.

"I'm Theo, by the way," the young boy suddenly said as we walked in silence.

"I'm—"

"I know who you are," Theo interjected. "The girl we're about to run into is Amy and the boy is Lock. We don't have much time so Light will teleport us a soon as we all make contact."

Sure enough as we turned the corner I caught a glimpse of a brown-haired girl and a dark-skinned boy.

# CHAPTER 20

# CYRUS

When we reappeared it was raining. Below us was a large blotch of land. I looked around and took in the airship. It was massive and stretched at least half a mile. The shape was like that of a dinner plate. I had to brush away the wet hair drooping into my eyes.

"Sorry! I can't go to places I've never been so I couldn't take us inside the airship!" Light shouted over the rain.

"Does that mean you've been on top of the airship before?!" I shouted back.

"Maybe," He muttered quietly.

Light then merged through the roof of the airship and felt inside.

"Follow me!" Theo suddenly shouted.

He jammed his hand into the airship and tore a hole through it with ease. He was stronger than he looked. Amy dropped down first, shouting, "This room's empty!"

Lock and Theo dropped in. I followed suit.

The room we entered was just white walls and an equally white floor. Then, suddenly, the door that left the room slammed closed. The white walls turned red and an alarm system began to blare.

"What's going on?!" Amy shouted over the noise.

"Get ready," was all Theo said.

I wasn't sure what to get ready for, but there was a problem. I didn't have any of my weapons. I'd left everything in my room. Then I felt Theo tap me on the shoulder. I turned and he was holding up a Beretta M9 pistol and a utility belt with four clips of ammo. I was surprised anyone still had a gun as old as the Beretta.

"Take it quickly," Theo said, stone faced.

I didn't ask how he knew I was totally unarmed. It didn't really matter either. I cocked the handgun and clipped on the belt. As soon as I did, the walls opened up like garage doors. Skeletons began to flood out of them and charge at the four of us. They stopped suddenly and surrounded us in a circle. Lock shifted back and we made contact, back to back, with one another. I felt Amy push into my shoulder and Theo push into the other. They all were holding guns, but I couldn't tell what kind at the moment. I just knew everyone had a different one. The skeletons were holding various melee weapons, clubs and swords. Everything stood still in the room, and I shifted my footing nervously. Then Theo fired his handgun. The recoil on the gun seemed massive, I could feel the vibration through Theo, but Theo's arm didn't even move. The bullet went through one skeleton's head into another and then another. After that, the creatures charged. I fired into the crowd of bony bodies. It didn't take long to realize only head shots would kill. Shooting their exposed spine would only leave them dragging their bodies with their arms. We were getting tighter and tighter together as the skeletons began to close in. Amy threw the black marbles she carried around the room. They, however, didn't exploded like the ones I had seen previously. She must have been setting up something. I saw a bright flash of purple coming from behind me. I turned to see Lock's fist glowing brightly. When he threw it forward at a large clump of skeletons, it exploded into a purple flash.

"Cool."

"Thanks," Lock replied.

That blast had cleared out all the skeletons on one side so we could finally move around. I kicked back one of the skeletons that had gotten too close. When I kicked it, it was the sound of hollow metal instead of crunching bones.

"These things are robots?" I asked aloud.

"Explains a lot and adds more questions," Theo replied.

"We don't have time to answer questions." Lock punched his fist clean through one of the heads of one of the machines.

One skeleton bot swung its mace-like weapon, connecting it with the back of Amy's head—or so I had thought. She had disappeared and reappeared near one of the black marbles she'd thrown. From that position she shot a hole through the back of the robot's head. At this point the robots had thinned out. One of the skeleton robots charged me with a broken sword. I batted its lunging arm down and ripped off its head.

*Strength multiplication times five,*

I saw Theo calmly punching holes in the robots' heads with simple quick jabs. We were clearly going to win this.

"Guys, what's that?" Amy suddenly asked.

Another robot came lumbering out of the garage-like walls. It was, however, much bigger and didn't have bony metallic parts. It looked like the Robocop from that old 2014 movie. The face was a skull, however, and blazed kind of like that old DC superhero. It easily tossed aside the other metal skeletons as it made its way toward us. The other skeletons stopped attacking us and retreated back into the wall, which closed behind them.

"Targets acquired. Amy, Lock, Jonathan, Theo. Target Cyrus is not present. Commencing extermination," the robot spoke.

"Wait, who's Cyrus?" I asked, confused.

"That's not important!" Theo shouted. "Just run!"

The tall robot's arm transformed into a Gatling gun. As it did, we ran with Theo leading us. The door that had previously been closed had opened. As soon as we left the room bullets came tearing through the walls. We ran straight down the hall without stopping to inspect the other rooms that could have been of some importance. I saw bullets hit Theo, but they ricocheted off him. One of the ricocheting bullets caught Amy in the side. She cried out, stumbled, but didn't fall.

"Are you ok!" I shouted over the loud blasting.

Did this guy ever run out of ammo?

"I'll live ... probably." Amy grimaced.

"Next left," Theo suddenly said without acknowledging Amy's injury.

When we reached the left we turned as directed. It was a dead end.

I looked around. "Uh, Theo, this can't be right."

"Don't worry, this has a seventy-seven percent chance of success," Theo replied.

Theo took off his glove to reveal his hand. Then he pulled the skin off of it. The skin, however, was more like a glove covering a metal hand with different buttons and wires on it.

"Theo, what—"

"I am a cyborg and no more questions." There was a short silence before Theo said, "Thank you."

We heard the robot making its way down the hall. It was slow and anxiety inducing. I knew nothing about Theo's plan so I wasn't feeling very safe. When the robot walked into our field of view it stopped. As it turned slowly, Theo's hand transformed into a spearhead. The robot raised its arm, but at that same time Theo jabbed his pointed arm into the machine. It made a click instead of the sound tearing of metal. Then both of them stopped moving completely.

"Uh, Theo?" Amy asked, concerned.

Gripping her side, she began to walk slowly toward Theo. Lock thrust his arm out in front of Amy, stopping her in her tracks.

"You don't know what'll happen," Lock said, justifying his actions.

I, however, walked past Lock, unafraid of the possible outcomes. I slowly crept onto the side of Theo and the robot. I looked into Theo's eyes. His blue eye had scrolling text that moved so fast it looked like gibberish. I waved my hand in front of his eyes, but he didn't react.

"Hello?" I asked confused.

I couldn't tell where this was going. We all stood awkwardly and silently for a couple more seconds. Theo suddenly dislodged his spear-hand from the robot. The metal giant fell to the ground with a thud. Theo shook violently before stopping all movement completely. His spear-hand transformed back to normal, and Theo silently slid on the glove.

"I know where Julian is, so I'll lead the way," was all he said.

Theo began to walk forward. He stepped over the deactivated robot.

"What did you do to it?" Lock asked, searching for answers.

"Him. What did I do to him?" Theo sounded bothered.

"Okay … what did you do to him?" Amy asked.

Theo stopped walking and tapped the side of his head. I assumed he was gesturing to his brain.

"I placed his AI into my storage center. At the moment I'm using his guidance system. Making him a sentient AI gives him power to do what he wants," Theo explained.

"You can make an AI sentient?" I asked, surprised.

"Nowadays. Most AI units were human at first. They had their brains converted into a robotic intelligence. I am one such unit who was created with sentience and the ability to transfer it. No more questions. We must be going," Theo explained as he began to turn down the hall.

I'd heard of alternate intelligence being made. Sentient technology, as far as I knew, was still under development. Amy, Lock, and I followed Theo down the hall after having shot concerned glances to one another. We walked for a short amount of time before Amy suddenly collapsed. Theo, however, kept walking. Maybe he was going to scout ahead.

"Wait, we forgot to wrap that shrapnel wound!" I suddenly remembered.

"What? What shrapnel?" Lock gave a concerned look.

Lock conjured a roll of medical tape from his magic item storage. Lock moved Amy's body so she sat against the wall. Lock lifted just enough of her pink tank top so he could dress the wound. I just couldn't believe all of us, including Amy, had forgotten about her wound.

"Dat blade was small, but did damage through," Lock randomly said while patching Amy up.

"Blade? It was shrapnel from the explosion if I remember correctly," I said, correcting Lock.

"Amy was shot by a bullet that ricocheted off me. I'm sure the robot had shot me, which ended up hitting her," Theo said when he returned.

Something was wrong. Why did Lock and I remember something different? Now that I'm thinking about I'm positive I saw Amy get shot. Where did the idea of shrapnel come from? When Lock had finished wrapping the wound, Amy suddenly woke up.

"Quit touching me, pervert!" she said angrily.

She pushed Lock away and pulled her shirt down over her body. She crossed her arms, hiding herself out of embarrassment.

"Sorry, I was just tryin' ta help." Lock scratched his head.

"Help with what? Also, why does my side hurt so much?" Amy was oblivious to her bullet wound.

"What's exactly going on?" I asked aloud, searching for answers.

"My data banks have informed me of a Strain named Chloe. It appears she can alter memories of compatible within a certain pre-established area," Theo explained.

"Apparently she's been seen with Julian on multiple occasions."

"We should find them both as quickly as possible, then," Amy held her side.

"Follow behind me," Theo said as he walked off.

## Light

"How long do you think you would last?" Julian asked.

I'd challenged my older brother alone. I was sure I could beat him. He wasn't this strong forty years ago.

"Why ... can't I beat you?" I asked, huffing and puffing.

Julian slashed the golden sword Excalibur through the air. He stood wearing a powerful golden armor and the crown of immortality. With gear like that, he could truly be invincible. The wreath crown and golden armor plates shined, along with the white cape draped over his shoulders. Where did he get these legendary artifacts?

"By now you've probably figured out what exactly I am wearing. The impenetrable armor of Achilles and the wreath crown of immortality. You couldn't have missed Excalibur either. The question is, can you still find a way to kill me?" Julian asked.

"I ... I will!" I shouted.

I grabbed for my own weapon. I used my sword to prop myself up as blood dripped from the side of my head. The blood, however, was gold. I stared at it in shock.

"Ah, it's working," was all Julian said.

"What did you do to me?" I replied, confused.

"Didn't you know? When Excalibur cuts people, their magic energy is turned into liquid energy. And now, I'll extract it from you."

He slashed Excalibur, drawing a pentagram through the air. He then punched his fist through the floating image. The pentagram warped and wrapped around his arm and changed from white to black.

"Don't fret. This won't kill you," Julian said.

I didn't know what to do, but I did know what that was. Projection sorcery.

"What are you—" I began but hacked up some gold blood. "...doing?"

"Restriction spell!" Julian conjured a magical series of ropes and vines that flew in my direction.

I jumped to my side, but the vines followed. I thrust my sword foreword and attempted to block the magical conjuration. It wrapped around the sword and snaked up my arms to the rest of my body. All my movement was restricted.

"You ... bastard ..." I managed despite any movement causing me extreme pain.

"That's in poor taste, Cyrus. We are siblings after all," Julian said.

He sat on the throne that had oddly shaped and colored swords sticking on and around it.

"Now then, Cyrus ... or should I say Light ... we wait." Julian smirked.

"For ... what?" I grunted.

"For your friends to arrive so they can watch you die!" Julian laughed heartily.

"You bastard ..."

"Can't you think of a better insult?" Julian asked, laughing.

"You're as useless as a knitted condom!" I shouted in defiance.

It was the first thing that came to mind. Now that I think about it the insult was pretty childish.

"Wow, how scathing," Julian replied unfazed, but laughing.

"Brothers shouldn't fight like this," a voice suddenly said.

Despite the burning sensation, I managed to wriggle my head toward the direction of the voice. A small girl wearing stereotypical witch clothing was suddenly standing next to Julian.

"Chloe, I told you to stay hidden until it was time to harvest Cyrus's magic," Julian said.

Harvest my magic? He must be planning to use me to power the light cannon. That or he was more selfish than I thought. It would explain why he never shared anything with me and Lazarus.

"I know, but I had to tell you a couple things. First, my trick room is failing because the one named Theo's mind can't be swayed. Secondly, they'll be here in about fifty-six seconds," Chloe said.

"Good. Now hide until I request you," Julian commanded.

"Understood." Chloe replied, but she seemed almost reluctant to do so.

I watched as the blond-haired girl disappeared in a puff of smoke.

"Strains really are the best companions, aren't they? You have a couple Strains in your little club don't you?" Julian asked.

"They have names, you know that. Lia and Sara. I'm sure Chloe has told you about them," I said, annoyed he didn't care enough to name my friends.

"Chloe tells me about all six of her sisters constantly. It's too bad that the youngest one doesn't know her sisters' names. In fact, I heard she just recently met Lia."

"They'll be here in sixteen seconds," Chloe's voice emitted from nowhere.

"Move Cyrus onto the machine," Julian replied.

"What machi— Oh, that one," I said, realizing where I was.

The light cannon's control panel and some sort of electric chair-like thing sat on the farthest side of the room. My body floated over and was placed into the chair. The odd glowing restraints snapped onto my arms and legs and the headpiece slipped onto me.

"Everything's in place," Chloe's voice echoed through the room.

Just then there was a banging sound against the large metal door. "This door is tougher than it looks!"

There was another loud banging the door, however, didn't budge.

"You're right. My hand hurts now!" It was a different voice now.

"Allow me," a third voice I recognized as Theo said.

Right after Theo spoke, the door was pierced by a hand which then grasped and tore open the metal.

## Jonathan

In hindsight we probably should have let Theo tear open the door in the first place. Clearly, hindsight is twenty-twenty so I can't say much now. Theo continued to demolish the door, tearing it off the hinges and flinging it into the center of the room. He stepped in and Amy, Lock, and I followed.

"That's not good," Theo said as he shifted his view.

Light sat strapped to a chair with black lines across his entire body. He was hooked to a machine which I could only imagine was part of the light cannon. It was painfully obvious because the end of the cannon was only a few meters away from Light's chair. It was also at least four meters wide.

"Hey, guys. Sorry. I failed to take him down," Light said, smiling as usual.

"Why did you try alone! We were worried about you!" Amy raged.

In all honesty we weren't worried about Light. Not only were we busy trying to survive, but I had figured he could take care of himself. This scene made me less confident in his abilities, however.

"He's stronger than I could have guessed. Stopping him from destroying Australia is looking harder as time passes," Light replied somberly.

"I still can't believe you would so easily slaughter and destroy the homes of those people!" I bashed Julian's plan.

Julian scoffed at my anger. In fact, he even began to chuckle. From there he broke into an incredibly withering laugh.

"What faulty information have you received? The Australian people have already evacuated! The rifts that have almost entirely consumed the continent threaten to release a demon more powerful than all of the kings combined could handle. Destroying the rift is the only course of action available," Julian explained his actions.

"You can't just destroy the homes of all those people. And what about the soldiers that are fighting the demons as we speak!" Amy argued furiously.

"As you can clearly see, I do what I want." Julian gestured to his doomsday weapon. "Besides, those men won't survive regardless of whether or not I kill them."

Light's eyes appeared to shine out of anger and frustration. He struggled against the restraints, but couldn't break free. Julian crossed his arms and leaned back to show his power. The throne he sat upon had a lot of weapons that I felt Yin would know the names of.

"I guess we'll jus hav ta take ya down," Lock said, raising the handgun he had used previously.

"With simple mechanical weaponry?" Julian laughed.

"Shouldn't be too hard." Amy also raised her pistol.

Theo didn't say anything. He aimed his gun in silence. Julian raised an eyebrow before standing slowly. His figure was towering even without the throne he had sat upon. Julian suddenly frowned before disappearing like a swift gust of wind.

"Where did he go?" I asked, confused.

"He hasn't moved. The Strain is messing with your mind," Theo replied with unwavering confidence.

I blinked a couple times and sure enough Julian stood in the same spot.

"It's pointless, Chloe. Theo will always know where I am," Julian addressed the girl behind the trickery.

"No fair. I'm useless here, aren't I? You won't leave me, right, Julian?" Chloe appeared to blink into view.

The tiny blond girl looked worried, staring up at Julian. She had a purple staff with a black diamond-like gem on top. It seemed to glow when she deactivated her magic.

"You're too valuable to abandon," Julian replied quickly.

"I could use some help!" Light shouted in an uncharacteristically taut voice.

"Prepare to attack. We don't have much time to waste," Theo said, heeding his friends call for help.

"I'll attempt to render all of you immobile instead of killing you. The rest of the world will most likely need your heroics." Julian leveled Excalibur.

"I'd like to see you try!" I replied, firing my Beretta.

I'll admit to not being the greatest shooter. With that being said, I should have been able to hit a non-moving target. Julian, on the other hand, was capable of more than I had thought. My first shot he tilted his head just out of the way. All of our shot combined were either slashed through or caught. Julian even opened the palm of his free hand, dropping the crushed metal pellets to the ground. The golden gauntlet he wore didn't even appear to be scratched.

"Dis is gonna be harda than we thought," Lock said.

His gun was smoking from the barrel. Amy and Theo's guns also looked as if they had just been fired. Julian had dodged and slashed through our bullets without taking a step.

"So, who wants to take a nap?" Julian asked, rubbing his hand down the faintly glowing blade. No one replied. We were still amazed he'd not even been touched by a single bullet.

"Ladies first, then," Julian said, snapping me out of my thoughts.

Julian dashed forward before any of us could react. He threw a corkscrew punch into Amy's abdomen and sent her flying back and slamming into the wall. In that split second of clarity I saw Amy do two things: she dropped one of the black marbles she'd been carrying and also managed to make contact, using her hand, with Excalibur. Amy's body collapsed to the ground with a sickening thud. Blood trickled out of a wound in the back of her head, and it also gently streamed from her mouth. Her body twitched and her arms flailed as if she was attempting to move. Amy coughed and tried to stand before falling awkwardly back into the same position. Suddenly she stopped all movement and lay silently in her own puddle of blood.

"Amy!" Lock shouted, rushing to her side.

"Don't move her! She could have easily broken her neck," Theo warned.

"I'll kill ya for hurtin' her like dat!" Lock threatened Julian as he began to stand slowly.

His left hand began to glow faintly as he removed his sunglasses. His eyes were a soulless black with no pupils.

"Don't worry. Not only will she live, but you'll be joining her on the floor soon enough."

Lock charged forward, brandishing his glowing purple fist. He roared like an animal as he jumped and released the energy punch he'd charged up. Julian took it head-on, slashing through the projection. The giant fist exploded as it made contact with Excalibur. The explosion was rather small, but it was extremely bright. I held a hand to my eyes, but I looked through the cracks in between my fingers. I saw the shadowy figure of Lock make an attempt to punch Julian, who batted his hand upward. As Lock fell, Julian's knee met his stomach. Julian then quickly drew back his arm and knee simultaneously. He brought down Excalibur, but only the hilt made contact with Lock's head. The blow itself could be heard as well as the dull sound of Lock's body slamming into, and even cracking, the ground. A liquid had already pooled around Lock's head area. It wasn't red like normal blood, it was more a navy color.

"That shouldn't be enough to kill a demon like you," Julian said while cracking his neck.

Almost as if on cue, Lock groaned and began to attempt to push himself up. The navy blue blood streamed from the side of his head as he managed to climb to his feet. He stood half crouched, huffing, trying to regain his breath. The blood began to stain the white carpeted floor.

"I'll probably have to get that replaced now. Might as well wait until the rest of you people's blood stains my airship before I replace the carpet." Julian laughed.

"Were outmatched here. The number one priority has changed from defeating Julian to freeing Cyrus and escaping," Theo suddenly said.

"You can try," Chloe's voice echoed through the room.

I was suddenly lifted and tossed through the air by what felt like an invisible hand.

*Durability multiplication times five*

I crashed into the wall at sonic speed. I saved myself from taking too big of a hit with my multiplication. The wind, however, was still knocked out of me. When I fell, I noticed where I'd landed. It was the front of the light cannon, right at the part where the beam would be fired. I tried to move, but I felt pressure from some unknown power holding me down.

"He's immobile now," Chloe said, appearing next to Lock.

Even though Lock was still disoriented, and hadn't moved from his half crouched position, he noticed Chloe. He attempted to punch her, but his fist was stopped by an invisible wall.

"What?" Lock grunted in surprise.

"I wouldn't reappear so close to you if I didn't know I could stop you," Chloe replied.

Chloe then moved his staff and tapped it against Lock's chest. He flew back at blindingly quick speed and crashed through the metal wall. Luckily that wall just led to another room and not outside the ship.

"Chloe, please don't destroy my ship. It wasn't cheap, you know," Julian said.

"What! You won't leave me alone now, will you!?" Chloe suddenly cried out in fear.

"Why would I do that? Like I said, you're very useful to me," Julian replied quickly.

I attempted to get up, but I was still being held firmly in place by the invisible hand. I had to wait for my opportunity. I didn't want to waste magic struggling against something that I couldn't overpower. While I was thinking of an escape plan, Theo was thinking of an attack strategy. His skin gloves were suddenly burned off his mechanical hands. They glowed with a gentle green light. He aimed both hands at Julian.

"Analyzing targets. Lethal fire authorized. Preparing ..." Theo spoke, but his mouth didn't move.

"Targets, huh? What else are you aiming for?" Julian asked, quickly catching on to Theo's plan.

"Wouldn't you like to know," Theo replied.

He fired the first green beam at Chloe, who was occupied holding me down. At the same time he fired a blast in an attempt to destroy the light cannon. He had probably figured Julian couldn't stop both shots. He also must have known Chloe's ability wouldn't work on the energy beam. The plan didn't even half work. Julian, moving almost as fast as Amy when she teleported, sliced through the beam aimed for Chloe. He then moved and blocked the beam that would have at least damaged the light cannon. Theo stared blankly.

"You must have known that wouldn't work." Julian broke the silence.

"So far this has gone how I'd expected," Theo replied, acknowledging his words.

"How so?" Julian asked cautiously.

Theo raised his arms once more. They glowed extremely bright this time.

"You're in perfect position. You can't dodge, but you won't be able to stop this attack." Theo gave away his plan.

"Then I'll bounce it back," Julian replied confidently.

Theo fired a giant beam of energy. It was at least five times stronger than the two beams before combined. The green wave shot across the room at Julian, who stood firm in his path. He thrust out his hand and caught the wave like a baseball. The beam condensed and stopped in its tracks. All that remained was green glowing ball sitting in the palm of Julian's hand.

"A miscalculation ..." Theo muttered in realization of his failure.

Julian was more powerful than any of us could hope to match. Julian calmly drew his arm back and threw the ball at an incredible speed. Theo crossed his arms in front of his chest and took the blast. It sent him reeling back until he collided with the wall. Then the green ball exploded. I expected a cry of pain, but then I considered that Theo probably couldn't feel any. The dust and smoke from the explosion encompassed Theo's body, making him look like an immobile statue. In fact a couple seconds went by and he still hadn't moved.

"Theo?" I questioned.

I was met with silence.

"Theo, I kinda need you to move now," Light, who I'd forgotten about, said.

"I'd imagine that would have been painful for a human," Theo spoke suddenly.

The dust settled, revealing Theo's blond hair which was now stained sort of gray. The clothing he had on was tattered and charred. The skin suit he had worn had been completely burned off, leaving behind only mechanical parts. His body sparked and showed clear signs of damage. His left arm was missing a lot of the metal parts that were on it previously.

"I guess I shouldn't be surprised you survived a weaker version of your own attack," Julian said.

Theo didn't reply, but he grabbed onto his left arm at the bicep. His fingers jabbed into his arm like a cord in an electrical socket. The arm then transformed from the forearm down into a blade. It radiated the green energy Theo had appeared to fire before. The metal seemed to be vibrating softly and made a quiet, humming sound. As if he was testing something, Julian pulled a small knife out from a pouch he wore behind him. He calmly flung the knife at Theo. In response, Theo slashed the knife out of the air. The tiny blade was destroyed on impact. Theo's weapon-arm made a sound akin to that of those light blades in that old 2015 movie. Julian's eyes lit up after the events transpired.

"This might be fun," Julian said, spinning Excalibur.

Theo didn't reply. He charged forward without making a sound. He slashed horizontally and Julian blocked. Julian took advantage of his height advantage and rained downward strikes onto Theo. Theo bobbed, weaved, and blocked them. Julian faked a slash and then drove his elbow into the throat of an unsuspecting Theo. Theo took the blow full force, but didn't back off. In fact, he was virtually unaffected. Theo's arm blade slashed upward at Julian's face. Julian hopped back before slashing Theo's right arm clean off. Sparks and wiring flew out of the open hole, but Theo pressed on. He slashed once more at Julian and managed to slice his chest. There was no spray of blood; the cut wasn't deep enough. Julian grasped the back of Theo's head and slashed his head off before he could react. I stared in shock at Theo's defeat.

"Theo!" I feared the worst.

Julian tossed his head and it rolled near Amy's body. The room was filled with silence. I closed my eyes and punched the ground as hard as I could. I was furious due to my inability to be of any use.

"Amy, you're going to have to move soon," I heard Theo say, cutting into my thoughts.

Even as a head, he was still operational. Go figure. I didn't know why he was commanding Amy to move. She was clearly unconscious. Just as I thought that, Amy's body twitched a little, like she was slowly waking up. Julian, who hadn't heard Theo, walked over to where Light was tied up.

"Well then, Cyrus, prepare to use your life force to fuel my light cannon," Julian said in an oddly modulated voice. "Any last words, dear brother?"

"I've got a speech really," Light began. "It's been fun. These past couple years with you three. Sorry I didn't get to spend much time with you, Jonathan. We probably would have made good friends. Amy, I uh …" Light paused, wobbly. "You probably can't hear me, but I … uh … loved you … I know you don't like guys, so then I fell in love with Rylen, but you were my first crush," Light finished quietly.

"Light …" was all I could manage.

I felt not only useless but sad. I struggled to move, still pushed down by Chloe's power. You know what, screw saving my magic. This was what I was saving it for anyway.

*Strength multiplication times ten*

I pushed down on the ground, trying to push myself up. After a couple seconds of pointlessly struggling against Chloe's invisible hand, my arms gave out. I just wasn't strong enough to force my way out.

"Even though I'm sure you were just stalling, that was well said." Julian aimed Excalibur at Light's heart.

As Julian drove the blade forward, Amy's body suddenly disappeared. It was clear she had teleported, but I wasn't expecting her to do what she did. There was the sound of metal cutting through flesh, a spray of blood, and a cry of pain. It wasn't the gold blood associated with Excalibur draining someone's magic. The red liquid dripped onto the floor, streaming from Amy's impaled body. She'd teleported and forced the blade to change directions as it stabbed her. Amy quietly groaned in pain, but for some reason didn't cry out.

"Clever girl. You knew that Excalibur would easily slash through your skin and make contact with Cyrus. So you let it severe your lower spinal cord in order to slow the blade down. I commend your strategic mind and unshakable resolve, but sadly you won't live for much longer," Julian said matter-of-factly.

As if on cue Amy's knees began to buckle. She leaned her body onto Light, dragging the blade downward cutting into part of the cannon. Amy moved her hand onto Light's furthest shoulder and spoke into his ear. I could see the events play out so clearly and yet I missed it. Her body went limp. Light stared wide eyed at one of his best friends who had just died in his lap. The room was so quiet you could have heard a feather touch the ground. It was like the emotions were sucked out and left behind only rage and quiet agony. All those involved looked down. Chloe even removed herself from the room. She disappeared like a wisp of smoke. I tried to move immediately, but the invisible hand still held me down. A ray of light cut through the tense, but depressing atmosphere. The bright gold radiated from Light's body. A golden figure with no defining features seemed to come out of Light's body. It moved downward and then seemed to step into Amy's. There was a flash so bright I had to cover my eyes with my hand. When the light faded Amy stood alive and well. There was a few major changes, however. Her brown hair had been exchanged for a long, golden mane. The hair moved like wind was blowing through it. It looked alive. I could only see her back, but I saw her arms move. She appeared to grasp onto Excalibur and then vanish along with the legendary blade. She reappeared back where she had dropped the black marble before. Even with the sword still shoved in her back Amy stood firm. She suddenly held her hand out to the side, open, as if she was waiting for something to fly to it. And something did fly into it. Excalibur disappeared and reappeared in Amy's open palm from inside her body. I'd observed Amy could only teleport to objects she'd touched and couldn't teleport anything to her. Those limitations seemed to have been lifted. Even with the blade removed, Amy didn't bleed anymore. The wound appeared to have closed itself up.

"Cyrus, you're making a big mistake delaying me like this. What I'm doing here is bigger than all of us!" Julian said, irritated.

"There has to be another way!" Light's voice rang but was synchronized with Amy's.

When Amy spoke it sounded like Light was matching her tone. Light also said the same words from his chair. The whole process was very trippy. I sat dumbfounded, not sure what to make of the odd fusion between Light and Amy.

"Give me back that sword!" Julian stomped the ground.

Amy smirked, leveled the blade, and switching her stance.

"You want it? Come and get it!" both Amy and Light's voices resonated.

He was fast as wind, but Amy teleported faster. Julian punched and Amy dodged. This continued for a while with Julian just barely missing Amy as she teleported. After a wide punch, which Amy ducked under, she slashed Excalibur, but the blade was slapped down by Julian. Julian then grasped Amy by the throat and slammed her onto the floor. She hadn't dodged that one. Julian reached down at her unmoving body, but she teleported once again. When she reappeared, however, her hair had lost color and was more brown than gold. Amy was leaning against the wall, but she looked lost. Her eyes were searching and she looked frightened. As she tried to stand, her legs didn't cooperate. She flopped to the floor before using Excalibur to force herself onto her knees.

"Poor girl. The power Cyrus gave you must have worn off." Julian said, quickly stepping across the room.

He grabbed Amy by her chin and forced her head upward. Amy didn't appear to be able to put up a fight and helplessly stared up at Julian's towering figure. He appeared to search her eyes for something. After a couple of seconds, he seemed satisfied and released Amy. Her head dropped low as if she'd fallen unconscious. She remained on her knees with Excalibur still supporting her upper body.

"Sorry about this," Julian coldly spoke with his naturally dead eyes.

He then proceeded to kick Excalibur out from under Amy's arms. Her body flopped forward as the blade flipped into the air. Julian quickly caught it, but made no effort to stop Amy's fall. Her head banged against the floor, creating an awful, gruesome noise. Even though Amy's previous wounds had healed, the new one didn't. She bleed gently from the abrasion her skull. Her brown hair began to soak up the small blood puddle. As Julian walked toward Light with narrowed eyes, Amy remained still.

"Amy, are you ok!" I shouted in worry.

A groan escaped her mouth a couple of seconds after I had cried out and only fueled my concern. I scanned the room for anything I could use to fix the situation but to no avail. I was utterly useless. Julian had made it to Light and pointed Excalibur at his heart once more. Even with nothing to hinder him Julian just kind of stood there.

"What are you waiting for? You of all people can't be having second thoughts, right?" Light asked, provoking Julian.

"My will and resolve are absolute," Julian replied, unshaken.

"Then what are you waiting for?" Light asked.

No reply. Light leaned forward so the point of Excalibur pricked him. "Just do it already!" Light commanded.

Julian stood unwavering. To others it may have looked like he was second guessing, but to me it looked like Julian was torturing Light.

"Just kill me!"

Still nothing. Julian's face remained stone cold. Suddenly, Light stopped raging. He even began to cry.

"Just do it ..." Light muttered in a shaky voice.

Then it was over. Julian impaled Light without warning. Before the bright flash of light, I saw something unforgettable. I watched Light fade away into the bright glow that consumed the room. When the flash began to fade, I noticed Light's outline was missing. When I could finally see again he had disappeared, leaving specks of gold floating through the air like fireflies. Julian began to walk away, dragging Excalibur on the ground behind him. Julian sat on his throne and began to interact with the holographic screen that appeared in front of him. I heard the roar of a machine coming to life. I craned my neck and looked down the dark tunnel which was the light cannon. In the far back I could see a faint light. It appeared to grow brighter the longer I stared. As I observed the cannon being powered on, I felt the invisible pressure be removed. I stood in confusion, not sure why I was released.

"We have no intention of killing any of you. In Cyrus's case, there was no other way," I heard Chloe's disembodied voice resonate throughout the room.

"There's always an alternative! You didn't look hard enough!" I shouted, directing my anger at the air.

"If only that were true. I spent months looking for a power source that equaled Cyrus's soul. When the time came, I had no choice but to use him as a battery. I'm sorry to have even involved the rest of you," Julian replied, unfazed by my rage.

I had wanted to scream at him before. To tear him apart for killing my friend. And yet his apology was so sincere. It was also rather sad. I lowered my arms, defeated. He had some odd way with words.

"What could possibly be so powerful that you had to sacrifice your brother's life to stop it?" I asked, drawing into myself.

"There's a demon that's forcing its way through that gaping rift as we speak. It's a hunter whose name and strength I do not know. I only know hunters like him come, kill anyone, and fulfil any deeds that Death has appointed them," Julian spoke calmly.

The idea of a monster that Julian couldn't handle interested me.

"A hunter? Just how strong are they?"

"You ask a lot of questions. I fought a hunter once. His name was Apolonios. We fought for seven days and seven nights. He defeated me during the seventh night. I only still live because his target was Chloe, who had escaped to somewhere he couldn't follow."

A being strong enough to defeat Julian? He had dispatched all of us with ease. Not only that, but he'd found an enemy that he could fight for a week.

"What are they like? Are they humans? I still don't like you, by the way."

"You can hate me for all I care. What's done is done."

I stood glaring at Julian, but found myself unable to hate him. Why? Why couldn't I hate the man who just killed and critically injured my friends? I clenched my fists so hard my untrimmed nails drew blood.

"I'm going to fire the cannon now. You should probably get off there," Julian said, snapping me back to reality.

"No …" I replied after a short silence.

"That's your life you're wasting. Don't blame me when this kills you," Julian replied coldly.

I shrugged off his words while turning to face the steadily growing light. I inhaled deeply before holding my hands in front of me.

*Durability multiplication times ten*

*Fire resistance multiplication times ten*

I figured the fire resistance might protect me against the burns. The destructive beam was getting closer. I could feel my skin beginning to burn and it wasn't even upon me yet. I shifted my feet out of fear. I was second guessing myself now, and I backed up slowly. Then all at once the light beam shot forward and collided with me. I stopped part of it with my hands, but it bent through my fingers and underneath my arms. My shirt was gone in seconds as the beam burned it away. I grunted in pain and frustration. The beam had now surrounded me and was beginning to push me back. Julian had been right. It was idiotic to think I had a chance to stop this. I crossed my arms to shield myself from the burning light that charged my skin. The pain wasn't intolerable, but it hurt a lot.

"I tried to inform you of your imminent peril, but you were too naive to heed my warning," Julian said over the loud humming of the light cannon.

The power from the cannon began to carry and force me out of the airship as I tried to reply to Julian. As I fell to my imminent demise, I felt warmth instead of terror.

# CHAPTER 21

# MEMORIES

## Sara

I sat on the stool with Mia's arms wrapped around me. Even though her mechanical arm was cold, I didn't mind being close to her. With Jonathan gone, she and Yin were the only people I could talk to. Mia stroked my hair with her real hand, and I leaned into her in response. We both were silently watching Yin work in the forge. It took a lot of begging, but we convinced Jacob that we would be fine so he allowed us to explore Paris. While we were walking around town, we discovered this magic forge. Quietly and diligently, Yin hammered away at the metal before her. Blacksmithing had become a hobby for Yin, so she brought myself and Mia along with her. Since Yin was really sweaty, Mia and I kept our distance. The whole room was ablaze with others working on magic and non-magic weaponry.

"I really can sharpen magic blades, huh?" Yin said to herself.

She'd been hammering away at Nightfall for a while now. On her third routine strike, something odd happened. She broke the blade with the sludge hammer. The sound of the blade snapping drew the attention of everyone in the room. Yin stood in shock as half of Jonathan's sword clattered to the ground. The other blacksmiths stared for a couple more seconds before moving on to their projects.

I quickly pried myself out of Mia's grip around me. I rushed over to Yin who stood in shock at what she'd done.

"I … don't know how that's possible …" Yin muttered with wide eyes.

"It's not your fault. It just wasn't built to take so much damage," I said, trying to rationalize Yin's blunder.

"This has to be some kind of bad omen. It shouldn't have been that easy," Yin replied, still baffled.

I opened my mouth but the crescent moon symbol on my forehead began to glow. As it did, my head began pounding and my forehead felt as if someone was pressing a hot piece of metal to it. I cried out in pain and dropped to a knee. My vision became hazy, and I lowered my head between my knees attempting to ease my headache.

"Sara, what's wrong?" I heard Mia's voice, but it sounded far away.

It was like had been submerged underwater now. I felt something escape from my body. I didn't know how to describe it. Part of me had gone missing. Then I blacked out.

## *Jonathan*

The sun symbol on my chest glowed and burned my skin for reasons I didn't know. At the moment that was the least of my concerns. The whole "life flashing before your eyes" thing began to seem like bull as I descended toward Australia. The raging storm had calmed, but the sun was still hidden by clouds. As the ray of light penetrated the cloudy atmosphere, it might have looked like a beam from Heaven to the unsuspecting person. To me, however, it was death and destruction. I looked at my hands, which had begun to turn black and break apart like a mannequin made of dust would in the wind. My entire body had disappeared, and I was simply a floating hand. Then I stopped breaking apart. I watched in awe as the body of a tiny, unidentifiable person reformed my missing body parts. The strangest part was my point of view. Not only could I not feel any of this, but I was watching from behind the figure. The glowing green figure worked their hands as if drawing my body back into existence. Then they stopped and began to blink as if they were fading. My torso and one of my arms and legs had been the only parts to return to me. As the green apparition began to lose shape, a glowing gold figure placed a hand on their shoulder. Even without facial features, I could tell the gold astral being was Light. I also noticed the crescent moon on the little one's forehead. That had to be Sara.

"My soul will be destroyed at this rate," Sara said, looking up at Light's golden body.

"Can Serena finish for you?" Light confirmed my suspicions.

Sara didn't reply, but the green projection become taller and more feminine suddenly. While it was still faceless and featureless, the green being was clearly no longer Sara. My body's missing leg began to reform as the golden projection of Light began to dwindle and fade.

"Too bad he won't be able to see what you're doing for him before you die. Especially in your case." Light said grimly while flashing sporadically.

"I will see what you did!" I shouted, but my words didn't seem to travel to them.

"He barely knew me anyway. He'll take good care of Sara when I disappear," Serena replied with an off-putting tone.

"Don't do this! Just let me die!" I shouted, trying to persuade Serena not to disappear for my sake.

My words were sucked up like the void in space. I watched sadly as Serena suddenly split apart with Sara returning in her astral from. Serena was fading fast and appeared to have given up on restoring my left arm.

"Goodbye, little one. It would be best if you forgot about me. In fact, I'll insure it," Serena said as she placed her palm on Sara's head.

"What, no don't—" Sara started before her projection dimmed and then quickly faded.

"I don't know how I feel about that decision," Light said.

"It'll be fine. Even if she remembered me, time would cause me to slowly fade from her mind. You know what they say," Serena replied.

"No, no I don't," Light replied as he began to shimmer and vanish.

"Once your life's over, time fades your photo," Serena replied as she too seemed to be blown away by the wind.

My body continued to fall as my saviors vanished from sight. I watched in shock and awe as Australia was impacted and erased by the light cannon. I made no motion to shield myself because I figured my body wouldn't survive. To my surprise, desolation wasn't left behind. The continent was just gone. Like it had vanished at the snap of a magician's fingers. My spirit didn't descended and instead hung in the air. I didn't know how to move, so I just floated. Alone. I gazed down at the red sea—not the place. Small pools of the ocean were red with what I could only assume was the blood of the millions of ocean dwelling creatures vaporized by the canon. The sight was repulsive, but I was too busy trying to see if my body was still intact. Then, I spotted it: my body lying on what I could only assume was the last remnants of Australia.

"Darn, there's nothing I can do, huh?" I asked the empty space around me.

I searched for the airship, hoping Julian might spot my floating soul and show some sympathy. Of course the ship was nowhere to be found. I gazed down at my hollow body, unable to do anything. Then I heard a roar. It was loud and ferocious, causing me to cover my ears. Although, something seemed wrong about it. The roar appeared to emanate from nowhere and no discernible object or beast was in sight. As I thought this, something rose out of the water. It was big, scaly, and glowed blue like the sky. A spiraling pillar of water shot out in all directions, drenching my real and spiritual body. I looked on in amazement at what I could only describe as a sea serpent. With all the beings that had appeared from mythology and folk tales, to my knowledge nobody had met anything like this. They were the only legend or myth that remained just that. A myth. The shock of seeing the beast must have been great because I blacked out and subsequently awoke in my body. I moved swiftly looking up at the beast that was now only a few meters in front of me. It was so large I would have only been a fly if I had stood on its head.

"You dare disturb the slumber of the great Jeevith, god of the sea?" the serpent asked.

It didn't roar and its giant mouth didn't move. It spoke directly into my mind. I stared at it without replying. I was still shocked at its very existence.

"Speak, human, before I devour your entire being."

I snapped out of my trance like state.

"I'm here by unfortunate circumstance, sadly," I replied, half grinning.

The serpent circled around my tiny island, staring deep into my soul. He suddenly stopped and then drew so close I could feel his hot breath on my skin.

"I assume whatever destroyed this continent also took your arm?" The serpent telegraphed the words into my mind.

"It was a giant light cannon." I hoped he'd understand.

"I've been dormant for a thousand years. What is a light cannon?"

I looked at him for a couple seconds without answering. He just gazed back into my eyes. His gold eyes might have been brighter than my own.

"Your eye color is indeed similar to mine," Jeevith intruded into my thoughts.

"Can you read my mind?" I asked immediately.

"Normally I wouldn't. Humans have the most ... unsavory thoughts, and I would rather stay away from them. You, however, weren't giving me affective answers so I am now intruding," Jeevith explained.

"Wait, what kind of thoughts?"

"The ones that are more subconscious. For example, you're always thinking about those girls you travel with. To be more specific you think about spending as much as your time with them as possible. I'll commend you, though. That's as far as those thoughts go," Jeevith explained.

"I don't follow ..."

"You fear being alone," Jeevith quickly stated.

"You're kidding." I laughed. "I've been alone for years at a time. I have always been just fine."

"Really, now? What were you doing those years?" Jeevith asked even though I was sure he already knew the answer to his question.

I didn't reply. He had gotten me to remember. To remember what it was like to be so ... alone. I clenched my remaining fist and tilted my head to hide my eyes.

"If you don't remember, then I'll make you remember," Jeevith threatened.

"Remember what?" I asked with an innocent smile.

"The night they died," Jeevith echoed in my mind.

"I ... don't know what you're talking about," I lied.

I knew exactly what he was talking about. I also knew he had easily found the truth. I didn't want to remember what I had done that night. I sat down on the remains of Australia and drew my knees to my chest.

"You lost it that night. You killed them both that night. There was no third party that killed them in front of you. You murdered both of them in cold blood. Do you know why?" Jeevith's voice shattered any other thoughts I tried to occupy myself with.

"Shut up …" I muttered, lifting my hand over my face.

"You didn't want to be alone. They wanted to go live together. Without you. So you did what you were made to. Kill all who went against you. You slit both their throats before they could turn the knob to the door. That is what you fear and it is who you are," Jeevith recounted my past.

"Shut up, shut up, shut up, shut up …" I muttered to myself, rocking back and forth.

"So, tell me, will you try to kill me if I leave you here?" Jeevith asked.

I stopped muttering to myself and stopped rocking in place. I stood calmly and quietly. "No, stop. Just stay inside …" I tried to talk to him.

I gazed into the blue beast's gold eyes. He poured his murderous intent into me. Except, it was … warm. That murderous intent was warm. Warmth with murder wasn't what I was used to. My malicious feelings were ice cold. Not only that, but I knew what was coming. I was snapping, and he was being set free. The barriers that I had spent those lonely years building began to shatter. I kept him contained for all that time. After all, I was just the outer Jonathan. Just a device made by the Holy Grail to contain the real one. The walls were closing in and forcing me to either free him or be destroyed. The me who enjoyed this evil, sickening world was set free.

"I'm finally free, after all that time," I said with my head tilted slightly and a wicked smile on my face.

Jeevith wasn't fazed at all. He slithered back and the water around us changed to a turquoise color.

"You can walk on it now," Jeevith explained the color swap.

"Why, thank you," I genuinely thanked the serpent.

I stepped onto the water and walked on it like land. I felt the cold water on my bare feet. Every emotion that had been locked away by the fake me began to return. The outer Jonathan had been wrong about me anyway. I didn't enjoy the sickness, disease, and death that circulated in this god forsaken planet. I just loved the bright red blood that dripped onto the floor. Yes. The taste and texture of blood was almost ... orgasmic.

"I like you. That malice is rare amongst even the coldest of humans. If you want your friends to survive the coming hunt, and if you want to join them in battle, then come. If you wound me at all, I'll help you."

"Wound you? It would be easier to kill you," I said, biting into my fingers and drawing blood.

"Doesn't that hurt you?" Jeevith asked, but he wasn't really concerned.

"I simply ignore pain. I ignore it because the pain keeps coming. It keeps coming, and I keep bleeding. Honestly, it makes me feel ... alive," I replied, smiling innocently.

"Your friends wouldn't want you take action this way," Jeevith said as he wrapped a slimy tentacle, which I'd missed before, around my waist.

Friends? What friends? The ones that the outer Jonathan made? What did I care for them? I snapped the tentacle with ease, causing dark blue liquid to drip into the ocean. The red liquid dripped into the water and mixed with the beautiful colors. I moved my bloodied hand back and used it to pull my long, white hair back. The blood matted it down, but also dyed parts of it red. I continued to shape my hair back onto my head.

"The white flower is dyed red ..." I muttered quietly to myself as the reshaping continued.

As I watched the colors mix, I heard a voice in the back of my head.

*"Why are we lying to ourselves? You and I know darn well we don't want to kill our friends,"* the voice called reason spoke.

"What do you know? You're the fake me. I'm the real Jonathan. You're just a being created by the grail to hide my true personality! Besides, they're *your* friends!" I snapped.

*"Yeah, I am fake. Everything we do is done by me, though. I'll tell you what, given the chance, I'll let you fight our enemies for a change,"* the other me spoke.

He'd never let me fight if he could control himself. To be able to fight and not have to suppress either side of myself would be …

"Yeah … you're right," I replied aloud.

"You've reached an ultimatum?" Jeevith asked.

"I think so. I want to kill all those who get in my way. All those who I don't consider friends but the other Jonathan does will remain," I explained while simultaneously calming down.

"It's a start," Jeevith began. "But now I know one thing. This test of strength is meaningless."

I stopped walking toward the serpent. I rolled my neck, cracking it, and stared at Jeevith. I had only seen one facial expression from him, but he still seemed serious to me.

"What do you mean?"

"I was testing you mentally to see if you'd survive a fusion with me. I'm positive you could. Therefore, this fight between us has no stake."

"Afraid I'll kill you?" I asked.

I'd gotten myself all hyped up to fight. Now Jeevith was backing out. I couldn't stand the thought of not hitting something.

"Come then. I'll show you the gap between our powers," Jeevith replied.

A torrent of water began to pool around me and forced me into the air. One of his large tentacles also raised with the water and smashed me out of the air. I bounced once on the soft water before skidding to a stop. Another tentacle came, but I caught it and pulled it apart. Jeevith brought down a storm of rain as sharp as icicles. I blocked the attacks, even though the small rain drops cut into my skin. After a while, I dropped to a knee from the cuts on my legs. The rain ended when Jeevith thought I'd been defeated.

"Is that all?" Jeevith asked as he serpentined closer to me.

As soon as he was within range, I jumped into the air and bashed his head with my fist. Jeevith reeled back, and I dropped like a rock onto the watery surface.

"No. How about you?" I asked, egging it on.

Jeevith began to bring in a storm, but I was prepared to fight. Winning, however, I could tell was out of my reach. Oh well, this was just for fun.

## Sara

The headache was gone and my fever died down. I had awoken in a bedroom with white walls, white floors, and the door was also white. I hated it. It was too bland without any architecture showing. I rubbed my index and middle fingers against the moon on my forehead.

"Is something eating at you?" Yin, who I hadn't even noticed, asked.

"I don't remember. I feel like I forgot something really important," I searched my thoughts but came up blank.

Yin looked puzzled for the moment before looking out the window.

"Hey, Mia, what time is it?" Yin ignored my dilemma.

"Like, four in the afternoon. Why?" Mia, who I also didn't notice, said.

She was playing with her metal arm while sitting to my side. She calmly scratched at the metal, chipping it in places, before smiling at me. I looked over at Yin, who was staring out the window.

"I have three questions. Why is the moon out? Why is the moon full? Last, but certainly not least, why is it so dark outside?" Yin asked us.

Since I was feeling better, I hopped out of the hospital bed and made my way to the window. The window was higher than I thought. For that reason I had to get on my toes and pull myself up using the windowsill to see out. She was right. Not only was the moon full, but it was pitch black outside. I could, in fact, only see the moon and the darkness eclipsing the rest of the world.

"What is going on?" Yin asked, resting her chin on her fist.

Then the lights in the hospital dimmed. It wasn't hard to see, but our vision had diminished. As I looked around, I felt something akin to a spider crawling up my spine. I knew there was nothing there, but the feeling was terrifying.

"Something's coming." I scanned the small room.

Yin heeded my warning and equipped a cyan blue set of armor I hadn't seen before. It looked like something a videogame character would wear. The visor seemed to glow red from somewhere on the inside. Yin summoned Hope's End to appear before her. The blade complied and fell from the ceiling, stabbing into the white tile floor. She grabbed the hilt and as she did, a fog seemed to roll into the room.

"These are some of the targets, right?" a female voice asked from the fog.

"Kill with no discrimination," another voice replied.

Mia stepped in front of Yin and me. She, without thought, fired a flame ball which blast into the fog. The fog was dissolved in that part of the room, but the voices we had heard hadn't been eliminated.

"You shouldn't allow even a measly beast tier hunter like me behind you. It could mean your doom," the female voice said.

I turned and was face to face with an extremely pale, blond-haired woman. Her eyes seemed to reflect the moon even though the glowing ball was at her back. She drove down a fist blade, which I wasn't ready to dodge. I panicked and froze. I felt the tip of the katana touch my throat. The cold point passed through the first layer of skin. Then it was jerked harmlessly to the side. Yin had shoved the woman's arm back and kept the blade from slitting my throat. As soon as I was safe, I dropped to a knee in a cold sweat. I grasped my throat and only a small amount of blood had dripped from it. I breathed heavily, still panicked from a near-death experience.

"Sara, I need you to move!" Yin shouted as she brawled with the attacker.

I didn't reply. I couldn't reply. My breathing was becoming erratic and I was shaking all over.

"Sara, help, please!" Mia, who was dodging another attacker, cried out for help.

They both blocked and dodged their two adversaries' attacks. I was sure I was hyperventilating, but I couldn't calm myself down.

"I'll get rid of the little one," a burly man's voice boomed.

I managed to face him and saw something I didn't expect. He was a stocky man with a cloak and bowler hat identical to those the other hunters wore. He walked toward me slowly. A grin spread across his pudgy face. He was holding what I could only assume was an ice pick made for the express purpose of cutting through my skull. I tried to move, but I could only stare at my executioner. As he brought the pick down, I closed my eyes fearing my death. There was nothing, but a quiet, strangled sound and the tearing of metal. I felt a liquid of some sort drip onto my head. I looked up to see Yin standing tall in her blue armor.

"Yin, I—"

I noticed the ice pick was through her shoulder and blood was dripping off its tip. One of the hunters was missing and the female one had lost an arm. The room was now covered in blood.

"Yin, are you alright?" I scrambled to my feet.

I rushed to her side, but she somehow thrust her injured arm out, signaling to stay back.

"Stay over there if you're going to be useless!" Yin shouted angrily at me.

I shrunk back and bumped into the bedframe. I looked to Mia for help, but her eyes were cold. Which was odd for her on so many levels. Besides that, I'd never been useless before. Useless. That sounds like the right word. I was so useless. I was such a coward. What was wrong with me? I could kill without remorse before, but now …

"I'm so sorry," I said, panicked.

I rushed into the hall leaving my two friends behind. Why? What am I doing? Why am I running? I turned into a room down the hall and locked the door behind me. I leaned against it, trying to calm down but wasn't very effective. I slid down the door and assumed fetal position. Every crash, bang, and shout I heard echo through the hospital made me shiver with fright. I started crying, as quietly as possible, to myself. I distinctly remember being alone before, but I'd never felt so lonely. I played with my green hair, which had grown far too long. Surprisingly enough, the soft texture calmed me down. Now I'd gone from sad to angry. I stood up and paced around the room. I gripped my hair but made sure not to pull it out.

"Darn it!" I shouted aloud.

I made an attempt to punch the wall, but my fist was stopped mid punch.

"This must be the repercussions of what Serena did." A girl with golden eyes and hair stood before me.

She looked familiar, but I didn't know anyone like that.

"Who are you?" I asked as I pulled my fist back.

"You don't remember me?" She seemed upset.

Her voice echoed throughout the room. I searched my memory for her face, but everything seemed kind of fuzzy. I shook my head. The girl pouted before walking over to me. She bent down slightly and stared into my eyes. We stayed like that for a couple seconds.

"This is awkward." I said, breaking the silence.

"Shut up," she snapped, but didn't shouting or seem angry.

"Yes ma'am!" I replied quickly.

As she stared into my eyes, a name popped into my head. Amy. I heard the name echo throughout my conscious, pushing through my other thoughts.

"Amy?" I asked aloud.

"So that does work," the woman said more so to herself than to me.

"What do you mean?" I asked, confused.

"I figured in this form I could teleport anything. I turned out to be right, so I teleported memories of us together into your thoughts." Amy explained.

As she did, the golden glow of her eyes and hair began to fade. Then she vanished.

"What—" I began before she reappeared.

Amy was now back to her brown hair and she sat in a wheelchair. Her eyes looked distant and faded. She looked at me but didn't say anything. I inched over to her cautiously. She didn't react at all. Eventually I was so close to her I could feel her breath on my face.

"Amy?" I asked.

She didn't react at all. I put my hand to her face and waved it to get her attention. Finally she reacted.

"Sara, hey ..." Her words were slurred as if she was drunk.

There was a bang on the metal door followed by the sound of a firearm. The bullets shot through the door and hit the wall behind us. I wheeled Amy to the side safe from the hail of bullets. I then held my hand out and mentally prepared to attack. Except I wasn't ready. I started to sweat and panic again. I felt a hand on my shoulder and looked back to see Amy back to normal.

"Just concentrate on survival. Hunters aren't human, and when you kill them they won't stay dead. Don't think, just act," Amy said, trying to calm me down.

"Yeah. Yeah, ok, I got it," I replied confidently.

Except I didn't have this. I hadn't even decided which element to use. There was another gunshot and the door was sent crashing to the ground. A hunter came in and turned to face me. I looked at his face for a second. His mouth was hidden by a black facemask and his eyes were dark and unreadable. His bowler hat hid them well. He pointed a huge revolver at me, but before he could shoot, I froze him. I still hadn't decided on which element to use, but my body appeared to have made the decision for me. With the danger having passed, my breathing began to regulate.

"You've got to melt the ice," Amy suddenly said.

"What! That would kill him!" I shouted angrily as I turned around.

"Even a lower-level tier beast hunter will break through that thin ice in a few seconds. You've got to finish him off," Amy urged.

We both glared at each other, but I didn't have the heart to get mad at her. It made sense, of course, to stop him from coming after us again. I was about to melt the ice, but suddenly Amy's eyes lit up.

"Move it!" Amy said as she thrust me to the side and into the closet.

Amy pulled out a plasma gun I didn't know she had. I saw the hunter break free of the ice but as he moved to shoot, Amy fired. His hand was vaporized by the plasma gun. His giant handgun was gone, along with his arm. He dropped to a knee, holding onto his missing appendage.

"You bi—"

Amy wheeled over and shoved the plasma pistol into his mouth. "Don't speak. Just die." Amy commanded.

She fired the gun without a second thought. The man's head shot back and dissolved into dust, along with his body. Amy exhaled before maneuvering the wheelchair toward me.

"I can't walk and aiming while rolling this chair won't be easy. I need you to push me." Amy explained, adjusting the gauge on the side of her firearm.

I nodded in agreement and climbed to my feet. I got behind Amy and pushed the chair toward the door. Then I remembered something. Amy could walk before, right?

"What happened to your legs?"

The memory seemed to make Amy wince. She, however, told me anyway.

"We went up to Julian's warship as planned. At first everything was alright. Then Lock got put in a coma, Theo became a bodiless head, and I got my lower spine severed."

I didn't know how to reply. I remembered all those people except for Theo. Still, to have all three of them defeated so easily was ... unreal. I stopped pushing the chair and Amy didn't complain. Wait, didn't five of them go to stop Julian?

"What happened to Light and Jonathan?" I asked.

Amy took a deep breath, exhaled, and repeated the process once more.

"Light's gone. Julian used his life force to power the light canon. That same light cannon vaporized Jonathan. Both dead. And I was powerless." Amy's voice shook.

I reared back until I slammed into the nightstand adjacent to the closet. I slid down until I was sitting with my back against it. This was too much. No way both of them died. Those two were—no, *are* so powerful. I refused to believe it.

"If you wanna cry, go ahead. I'll guard the door. Just do it quietly" Amy managed in a low voice.

She was serious. They really were dead. So cry I did. I cried as quietly as I could, burying my head into my knees. My sad state of mind was, however, quickly interrupted.

# CHAPTER 22

# HUNT

**＊＊＊**

## *Mia*

"Hey, Sara?!" Yin shouted in a panic.

We had dispatched five hunters now, but there had been no sign of Sara. Despite Yin's numerous wounds, she still remained as hyper as possible. I really envied her. I kept a hand on my cracked ribs as we continued searching. Every step sent shock waves up my spine making me wince in pain.

"Sara, I'm sorry! Please come out!" Yin continued to urge.

Her words fell on deaf ears. She bashed in every door we passed, and I would check them. Mostly since Yin would barely even glance into a room when she checked it. Then we came across a room with an open door. There was the faint sound of crying, but it was unidentifiable. I cautiously took a painful step forward. Yin, however, shoved into the room.

"Yin!" I shouted in surprise.

As she rushed in and turned the corner, she got blasted by something. The already cracked blue helmet was blown off, but it didn't seem to slow Yin down at all. She began to surge forward, but stopped.

"Brown-haired girl?" Yin asked someone.

I gingerly walked into the room to see Amy, although she was in a wheelchair. That was new.

"Yin and Mia. We're so screwed." Amy said, smirking.

"What's that supposed to mean?" I asked.

"It means we're probably going to die now. Grouping together means more hunters will come for us. They'll be stronger too," Amy explained.

She was more pessimistic than I had remembered. I was about to respond until I noticed someone behind Amy. I wandered deeper into the room and around Yin. Sara sat behind Amy, but her face was buried into her knees. Her body shook and she was definitely crying. I walked past Amy who didn't bother to stop me.

"Way to go, Yin," I joked, kneeling down next to Sara.

I poked Sara on the shoulder, and she looked up at me. Her eyes were red from crying and when she saw me, she buried her face in her hands. I sat down next her and put my arm around her. She immediately snuggled into my body.

"What? Is she still crying about that?" Yin fretted while her eyes darted throughout the room.

Amy wheeled her old-fashioned chair toward Yin and grabbed Yin's arm, pulling her down so she could discreetly speak into her ear. I was busy attempting to comfort Sara so I wasn't paying much attention to them. Whatever Amy had told Yin made her eyes wide. She said something back that I didn't care to listen to. Amy replied, and Yin seemed to compose herself.

"What's wrong with you?" I asked Sara after shrugging off Yin and Amy's conversation.

"Jonathan … died," Sara bluntly reported with a thick voice.

I sat stunned for a second. Then I laughed. Out of pure disbelief or just out of insanity, I didn't know. Sara stared at me in confusion.

"Did you see him die?" I asked.

"Amy, did you see him die?" Sara said, sniveling.

"Which one?" Amy asked as she halted her conversation with Yin.

"What do you mean which one? Only Jonathan died right?" I inquired.

"Uh, yeah …" Amy replied suspiciously.

I, naively, thought nothing of it. I figured there wouldn't be anything to hide from me at this point.

"No, I didn't actually witness his death, but surviving a light cannon of that size is unlikely," Amy explained.

"Have you ever watched a movie where a character is assumed dead, but they died off screen?" I asked no one in particular.

Nobody answered. I was beginning to rethink my idea.

"Yeah, so?" Yin asked after the awkward pause.

"If you aren't one hundred percent sure that he's dead, he's probably not," I stated confidently.

"That's far-fetched and wrong on so many levels." Amy looked annoyed.

"It's better than assuming the guy I …"

"You like him, don't you?" Yin asked quietly.

I didn't reply and grabbed at my mechanical arm. I scratched at the metal, peeling the paint a little. It had become a habit at this point.

"It won't matter how much she likes him. He's dead either way!" Amy suddenly snapped.

She didn't seem angry, though. Just somber and depressing. The steadily increasing sound of her voice backed her emotional unease.

"I know this is the longest conversation we've had, but have you always had such a pessimistic attitude?" I asked.

I knew Amy was hurting inside, but I didn't care. She had no excuse to crush our hopes over her assumptions. Amy didn't reply, but she quickly turned the old wheelchair toward the pitch-black window.

"We should continue this conversation later," Amy more commanded than stated.

"You can feel him too?" Yin asked.

"Feel who?" I asked before Amy could answer Yin.

"There's an especially strong hunter outside this hospital right now. I can sense his aura," Yin explained.

Why couldn't I do things like that? I groaned in annoyance of their advanced abilities.

"Yin, you need to teach me how to do that."

Yin opened her mouth to reply, but Sara cut in.

"Hey, guys," Sara began, "Why is there a silhouette of a man on the moon?"

She was right. I saw the shadowy figure on the moon staring at me. Then it vanished.

"We need to move. If that thing catches us, it's game over," Amy said, panicking.

"Move where?" I asked.

"Yeah, I mean, we're in a labyrinth disguised as a hospital at the moment. Can't really go anywhere." Yin proved my point.

"What? Did you try to leave?" Amy seemed confused.

"The hallway is endless and all the doors either lead to other hallways or more rooms like this. If there is a way out, I haven't found it yet," Yin explained.

She was right. We had gone down two other hallways and ended up here by sheer luck. All in all, there wasn't much of anything we could do now. Just wait for whatever is out there.

## Flyx

These freakin' hosiers are getting on my nerves. One after another, they came flooding into Outcast Corner. Marguerite and I held them back with plasma rifles, but no help had come for us. It had been hours and sure enough the only ones defending the outside were Marguerite and myself. These beast hunters had interrupted my drinking. Not only that, but they spilled my mickey. Unforgivable.

"I a-am al-almost out o-of ammunition," Marguerite stuttered like always.

"Switch to silver bullets when you're empty," I shouted over the zapping of the plasma rifles.

I carried more than five silver-bullet guns. The first two were Colt Python revolvers. Two more were Colt Anacondas, and the last was a beauty. It was an older double-barrel shotgun that had been modified to fire explosive rounds instead of shells. Found this baby in a pawn shop and bought it immediately. I fixed it up and tweaked it with a quadruple barrel. It reloaded quickly with a quick swap magazine as well. I named it the Raging Demon. After blasting the last shot of my plasma rifle, I snapped out of my thoughts. I whipped out the gun as a hunter got a little too close for comfort. He slashed at me with a blade, but he was slow. I casually ducked under his sword and strutted over to him. He was so slow he hadn't moved from his position. Well, it wasn't so much as he was slow more so that I was slowing him down. Mixing Holy Grail water and alcohol had its perks. Every day that I don't drink, I have gnarly hangovers ... but when I do time slows down when I want it to. I whipped out the Raging Demon and blasted the hunter's stupid bowler hat off his head. Then I shot him right between the eyes. His body dissolved quickly, and I caught the ridiculous bowler hat out of the air. It too disappeared into black smoke.

"Pretty rad, eh?" I asked out loud.

"What?" Marguerite answered my question with a question.

I didn't reply and Marguerite didn't press any further. The wave of hunters kept on coming. Eventually they were getting too close for us to keep at a distance. I had no problem dispatching the hunters with my slow-time power. Although, Marguerite wasn't as fortunate. I was too caught up in quickly dispatching the dozens of hunters attacking me at once that an especially strong one slipped past me. The female hunter caught Marguerite off guard and slapped her firearm to the side. Marguerite, however, wasn't ready to retaliate at close range. The hunter gut punched the pink-haired girl, collapsing her body onto itself. Marguerite sat, coughing, doubled over. The hunter pulled out a small crossbow and pointed it to her head. I made a move to assist her. My path was blocked by an especially tall and armored hunter. I tried to shoot past him, but he blocked the silver bullets with his gauntlet.

"Get the hell out of my way!" I shouted.

"Move me," the giant hunter calmly replied.

I switched between firing at him and past him while slowing down time, but his frame was too wide for me to get an accurate shot. I watched in utter helplessness as the bolt was released from the cross bow. Suddenly, the ceiling was blown open. Then there was a flash of purple light followed by a loud zapping sound. The hunter, the crossbow, and the bolt had all been reduced to ash.

"Backup has arrived!" I heard a booming voice shout.

"Why the frak do we have to play ishy backup?" another high-pitched voice asked.

"What took so long?" I asked, smiling.

"There was traffic." Lia, who came riding in on her broom through the gaping hole in the ceiling, joked.

Her signature purple fire swirled around her and she was systematically firing it at the hunters below. While I watched Lia soar, I had forgotten about the giant hunter. He made an attempt to punch me, but I easily side stepped him in slow motion. At least I thought I did, but his fist turned at an impossible angle and nailed me in the jaw. I lost connection with myself as soon as my head began to turn from the impact. My body fell as I dropped to a knee. I'd had a glass jaw since my boxing days.

"Flyx," I heard a worried Marguerite's voice echo inside my skull.

I knew what she wanted from me. To move. I slowed down time and dove to the side. His giant fist collided with the earth, but as soon as it did it seemed to shift direction. It came flying toward me at a ridiculous speed, but I managed to duck underneath it. I watched in awe as the hunter's arm had appeared to stretch all that distance. Then it began to retract.

"Wait, hold on," I said aloud and to myself.

I glanced over my shoulder and the fist was within licking distance of my face. I slowed down time once more and managed to flop to the ground before it knocked me out cold. As I was down, I noticed a half-empty bottle of rye rolling across the floor. Despite the many unsanitary factors the bottle may have possessed, I downed it in one gulp. That restored all my energy. I kicked up and reloaded the Raging Demon. Darn alcohol was good.

"You are gonna be one tough son of a gun, eh?" I smiled with blood and alcohol stained teeth.

"Seems stronger than the other hunters," Virgil, who had just dropped down, said.

The giant man smiled so wide his face seemed to have to stretch to compensate. His skin seemed elastic and snapped back into place as the smile faded.

"My name is Sark. The other hunters you have faced so far are low class. They are beast hunters to be exact. Only capable of killing the average human." Sark jabbed his inordinate, and frankly grotesque, thumb to his chest and laughed heartily.

"So what are you then?" Lia asked as she returned from torching the remaining beast hunters.

"When a hunter kills his first demon, he absorbs its power. We call ourselves demon hunters." Sark smirked and his face glowed.

There was a brief silence.

"Did you expect us to be in awe or something?" I asked, confused.

"I killed a skin-hunting demon. They tear the flesh off of humans and stockpile it onto their own. They are stronger than all of you combined. And guess what? I kill them for sport!" Sark boasted.

To be honest he didn't seem all that impressive. Especially because I had no idea what a skin hunter was.

"You, sir, are bluffing. Let me show you true strength!" Virgil suddenly shouted.

The purple hydro shot out from all over his body and made the floor spark. He fired a bolt of lightning, but Sark's body seemed to stretch around the attack. Sark flung his fist out like a mace and it hammered into Virgil. Virgil, who had been unprepared to dodge an attack, was flung back like he'd been hit by a truck. Blood shot from his head as his body hit the rack of bottles behind Lia and myself. I was looking over my shoulder to see if Virgil, and the alcohol, were ok.

"Wa-watch out," I heard Marguerite's voice echo throughout my head.

I turned around but had no time to dodge Sark's attack. I didn't even react in time to guard, but something thrust itself between the giant fist and my body. Still, the impact sent both me and the object rocketing back. In midair I noticed pink hair fluttering in front of me. I quickly wrapped my arms around the object because I recognized it as Marguerite. Surprisingly, I leveled out in midair and dug my heels into the ground. I skidded back until I slammed into the quickly approaching bar. It hurt, but physical damage had always been easy for me to overcome. I was, once, the Canadian champion across all weight classes. I began to lean forward but quickly stopped myself. I didn't want to fall onto Marguerite. I flopped onto my bum, closed my eyes, and took a deep breath. When I opened them I was treated to the sight of Lia kicking the guy's arse. She was flinging all kinds of objects at Sark, and they appeared to be doing considerable damage. Then, I remembered Marguerite was sitting in my lap.

"Hey, you alright?"

She didn't respond. I poked her in the cheek, but she didn't even flinch. I panicked a little. I reached for her wrist to check her pulse, but when I did she cried out in pain. When I looked at her tiny hand, I noticed something chilling. I was pretty sure a person's hands weren't supposed to bend that way. She whimpered the next time I lifted up her arm.

"Sorry about this," I muttered before I grabbed her forearm and wrist.

Despite her hair-raising shrieks of protest and pain, I twisted her hand until it faced the correct direction. There were a series of grotesque cracking noises as I did so. When I was done, Marguerite began to cry quietly and steadily. I slowly moved her body off of mine and lifted her up and over the countertop. As I left her safely behind the counter, I heard Virgil began to stir.

"Hurry up and get up," I spat before returning my attention to Sark.

The raging demon was too far away to get to now. I assumed it was because Lia had gotten a little telekinesis crazy. My steel-laced gloves would have to do since bullets had proven ineffective. I pulled down on my glove on my right hand to be sure it was on good. As I began to approach him, Sark seemed to have figured out Lia's attack. She's was flying quickly, but there was a pattern. I didn't have time to decipher it, however, because he threw a punch sending Lia flying through the roof and into the night. She cried out in pain, but mostly surprise, as she was suddenly thrown away.

"At the moment it's just you and me." I grinned widely.

"Maybe you'll prove challenging," Sark boasted.

I charged headfirst with my hands up like my boxing guard. Sark shot out his elastic fist, but I slowed down time and dodged it. I knew it would be back, but I got an idea. I grabbed onto the stretchy flesh and tugged on it as hard as I could. I ended up yanking Sark off the ground and toward me.

"What?" Sark said in surprise.

"I was a boxer, ya know. So I'll put you down with one punch," I taunted.

He was near enough to hit now, but I was ready for his tricks. I threw a wide haymaker on purpose hoping he would shoot his head back. Naturally, my enemy did as I wished. Sark stretched his head back, but as he did I slowed time to a crawl. I jumped into the air and brought my leg down like a super axe kick. I collided with his giant, muddy-looking nose. The helmet he wore didn't compensate for his giant nose so it made a good target. Time returned to normal as soon as I made contact. Sark slammed into the ground, making a small hole where his head collided. His helmet was destroyed either by my kick or the collision with the floor. He immediately tried to rise to his feet, but I let loose another jumping, super axe kick. Sark, however, tried to move again. Even though he was clearly injured, I didn't let up. I brought my knee down and smashed Sark's head into the ground. He cried out in pain, but I didn't stop. I rained down blows on the giant demon hunter until, eventually, he stopped making any noise at all. I raised my fist once more, but it was stopped by another part of my mind.

"He's done. Let him die peacefully," Marguerite, without a stutter, said inside my head.

I turned to where I'd left her battered body. She was standing and leaning on Virgil's muscular frame. Her eyes were glazed over and her breathing was very strained. Virgil's face was bloodied from the blow he'd suffered from Sark's hand. Lia had returned from being flung into the night and looked madder than in pain.

"Do you have to use telepathy right now?" I asked out of concern.

"Yes. I can't breathe properly yet," Marguerite explained, echoing her voice throughout my mind.

"Well, he won't die peacefully. I didn't do enough damage to kill him. He'll get up if enough time passes."

As if on cue, Sark groaned and his body experienced a short spasm.

"Let me burn him then!" Lia shouted as the purple fire materialized around her.

"No, I've got a better idea," Marguerite's voice traveled throughout the entire room.

She managed to half walk, half stumble over to Sark. She dropped, painfully, to a knee. She placed her hand on his head and a small pink glow encompassed her hand. The light, however, faded almost immediately. Marguerite used her uninjured hand to then hoist her body up thanks to a somehow still standing table.

"What'd you do to him?" I asked.

"He'll experience a dream. One in which he dies, calmly, at its ends," Marguerite explained through telepathy.

"That's kind, but also terrifying. Well done!" Lia laughed maniacally.

Marguerite managed a grin, but didn't say anything more.

"Hey, Lia, how are Jacob and Azazeal doing on their end?" I asked.

"I'll check," Lia simply stated as she closed her eyes.

I had remembered Jacob and Azazeal were somewhere in Paris searching for Jonathan's little posse. They were going to give them the bad news they'd received from Julian. That Jonathan and Cyrus were both dead. Lia suddenly opened her eyes and her facial expression displayed her confusion.

"Did you guys know Azazeal was pregnant?" Lia asked calmly.

"What?" The remaining people in the room replied in unison.

"Let's hurry and head to the hospital down the street. They'll probably go there," Lia quickly commanded without explanation.

## *Rylen*

The lower floors of Outcast Corner were emptier than usual. I had been wandering aimlessly for hours but hadn't run into anyone. The lights had gone out, and I was breathing fire every once and awhile to see my way around. I stumbled around in the tunnels, occasionally tripping over things I couldn't see. I turned a corner into an especially narrow hallway I didn't recognize. I didn't really venture through Outcast Corner that much, though. At the end of the hall I spotted two shadowy figures. I immediately recognized Gabriel because of his long wings, but I couldn't see the other person.

"Hello?" I called down the hall.

"Rylen, is that you?" A gruff, German accent asked.

I spit some fire onto the floor in front of me instead of speaking. The light from the flames allowed me to see their faces. I was quickly able to identify them as Carl and Gabriel. They had pained expressions on their faces.

"What's wrong?"

Gabriel and Carl exchanged a glance as if considering the pros and cons of divulging their secret. In fact, they seemed to decide against telling me.

"It is nothing," Carl lied.

Whatever was going on was not nothing. I stepped through the fire, which couldn't burn me and began to walk toward my two allies. They made no attempt to move out of my way or hide anything. Whatever they were hiding wasn't here. I wasn't one to become angry or impatient, so I waited calmly for an explanation. Everyone remained silent until another voice spoke.

"Light's gone, Rylen." I turned to see *him* standing behind me.

I hadn't heard or smelled him arrive. *He* had never had a particular scent anyway. His witch doctor mask still covered that disgusting face of his, but his outfit was different than usual. It was some sort of trench coat that made him look larger than he really was.

"Sorry, what did you say?"

"His soul's been split into three pieces, but the main one was destroyed. Unless he's found bodies to hide in, he's dead, Rylen," he explained.

My eyes widened in shock and fear.

"No way, not Light. He's too strong." I tried to make sense of his words.

I began to cry for the first time in … I couldn't even remember how many years it had been. I took a glance at Gabriel and Carl who must have known. Gabriel's face was full of sympathy, but Carl's expression was hardened. We locked eyes for a moment, and he frowned before looking away. That's when I realized I'd never cried in front of them either. I wiped my eyes quickly and stopped my crying. At least I did until I remembered the last thing he'd said to me.

*"I'll be back, I promise."*

"He … he promised …" I cried aloud before going into my flaming cocoon.

I had no plans to transform, but I didn't want to be seen crying anymore. I continued to sob, but recalled what *he* had said earlier.

Even if there was a small chance part of him was still alive, I needed to check it out. I let out a last howl of despair before wiping my eyes and allowing myself to calm down. I exited the flaming cocoon and everything around me was the same as when I'd hidden myself. I did a three-sixty as I glanced at the people who surrounded me.

"So … uh … what now?" I asked awkwardly.

Gabriel opened his mouth to say something, but another voice spoke before he did.

"You all will be coming with me now," a child's voice said.

I looked all around the narrow hall but couldn't see anyone. Carl looked just as confused as I felt. Then suddenly we were falling.

"What?" I shouted in surprise.

I looked down, but we were falling into an infinite darkness. It only lasted for a couple seconds. I seemed to just feel the ground appear underneath me and the sensation of falling vanished instantly. I immediately began to take in my surroundings. Carl, Gabriel, and *he* had also landed in the wide hallway.

"I don't like this …" Carl suddenly muttered.

Neither did I. The only light seeping into the room was from the glowing moon. The outside, however, was dark and foggy despite the full moon.

"Where are we?" I asked, but nobody gave me an answer.

I looked down the hall behind me but there was nothing but darkness. I turned the other way and paused all movement when my eyes fell upon a little girl. On another glance, it may have even been a boy. He favored both Jacob and Azazeal, but I didn't think there was any relation. The child's hair was a mix of red, black, and blue. It hung messily over the child's face, hiding everything but his mouth.

"And who are you, young one?" Gabriel asked out of curiosity.

He floated closer but immediately retreated. His eyes widened with fear. I'd never seen Gabriel afraid of anything.

"You … what are you?" Gabriel asked.

He was met with a child's laughter, but one without a distinguishable gender. The kid raised its hand, but nothing seemed to happen. At least, until his shadow seemed to move and become 3D. At first it was the same as the kid, but then it began to grow larger and its frame became more muscular. The shadow slashed a large battle axe through the air as it advanced past the child. Gabriel jumped back as the deadly shadow attempted to cleave him in two. I moved into my flaming cocoon so my dragon transformation could begin. I couldn't see what was happening outside of my flaming shelter, but I could hear everything. I heard the sound of metal clashing with metal and child's laughter.

Someone said, "We have no chance until Rylen transforms!"

They would have to wait ten more seconds, though. The sounds of the scuffle had begun to diminish as my transformation completed. The flame cocoon faded as I began to rub at the red scales that covered my body. They were stronger than a lot of bullet-stopping alloys, but were also rather uncomfortable. They stabbed into my skin lightly, but were great for defending me against many forms of damage.

"Aw, it's no fun if you run away," I heard the child say as Carl bolted in the other direction.

I didn't see *him* anywhere, but Gabriel was sitting up against the wall, his mouth agape with blood trickling out of the corner of it.

"G-Gabriel?" I hoped for a response.

I began to walk closer to my friend, but Carl returned and grabbed me by the arm.

"We have to go, right now!" Carl explained in a frenzy.

I looked at him in confusion before returning my attention to Gabriel. I searched lower on his body and my eyes fell on the gaping hole in his stomach. It looked as if something had jammed its arm through him.

"I ... don't understand ..."

I stood in shock as another person I cared about died because I couldn't do anything. Carl continued to tug on me, but I remained planted. Gabriel's blood began to pool underneath him and a bit of it touched my bare foot. I watched the crimson liquid spill in between my toes before quickly jumping away. The white claws on my foot, that replaced my fingernails, were covered with blood now. I searched the hall for the child and his shadow, but they were gone.

"Where did they go?" I asked, grabbing Carl by the collar of his shirt.

He looked down at me with emotionless eyes. Carl then adjusted his gaze down the hall before pointing and speaking.

"Some members of the Amethyst division arrived. They said they'd give us time to escape ..."

I followed his gaze and spotted the child and his shadow. The shadow was dragging the headless body of a soldier behind him. There was blood covering both of them. In fact, there was a large amount of blood specifically on the shadow's left arm. I clenched my fist and the claws dug into my scaly palm. They could hardly break the surface, but I was squeezing so hard blood began to trickle from my hand. I did everything I could to contain my rage, but steam began to shoot out of my nose and the fire burned in my throat. I finally gave up on holding back and shoved Carl behind me. My wings shot out of my back and I used them to propel myself toward the child. I roared as flames shot out of my mouth. I slashed at the kid, but the shadow grabbed him by the back of his neck and threw him further down the hall. I caught a glimpse of its face in midair and wished I hadn't. Its smile was grotesque, covered in blood, and huge. The kid had no nose, but its giant, hollow, eyes made up for the missing space. That all happened in an instant, but it froze me for long enough to take a hit. The shadow slashed his axe into my shoulder, but the scales kept it from penetrating deep into me. It did draw a lot of blood, however. I cried out from the pain, but didn't stop to grab my wound. I turned and slashed my claws across the shadow's chest, except I didn't hit him. They phased through his body, leaving me wide open for another attack. The shadow swung its axe and the blades caught me in the side. The scales stopped most of the hit, but the force of the weapon still sent me crashing backward and to the floor. I slowly rose to my feet only for the shadow to hit me with an upward swing from the axe. I flew upward and crashed into the ceiling. Still, no deep wounds had been made. I began to crawl to my feet again, but the shadow stomped on my head. He was so strong I was suddenly seeing the floor below, the one we were fighting on. I tried to get up again, but I felt something tug on my braids. I yelped in surprise and pain as the shadow pulled me up and off the ground.

"Any last words?" I heard the child giggle.

"Just one," I replied.

I then proceeded to blast the shadow with smoldering flames. He dropped me, and I immediately stabbed my claws into his chest. They didn't go through him this time, and gray mist began to spill out of the shadow. It screamed in agony, but didn't stop trying to kill me. He wrapped his fingers around my throat, effectively stopping my fire breath and my breathing. I literally clawed at the shadow's arm, but I couldn't get it to let go. If only I'd had more time to transform further. I was fading fast and already began to falter in my attempt to escape. My vision began to blur and darken as my struggling ceased. I hung limply, awaiting my death, when I was suddenly dropped. I immediately began to cough and gasp for air. I blinked the tears out of my eyes as I looked up to see Carl. He'd somehow managed to knock the shadow onto the floor. The dark figure hadn't moved since Carl had done whatever he did. I coughed a couple more times before speaking.

"Thanks, Carl."

He nodded in reply and offered me a hand. I took it and was immediately yanked to my feet. I hadn't expected him to be so strong and almost fell over again. Carl made no motion to stabilize me, but I remained on my feet despite that. I grabbed at my stomach wound, which had already begun to heal.

"Should we retreat?" Carl grunted as the shadow began to move again.

I thought about continuing to fight, but the shadow didn't look very damaged at all. Me, on the other hand ...

"Yeah, we should run," I replied as I began to back away.

The shadow began to advance when he heard me, but Carl and I bolted in the other direction. Then, suddenly, something seemed to come through a sort of portal just in front of us. A blazing, red horse clopped out of it with two riders on its saddleless back. I was amazed the riders weren't burned, but the idea was far from my attention at the moment. The girl jumped off first and the boy rode past us at the shadow. He slashed with his glowing blade, and the shadow countered with his own weapon.

"Hey there, how's it going?" the girl asked, her gold eyes glowing brightly.

Her brown hair was combed neatly down her back and her skin was a light tan. She had on an old, beat-up hat that clashed with her golden dress.

"Not well, actually. We're being attacked by—"

"I can see that. You two should get going," she said, walking past Carl and me.

I watched her go as a bow made of light appeared in her hand. She notched an arrow and aimed it down the hall. At the same time, the boy she arrived with smacked the sword out of the shadow's hand. It slapped him to the side as the girl fired her arrow. It blew off the creature's arm on contact. I wanted to continue watching, but I was interrupted by Carl grabbing my arm.

"Come on, let's go," Carl said as he dragged me away from the scene.

I said nothing as we ran away. My breathing was heavy, and I could hardly keep up with him.

"What was that?" Carl asked, seeming scared.

I continued to catch my breath but couldn't have offered him a reply if I'd wanted to. I didn't have the slightest clue either. I coughed again, like before, but when I drew my hand away my palm was covered with blood. I also hadn't noticed it happen, but I had reverted back to my human form. It wasn't a good idea to stay here in my weakened state. If I'm forced to transform, then my human body becomes a lot weaker than normal. I was going to suggest that we return to Outcast Corner, wherever that was, but suddenly we were back in the narrow hall. It was like whatever had just occurred had been a dream. Except both *he* and Gabriel were gone ...

## *Jacob*

"I knew you had been slower than normal for the past few months, but this was not what I was expecting," I said calmly.

Azazeal and I had been scurrying through the streets of Paris for hours now. I carried Azazeal on my back and allowed her to use Brimstone. She had, untimely, gone into the demon equivalent of labor.

"Yeah, but I didn't think humans could get demons pregnant. Shows what I know," Azazeal halfheartedly laughed.

I jumped over a car, off of a bridge, and into a small sewage tunnel.

"Will this do?" I asked.

"I have standards, you know. But, seriously, no, I'll need a room's worth of space. It's not like human birth where I push out a baby. Although, you could have guessed that from my lack of an enlarged stomach," Azazeal explained while sounding sleepy.

I didn't reply, but I searched the surrounding area. I skillfully jumped out of the sewage drain and returned to the road. A few hunters approached us immediately, but Azazeal shot them all before they even knew what happened. It looked easy, but Azazeal's breathing seemed strained.

"Have you ... spotted a place ... for us to go?" Azazeal managed through small breaks.

Even in the dark these eyes of mine could see. I had indeed spotted an area that would be perfect for childbirth. A hospital. I must have wandered toward it, because we were already close. I quickly walked toward the hospital building, but stopped when I saw a strange figure. The being was standing in the air just outside of the fourth floor of the hospital. I assumed it was male because of its large, sturdy frame. Everything about him was too dark for even me to see. He was wearing all black with a trench coat. His head was hidden by some sort of hood or cowl. It was too dark to see his skin color or any other features. Then, suddenly, he vanished. I blinked and he reappeared. He was standing a few lamp posts in front of us. I saw his shadowy figure just out of the range of the furthest light. We would have locked eyes if he'd had eyes. His face was like an unused canvas. A black, empty canvas. Then the farthest light went out. The being got closer. Then another light went out. He got even closer. I tried to move, but I was locked in place. The last light went out and it would have been pitch black for a normal person. I could still see. The figure didn't seem to walk, but rather glide with his feet still touching the ground. He made no sound at all. I couldn't hear his breathing, heartbeat, or anything else about him. He got right up to me, but he was considerably taller. The being reached his hand down and jabbed my forehead with his finger. I stood confused at his odd behavior. It would be child's play to kill Azazeal and me when we couldn't retaliate.

"As you are now, you have no hope of posing a challenge to me," the being simply stated.

I opened my mouth to reply, but no words came out. No, I said something, but the words faded away from my mind. I scrambled inside my head to remember them, but there was nothing. The being then returned to where he was in front of the hospital. The wall of the hospital seemed to disappear and the creature just floated in. I heard surprised shouting and the sound of metal on metal. As I wondered what was going on up there, the streets lamps flickered back to life. I could suddenly move again. I continued toward the hospital to confront the monster.

"Forget him. He's Second Earth's or Hell's equivalent of the boogie man. We can't do anything until I have this kid," Azazeal explained desperately.

I stopped in my tracks and looked up at the upper hospital room. I heard cries of pain, but still saw flashes of fire and light. Whoever was up there was battling it out with that thing. I believed the people would be able to at least survive in combat with him so I switched plans.

"Alright. We'll go to a lower floor of the hospital." I replied.

Azazeal didn't reply, so I began to jog toward the hospital. As I did I could hear Amy's voice, but it sounded drowned out. I heard other names begin shouted and more shouts of pain, but it didn't concern me. Though, Amy must have been in the room the creature had entered. As I entered the hospital, I quickly picked out an elevator. I quickly moved to it and hit the call button, but there was no sound or glow.

"The power must be out," I muttered.

Azazeal made a delusional giggling sound. "Just our luck, right?"

I didn't reply. The stairs were right next to the lift so I followed them up to the fourth floor. I had thought of an alternative way to do this.

# CHAPTER 23

# BERSERKER

*Jonathan*

He wasn't kidding. Jeevith had dispatched me quicker than I'd ever lost in my life. My body wasn't bloody, but I had bruises all over to the point where moving just a little hurt. It was my loss. Although, my handicap didn't exactly help me win.

"You blame your missing arm on your quick defeat?" Jeevith intruded into my thoughts.

"Can you not do that?" I breathed, exhausted.

"Regardless, we can fix that handicap of yours," Jeevith spoke.

I raised an eyebrow.

"How so?"

"We can do as god tier hunters do. I can become your arm and give you my power," Jeevith explained.

I cracked a smile, expecting a condescending comment but it never came.

"What, like, seriously?" I asked.

"Do I look like I'm joking?" Jeevith replied.

Jeevith's face and position hadn't changed at all. Then I realized what he meant.

"Oh, you can make jokes." I smiled.

Jeevith made a sound akin to laughter.

"So can we actually do this?" I asked.

"The hunt has already begun so we'll fuse and I'll take you to Paris immediately," Jeevith replied.

He began to move toward me. Probably thinking of starting the fusion.

"What is this so called hunt anyway?" I asked.

"You'll know everything when I become your arm."

I had no idea why I trusted this sea god, yet he seemed extremely reliable.

"Let's do this, then," I commanded.

"If you try and command me again, I'll kill you."

I flinched as his voice boomed and echoed inside of my head.

"Duly noted." I laughed halfheartedly.

## *Jacob*

I took Azazeal to a hospital room and quickly shut the door behind us. Azazeal immediately climbed off my back and moved to the approximate center of the room. Azazeal tossed Brimstone to me along with her black rapier.

"You'll have more use for them than I will," Azazeal said.

"Thanks."

I paused as Azazeal averted her attention to the floor. She grasped at her abdomen, underneath her tank top, and drew away a black liquid with her hand. She suddenly began to draw symbols, the meaning of which I couldn't discern. They were all drawn without her raising a finger. The figures were formed rapidly and with impossible correctness. After all, it wasn't easy to draw perfectly with a liquid. Regardless, I shut the door and left Azazeal alone.

## *Mia*

The wall the four of us stared at seemed to shake. Then it slowly peeled away to reveal a dark figure. No bowler hat, but the being was wearing a trench coat. Nobody spoke or moved. The figure seemed to look as over before raising a long, boney finger. It seemed to point it right at me.

"You. I want you." Its' voice seemed hoarse, but commanding.

I looked around and all eyes were on me. What did this thing want from me?

"I'm not looking for a relationship with anyone, but a certain person," I replied.

The whole room seemed to stop a give me odd looks.

"What, I'm not …"

"Who then?" Sara asked, smiling oddly.

I opened my mouth to reply, I wasn't going to tell her who, but Amy interjected.

"Forget it, and get moving!" Amy commanded, wheeling herself in front of me.

"What?" I inquired.

Yin and Sara also stepped in front of me. The three of them created a wall between me and the creature.

"This thing wants you so get out of here. Well take it down to keep you safe," Yin explained.

She was pointing Hope's End at the monstrosity, but holding Sunrise in her left. She tossed the blade back to me and I barely reacted in time to catch it.

"This is—" I got cut off.

"Jonathan's not around to use it so I'm giving it to you. Just hurry up and go and give it back when this is over," Yin explained quickly.

"I ... don't die on me," I muttered.

I took a step back before running out of the open door. Despite my wiser thoughts, I ran and didn't look back.

## *Aqua*

I could see the destruction of the hospital from the rooftops. The seven-day hunt had begun, and I'd unfortunately ended up in the ring. I looked up at Julian's airship, which was hovering just above me. I'd already boarded it and been briefed on the situation. The hunters had come for the strongest humans gathered in a certain area. The hunt, however, only happened during the sixth and twelfth months of every year. What were the chances that the week they picked would be this one?

"Why did I happen to come here today of all days?" I asked myself aloud.

"You want to come here to see the Mia girl," he replied in heavy Russian.

"You don't have to be literal about everything, Roman," I answered, but in English.

"My apologies, princess, I'll try to be less literal," Roman vigorously apologized.

"Don't call me that!" I stomped the roof, cracking it.

"My apologies ..." Roman muttered.

"Don't apologize so much," I snapped, but quietly.

The sounds of fighting in the distance were growing louder. The combat on the streets and in the buildings below demanded my attention. I heard the sound of wings flapping through the air behind me. I felt the presence of water appear, first small then big. It felt like the amount the human body was made up of—a female one at that. I took a guess without turning around.

"Snow, report," I commanded my little sister and scout.

I'd sent Snow to find the bulk of Jacob's soldiers. It was all in the hope of finding Mia Alves. Who, according to Roman, had been transferred the berserker's magic.

"The bulk of Outcast's soldiers are either headed to or in the hospital. The Black King himself is there as well. Although The Snatcher is also present. Shall we assist, sister?" Snow asked in Russian.

"The Snatcher?" I inquired.

"He's like the underworld's equivalent of the boogieman. He can do whatever he pleases," Snow explained in English instead of Russian.

That changed things. I hadn't planned on helping them fight. Just showing Mia how to use the berserker's magic. And possibly saving her from being bed ridden for the rest of her life. I pondered silently to myself. Would even someone as powerful as myself stand a chance against The Snatcher?

"If we're going, we should go now, milady," Roman urged.

"I'm aware of that," I retorted.

"Then why do you hesitate?" I heard a voice in the back of my head.

"I ... don't know." I didn't have an answer for the questioning voice.

"Princess?" Roman asked, worried.

"I'm fine," I quickly replied.

"You were talking to something again. Are you positive that—"

"I'm fine!" I shouted.

"You don't look fine," a child's voice sounded.

I looked upward to the overhang just above us. The child stood, upside down. I wasn't surprised by his sudden appearance as it was common to me. His devilish smile, red eyes, and glowing blue body were normal.

"Why are you here?" I asked.

"Does it matter? I go where I want," the child replied.

"Not like you're real anyway …" I muttered.

The child said nothing to this, remaining in the air. He knew that he was some figment of my imagination. That didn't stop him from bugging me.

"Aqua, are you ignoring me?" the child asked, snapping me out of my thoughts.

"Does it matter? Also, do you have a name or something? I don't believe you like being called a child. You have been one for as long as I've known you." I changed the subject.

"You don't have time to worry about me. She's about to use it." The child pointed toward the hospital.

The building had begun falling apart. The walls on one side were mostly gone and the roof had been blown off. I saw fires and ice spikes filling some of the rooms, though it was obvious they weren't doing damage. I watched The Snatcher grab the almost motionless body of a barley armored girl. It wrapped its long fingers around her throat and began to squeeze. She wasn't dead, but didn't make much of an effort to free herself. Her eyes were wide with terror and tears streamed out of them from the pain.

"Snow, go!" I commanded quickly.

Snow's human body vaporized and out of the vapor came a falcon. Snow's bird form quickly flew toward the hospital. As soon as she was within striking distance of The Snatcher, she transformed into a white tiger. She clawed across The Snatcher's arm, causing it to drop the girl. I quickly created a stream of water branching from the building we were on to an empty room in the hospital. I was about to ride it, but something stopped me. I turned and searched for the child, but then it was gone. I quickly glided down the water slide without giving it a second thought.

## Yin

Saying this was unexpected would be an understatement. A white tiger stood over me, but wasn't facing me. It was pacing back and forth, growling at the creature that just beat me black and blue. I rolled over and pushed myself to my feet. This suit of armor was already demolished. That sucked, especially since blue was my favorite color. I managed to find a part of the wall that was still standing. After leaning my hand against it, I let my body rest. Despite my armor, I'd never been this torn up before. My shirt was pretty much gone and I could see my sports bra. My pants had been turned into shorts. I'd also never bled this much. In fact, there was so much blood I'd already stained the white wall by leaning against it. Then, suddenly, I laughed. No reason for it. It kind of just happened. Maybe I was losing it, or maybe it was because I knew there was something left for me to lose. I returned my attention to the tiger, which was somehow pushing back the demon that had inflicted more damage on me than anyone or anything else.

"Yin ..." I heard someone moan my name.

I recognized the voice as Amy's. I managed to look behind the pillar I was leaning on. The brunette was pinned from the waist down by a large piece of rubble. Although she seemed to be happy about something.

"What?"

"I can't feel my legs!" Amy shouted, bursting into laughter in reply.

There was a slight delay where I thought she'd gone crazy.

"Good one!" I heard Sara giggle.

Even though I couldn't find Sara from where I was, I smiled. We were beaten, bloodied, but our spirit hadn't died. Not yet anyway.

"So, how ya holding up there?" Amy asked me.

"Just bleeding out. Nothing much other than that," I replied.

The tone quickly became more serious.

"How bad is it?" Amy investigated out of concern.

I glanced at the pillar I was leaning on. It had become red like someone was painting on it. I was about to tell her but my body forced me to prioritize breathing a little more.

"This pillar … was white thirty seconds ago," I replied after rushing some breaths.

There was no reply, and I watched the tiger battle back the shadowy demon. The creature slashed, but the tiger's reaction time was unbelievable. It avoided the monsters attacks with ease. One of the tiger's claws somehow connected with the thing I hadn't been able to put a scratch on. Black blood sprayed in every direction and some of it got on my exposed arm. It burned a lot, but I didn't react to it. My body was hurting too much. Still, I brushed the sticky blood off with my hand. As I watched the epic battle, a golden glow intruded into my peripheral vision. I was about to turn around, but a golden-haired figure appeared in front of me. It was definitely Amy, but not only was she walking she was also a blonde. Amy placed a hand on my shoulder and the scenery suddenly changed. We were still in the hospital, but a different room. It was empty, minus a bed and a plate of surgical tools. As soon as my stand was removed, I began to fall. Amy caught me, but suddenly I was sitting on the bed. I blinked in surprise, but remained silent. Super Amy silently tied my hair up and began to examine my body. I didn't object, but mostly because the adrenaline rush was gone. I was in so much pain I couldn't speak or move. I wanted to cry, but even breathing hurt, so I kept that shallow. I was like a doll in her hands. Amy was getting a little close. She moved me by using my shoulders to get a better look at me.

"This looks pretty bad." Amy sighed, sometimes touching the cuts on my face with her open palm.

I leaned my head into her hand. It was oddly soothing. Amy moved her other hand and began to feel the cuts and gashes all over me. I whimpered and my breathing pick up. I was in a ton of pain after all. I wasn't dealing with it very well either.

"Calm down would you. I'll take care of you," she said, smiling.

I only groaned in reply. At this point I couldn't tell just how Amy was trying to heal me. I'd stopped feeling pain and could only feel pleasure thanks to her powerful aura. My body twitched from her touch, and I groaned in immense pain. Amy suddenly tapped me on the forehead. I was then lying vertically on the bed. I was also, somehow, on my stomach. I was still processing what had just happened as Amy peeled of what remained of my tattered shirt. I yelped in surprise as Amy undid my sports bra. I began to make a motion to hide myself, but then I heard Amy chuckle.

"Don't go all prude on me now. Just relax. There's no way for me to do this any other way." Amy pointed out as well as commanded of me.

I couldn't argue when she was right. At least she'd left my pants on. Suddenly I felt a cold, wet, rag being dragged across my bloody back. It must have had some sort of anesthetic because the pain flicked on like a switch. I gritted my teeth to prevent myself from crying out due to the intense burning sensation. Then she stopped cleaning. I could hear her messing with the tools on the table so I directed my attention to them. Amy was filling a syringe with a liquid I could only assume was a pain reliever. The wounds must have been worse than I thought if I need some sort of surgery. As she filled the syringe I quickly noted the size of the needle. I swallowed in fear. Out of all the things in the world, I hated big needles the most. Sort of odd since I fought with swords more often than anything else. Amy flicked the needle before looking my way. She must have noticed my worried face because she smiled.

"Don't worry, I may not have a degree, but I studied for medical school before all this. Also, everything else I know I've also been taught by Jacob," Amy attempted to reassure me.

Despite all logic that encouraged me. She then made a motion to administer the medicine, and I closed my eyes in anticipation.

## *Sara*

Despite Amy taking Yin somewhere, I remained here. I probably wouldn't have been much use to them anyway. I could only muster up ice magic. The ice hadn't stopped the demon from beating me within an inch of my life. Regardless, I was more bruised than bloody. The battle between the white tiger and that thing took my mind off it. The creature that had given Amy, Yin, and I so much trouble seemed to be distancing itself from the tiger. It didn't seem fully invested in the fight either. The white tiger lunged at the demon, but all the tiger caught was air. The demon had used some ability I hadn't seen before.

"Found you," the creature muttered before tearing through the wall.

I watched in confusion as the demon vanished from my line of sight. I then remembered why we were fighting it in the first place. It had somehow found Mia. I attempted to move, but my body and mind weren't in sync. I was trying to force my limbs to move, but to no avail. As I sat defeated, the white tiger transformed into a woman. She was pale, muscular, and tall and reminded me of someone, but I couldn't remember who. As I searched my memory for that person, a wave of water burst through and destroyed the wall. I only slightly recognized the Blue King as she slipped through the steady stream of water. She looked a lot less scary without that domino mask.

"Where did The Snatcher go?" the Blue King asked.

The shapeshifter girl pointed. "That way."

The Blue King started to give chase but stopped when she realized the other girl wasn't following her.

"What's wrong?" the Blue King asked.

The shapeshifter said something in a language I couldn't understand, but she gestured to me. The Blue King replied in the same language before leaving the room. My vision had slowly been getting blurry as their conversation ended. The closer the shapeshifter got, the more static filled my senses. She knelt down and said something, but I couldn't hear her. She seemed to notice I wasn't exactly coherent because she waved her hand in front of my eyes. I tried to move or say something to show I was at least still alive, but I wasn't able to muster up the energy. I managed to whimper in pain, though. Even in my pitiful shape, I felt the older girl lift me up onto her back. She then transformed into the white tiger again. I wasn't sure where she was taking me, but if it was for help we were in a hospital. Hopefully, that meant we weren't going far.

## Mia

I had officially gotten lost. I was trying to find the exit to the hospital, but I'd gone down two floors, up one floor, and down this seemingly endless hallway. The power was out so I had to use the glow of Sunrise to see. I hadn't figured out how to use the sword effectively, so the glow was pretty dim. I wanted to use my fire, but I was sure that whatever that thing was could sense me. Well, maybe a little wouldn't hurt. I messed around for a bit while trying to force my magic energy into the sword. After shouting obscenities, louder than I probably should have, I calmed down. I stopped moving and began to focus my scattered mind. Sunrise, surprisingly, lit up like it was supposed to. I used the glowing blade to navigate my way through the abandoned hospital building. I came across a square room with three paths. They were labeled, but in French. Too bad I hadn't been taught any language besides my vernacular.

"Eeny, meeny, miney, moe ..." I began, but then I noticed something down the left hallway.

That thing had found me. Its nonexistent face and trench coat were a dead giveaway. Not only that, but that could only mean one thing. That fraker had killed my friends! I lowered Sunrise so the tip touched the floor. I'd never wielded a katana, but I figured it wouldn't be too hard. Although, whether or not I could use Sunrise was in the back of my head. I was really mad, more than I'd ever been before. I felt a familiar power began to rise from the depths of my magic circuit. The last time I had felt something like this had been back at that ice guy's house. I could see the red aura rising off my body, but it was different from that time. It hurt. My skin and blood boiled to the point where small dots of blood appeared on my body. Even with that, I was too blinded by rage to care. I gripped Sunrise with both hands and charged forward. The creature, at first, didn't seem fazed by my sudden charge. That was until I slashed into its chest faster than I'd ever moved before. The black blood shot in all directions. Some of it splashed onto and burned through parts of my clothes and my skin, but I didn't care. Killing this piece of garbage was my one and only goal. I found myself roaring like an animal as I slashed wildly at the ghoul. Despite having my fire magic, it felt like a waste to use it. Especially when this was working fine. My wild slashing, however, wasn't as effective as I had thought. I had only made contact once and everything else had been just off the mark. While I attacked with endless combinations, the creature just bided its time. I had been doing ok for someone who'd never used a katana—that was until I underestimated the blade's length and slashed deep into a pillar. I tugged, but Sunrise remained lodged in the rock. I kept pulling and neglected to pay attention to the monster. The creature flung out its crazy long finger claw things, but I was too busy to react effectively. I pulled my head back, but its sharp appendages cut a gash above my left eyebrow. The strange magic was still present, however, so I didn't feel or react to the wound. I began to punch the pillar with my mechanical arm until it was destroyed. This building was pretty destroyed anyway, so I didn't think it would matter.

"Eat this!" I shouted at the top of my lungs.

I raised Sunrise and unconsciously fired a light beam. Both the creature and myself didn't expect the beam to be fired. Its grotesque arm was blasted off, causing more of the black blood to spray throughout the room. More of it splashed on me, causing my own blood to stream from parts of my exposed skin. That was when I noticed just how much blood I'd lost. There was more of my blood on the walls and floor than the ghouls. The demon gripped at its missing arm before shooting out its remaining arm like a whip. I was too in shock from the unbelievable amount of blood I'd lost to dodge. I did manage to block at the last second, but the sharp fingers bent around my mechanical limb. The disgusting fingers shot into my abdomen and pushed me back. As I was sent careening toward the wall, the creature turned its stretched arm up. I was now wedged between the thing's arm and the ceiling. I felt its disgusting fingers churning my insides, but it didn't hurt. At this point I was like a waterfall made of blood. The drops of crimson red painted the white floor a deep ruby. I watched in a seemingly disembodied state as the blood streamed into the grooves of the tile flooring. I coughed once and even more blood began to drain out of my mouth.

"Not ... like ... this," I muttered.

I didn't want to die here, but I didn't know what to do. My body swayed above the floor, but I was numb to the pain. The longer I remained up here the closer I came to death. I gripped at the bloody arm with my mechanical arm, but it didn't do any good. I suddenly realized my grip on Sunrise was beginning to give. At the same time I remembered I was still holding a sword in the first place. I slashed through the creature's arm and immediately came crashing to the ground. I knew I hit the floor, but I didn't feel the impact. My vision went red, but not because of exhaustion. The blood from my cut had spread over my face and into my eyes. I watched the creature grow nearer through blurry vision, but my body was unresponsive.

"Stay back ..." I croaked out.

Obviously the demon continued to approach despite my weak command. At this point I was essentially bathing in my own blood. Even though the strange magic was keeping me alive, it wasn't keeping me sane. The closer the creature got, the darker my surroundings became and the more I began to lose my mind. If the creature was trying to torture me without touching me, it was working. As the unknown magic began to fade, the pain and fear began to rise. With the adrenaline from my compiled fears building, I managed to roll over and sit up.

"I said get back!" I managed to shout.

I crawled back, painting the floor red with my blood as I scrambled away. I dragged my bloody body to the wall and scampered up it. Regardless of my pride and thoughts, I began to cry. I bawled like a child even as blood shot out of my mouth every so often. Shortly, the exhaustion and pain had caught up all at once. As soon as I calmed down and tried to stand, I doubled over because of it. I pushed my hand over my stomach to stop the bleeding, but I had no way of knowing if it was effective or not. With my hand positioned as it was, I thought about something I'd seen in a movie. I knew it would hurt, but I hoped some of the effects of that weird magic remained. I seared the wound closed on both sides while crying out in pain. To my relief, the pain died out quickly. My terror, however, did not. The creature drew closer, but without its arms I wasn't sure what it could possibly do to me. That was until it grew a new pair. They seemed to break through the stumps of the former limbs and sprayed more of the black blood. Some of it got on my face, and I could feel the burn this time.

My tears quickly washed the acidic liquid from away. The creature reached out its hand in painfully slow fashion as if to touch me.

"Stay away! Please just leave me alone!" I cried in terror.

I expected to have my throat ripped out or some other gruesome way to die. I sobbed into my arms and assumed the fetal position. I awaited my demise, but it didn't come. I opened my eyes and to my surprise there was a black blade through the chest of the demon. It began to scream in agony, but the blade was quickly drawn out and used to decapitate the creature. Its body dissipated into smoke which revealed a familiar face.

"Still alive, fire girl?" Azazeal asked.

As soon as I saw her, I started crying silently. I had been saved. She was smiling, but looked slightly worried. How worried I wasn't sure because she had just called me fire girl. I opened my mouth to reply, but only a strangled noise escaped. Azazeal raised an eyebrow, but as she did I noticed two little people behind her. I sniffed and attempted to talk again, but once again I only croaked.

"Can't talk, huh?" Azazeal caught on.

I nodded vigorously. Azazeal laughed at my movements, but said nothing more. Since my voice didn't work, I energetically pointed a finger toward Azazeal's legs, and she seemed to catch on.

"Oh, them?" Azazeal moved each of the kids in front of her.

I nodded while taking in the children's features. The eyes were the only difference. One had coal eyes like Jacob, and the other had red eyes like Azazeal. Wait. They were twins and resembled Azazeal and Jacob. I was stumped. Azazeal seemed to notice my struggle.

"I guess you wouldn't know, but these two are mine and Jacob's twin children!" Azazeal exclaimed.

I stared blankly at Azazeal, and she frowned at me. The children also stared at me. One looked confused, while the other looked annoyed. I opened my mouth to say something, but no words came out. As I was attempting to force myself to talk, I heard a few voices come from the hallway. Down another hall came more voices, but I didn't recognize any of them. The first person I saw, out of all the people on the way, was Virgil. He noticed us immediately and approached with the drunk guy, Marguerite, and Lia following closely behind.

"Are both of you alright?" Virgil immediately questioned.

I opened my mouth, but still no words came out.

"She's gone mute." Azazeal gestured to me.

I nodded in agreement. Virgil looked puzzled, and Marguerite came over and knelt down next to me.

"You to-took a be-beating." Marguerite inspected my various wounds.

Marguerite made me lean against the wall and began to check if I was at risk in any way. I winced every time her fingers touched any of the cuts and bruises. Surprisingly, the blood had dried on the smaller gashes. My stomach still burned from the makeshift healing operation. I whimpered when Marguerite raked her hands across the wound.

"That's no good. You should a put some alcohol on that," Flyx said.

He took a swing from his bottle as Azazeal frowned at him.

"One, don't drink in front of my kids. Two, alcohol doesn't solve all your problems."

"Whatever." Flyx began to chug the seemingly endless bottle.

Lia's eyes lit up when Azazeal mentioned her kids. She rushed over and grabbed onto the older girl's hand.

"Did you name them yet?"

Azazeal was about to reply until we heard a roar come from down the hall. Out of the darkness we saw Sara, unconscious, riding on top of a white tiger. Behind them strutted the Blue King with her usual condescending attitude. Nobody said anything as she approached. She walked past everyone but me. The older girl roughly picked me up by my shoulders and slammed me against the wall. I managed to cry out in pain.

"What are you doing?" Flyx shouted, enraged.

The Blue King ignored him.

"Did you use it?" she questioned me with wild eyes.

I didn't know what she meant, but even if I did, I couldn't talk. I just stared back and the Blue King slammed me once more. I cried out again and my knees buckled, but she pulled me back up. I tried to light my body on fire for defense, but I didn't have any magic left.

"Answer me, darn it!" the Blue King spat.

I only whimpered as a reply. She glared at me before wrapping one of her hands around my throat. She was incredibly strong and lifted me off the ground with ease. I kicked my legs trying to find the floor, but there was no chance of that.

"Aqua, stop it!" Virgil made a move toward Aqua.

The Blue King created a wall of water around us. Everyone was blocked out, taking away my only chance of survival. Her grip became tighter and my breathing was cut off even more. I grabbed at her arm, but my body was too weak to be effective. If only I could use the machine arm.

"Aqua, stop! Can't you tell she's mute?" Azazeal's voice barely traveled through the wall of water.

My vision had gone black, and I stopped struggling. I clawed once more at Aqua's hand before finally giving up. As soon as I did, the water shell dispersed and the water from it splashed down on top of me. I was only half-conscious, but I felt the water streaming into my wounds. Aqua mercilessly smacked my head against the wall once more before dropping me. I immediately began to cough and tears welled in my eyes. Marguerite was the only person to rush to my side.

She got down on her knees and pulled my head into her stomach. I sobbed into her like a child, despite all the people who were around. Marguerite did something to calm me down. Her hand glowed neon pink, and she stroked my red hair. I was instantly reminded of something my sister used to do for me. She used to sing to me and stroke my hair. I cried, but not because of fear or pain. The memories that Marguerite brought to surface put tears in my eyes.

"That's low, even for you," Azazeal suddenly said.

Aqua scoffed and didn't say anything more. She began to examine the battleground looking for whatever she had questioned me about. She seemed to have found it because she stood and walked back over toward Marguerite and me.

"You must not be aware, but Roméo passed the berserker's aura to you. I bet you fought The Snatcher and had unlimited energy and couldn't feel any pain. You probably healed pretty quickly during combat too," Aqua inquired.

I sniffed and tried to speak, but still couldn't. I nodded.

"So you did use it. Well, prepare for a bad night of sleep. After its use, the berserker's aura inflicts horrific nightmares on its host for six hours. Not only that, but you temporarily lose something after every use," Aqua explained.

The news should have upset me, but whatever Marguerite was doing made me feel warm. In fact, it made me feel sleepy ...

# CHAPTER 24

# GOD

## *Jonathan*

We had essentially water-skied for 10,000 miles, and I was getting bored. I sat atop Jeevith's head for the hours it had taken to get to France. As soon as we made it to France, after a long trek on land, Jeevith became my new arm. The scaly blue appendage still felt foreign, but Jeevith had already turned into it once. It was raining, but Jeevith informed me it was because of him. It rained wherever he used his power. As I traveled through the empty streets of Paris, I noticed the entire place was like an apocalyptic wasteland. I knew the hunters had arrived to kill all of the strongest beings gathered in one area, but I knew nothing of how this could go unnoticed.

"The hunters create a barrier. They only include the humans they mean to hunt. Everyone else is unaffected by the destruction of the designated area," Jeevith's voice echoed in my head.

There was no reason to reply since he could hear my thoughts. I wandered through a back alley and came across what I could only assume was a hunter. I was prepared to fight him, but something odd happened.

"They sent you in, milord?" the hunter asked, dropping to one knee and lowering his head.

I figured I'd play along. The god-arm thing probably threw him off.

"Raise your head and stand. You need not submit yourself to me."

I spoke as if I was entitled and used the same manner of speaking.

"As you command." The hunter rose to his feet.

"Now leave me. I'm hunting a particular prey," I commanded.

"As you wish." The hunter bowed before vanishing into the mist.

I exhaled and looked up at the drizzle of water streaming from the sky. Then I looked to my right and left. There were buildings in close proximity on both sides.

"This could be fun," I said aloud.

I used the buildings to bounce back and forth. After the short exercise, I could see the majority of the city from my perch. I noticed a giant hospital building that looked like an F3 tornado had torn part of its roof off. That would be a good place to start. I jumped from rooftop to rooftop in order to reach the medical building in optimal time. I basically used parkour to get there.

## *Flyx*

I had never liked that Mia girl. She had too much energy and was always so happy. People like that just kill my vibe. Regardless, I officially despised Aqua for abusing her. Nobody, especially someone who just fought for their life, should be treated like that. Now Mia was crying in Marguerite's arms. I took a swing of my mickey and ran my sleeve across my mouth. Aqua really was a fraked-up human being. Who hits a girl who's so banged up she's gone mute. Despicable. As I spent time keeping my thoughts to myself, the two Strains were catching up. Sara had been patched up by our friendly healer, Marguerite, so she was itching to talk. Lia, however, was the only person in the room who felt up to it.

"You haven't met any of the others before, have you?" Lia inquired.

Sara shook her head.

"That's too bad. You'd love Circe. She's just as spunky as you," Lia explained, cheerfully.

"Let's go see her after this is over!" Sara exclaimed.

She was excited about the opportunity to meet one of her seven sisters for the first time. The conversation between them was all about their siblings, so I averted my attention. I leaned against the wall behind me and took another large gulp of my mickey. The tension in the room was incredibly thick, mostly because those of us from Outcast Corner wanted to get back at Aqua. The worst part was we weren't allowed to unless we wanted to start a war between the kings. Aqua's smugness and condescending attitude were mostly because of that. Mia remained unconscious against the wall while the rest of us spread out. According to Sara, Yin and Amy were still missing.

"When was the last time you saw them?" I asked.

Sara scratched her head and seemed extremely puzzled. I was about to ask again, but Sara's eyes lit up.

"Amy teleported Yin somewhere. Yin was going to bleed to death so she had to help her."

"We are in a hospital, so they could be anywhere," Virgil pointed out.

"The only thing we can do is start searching and—" I stopped there.

Gabriel and Jacob approached from the hallway. Gabriel was a sight for sore eyes. Jacob was carrying what could only be his dead body. The angel's wings had been ripped off, and there was a gaping hole in his chest. Jacob's eyes were hidden by his jet black hair, but there was no point expecting a reaction from him. Although, he did seem a little off. Nobody knew how to react to Jacob's arrival. Gabriel's death was problematic, especially since he was almost as strong as Jacob and Azazeal using their second strongest fusion.

"How did this happen?" Azazeal placed her hand over her mouth.

She had crossed her arms over her chest then reached behind her and stroked her own wings. The idea of losing those precious wings seemed to terrify her. It was surprising because I had never seen her afraid of anything.

"I found him like this. It looked as though something with a lot of power blew a hole through his chest and the wall behind him. I have a couple theories about what happened."

There was an oddly deafening silence. Even Aqua and her sister remained quiet.

"Well, what are they?" I slurred.

Jacob didn't reply. He gazed down one of the hallways nearest to us, waiting for something to come.

"Yo, Jacob, you good?" Virgil asked.

Jacob snapped out of his trance and carefully laid down Gabriel's body. "The first theory is a tier god hunter has arrived. The second, and least likely, is she did it." he gestured to Aqua, but it seemed halfhearted.

She looked shocked that she was even being accused. "I would never do anything so gruesome to any man or woman."

"I'd be inclined to believe you if you didn't just almost choke a mute girl to death." Virgil jabbed a thumb toward Mia's bruised body.

Aqua opened her mouth, but Jacob spoke first.

"What did you do to her?" he asked, but walked toward Azazeal instead of Aqua.

Aqua didn't answer the question, though it seemed she wanted to but couldn't find the words. Jacob glared in her general direction while inhaling the nicotine vapor from his e-cigarette. He blew the vapor toward her, but even that didn't prompt an answer. Jacob opened his mouth, but Aqua's sister attempted to cut in.

"She was just trying to get informa—"

"I didn't ask you, and that's irrelevant now. There are more precious matters to attend," Jacob quickly interjected.

Both Russian girls stood with arms folded, enraged by Jacob's dismissiveness. He'd just asked a question and blew them off when they tried to answer. I snickered and Virgil laughed quietly.

Jacob approached Azazeal, who was still stressing over Gabriel, and put his hand on her cheek. Azazeal immediately placed her hand over his before pulling her husband into a strong embrace. Surprisingly, Jacob did hug her back. Their twin children hugged Jacob's waist. I guess demon children grew fast because they were already half his height.

"How touching," Aqua scoffed.

"Piss off, ya hosier!" I snapped.

"I don't know what that means, but I'll take it as a compliment." Aqua laughed.

"Do as you will."

"Like you could stop me anyway."

"I could always kill you," I threatened.

I stepped forward to confront her, but suddenly Jacob was in front of me. Even Azazeal seemed confused as if he suddenly vanished from her arms. I looked him in the eyes and saw what he wanted to relay without using words. Every fiber of my being was screaming "back off," so I did. Jacob continued to glare at me before turning around. Had he always been this scary? Something was very off.

"Did you name them?" Jacob suddenly asked.

Azazeal didn't reply at first. After a moment she spoke, "Oh ... uh ... the black-eyed one is Tetra and the red-eyed one is Petra." She ruffled the black hair of both children.

Jacob didn't say anything, but he had a soft expression that I hadn't seen on his face. He cracked a smile too, one so faint that I wasn't sure if it registered as one.

"I know this is a dumb question, but what are their genders?" Virgil asked.

It really wasn't a dumb question. They were either both girls or a girl and a boy, but I couldn't tell which was which. Tetra did look rather feminine, and Petra just had an aggressive air about him/her as well. I figured Tetra was a girl and Petra was a boy.

"Tetra is a boy and Petra is a girl," Azazeal replied.

Well, I was wrong. At the mention of his name Tetra seemed to cower behind his mother. Petra, however, put her hands on her hips and smiled.

"How do you do?" Petra asked, smiling.

She was like a carbon copy of Azazeal, aside from her hair being considerably short. She did have defining traits such as fangs and small black wings. This must have been what Azazeal looked like as a child.

"It's nice to me-meet you all," Tetra said quietly.

The kid seemed oddly shy, especially for a demon. He did have the same fangs and tiny wings as his sister, but his wings were white. I hadn't noticed before but the ends of his hair also had what appeared to be red highlights. When I looked back to Petra, her hair had white tips. The colors about the twins seemed almost swapped. The closer I looked at Tetra, the more he reminded me of Jacob. Maybe demons just recycled DNA or something.

"Hey, Mommy, I can feel something scary." Tetra cowered.

"Don't worry. There shouldn't be anything scary coming," Azazeal reassured her son.

I didn't feel anything out of the ordinary. Although, it had been oddly quiet for a while now.

"No, he's right. Down that hall," Lia pointed out.

I focused my energy down the hall. The demon twin had been right after all. Two crazy strong auras were making their way down the hall. I glanced over at Mia and Marguerite. With the opponents we were about to face, they would only get in the way.

"Marguerite take Mia and the twins someplace safe," Jacob commanded.

"But—" Marguerite met Jacob's eyes and immediately got up, hoisting Mia onto her back. She than began to leave down a different hall with both twins in tow.

"Now I can let loose," Azazeal said.

She cracked her knuckles and began to stretch. At first I thought she was just going to stop pulling punches, but she suddenly took out her rapier and cut open her hand. She pointed the black blade toward Jacob who raked his across it. The blood from their self-inflicted wounds splattered on the floor.

"Ready?" Jacob asked.

Azazeal nodded.

They grabbed hands and a storm of black feathers surrounded them. I'd only seen the fusion once before, but not with this kind of strength. When the feathers settled, a mixture of Jacob and Azazeal stood tall. Like actually tall. Around six foot five I'd say. Jacob's Brimstone had been replaced with a sawed-off shotgun of sorts. Azazeal's rapier had been exchanged for a black scythe. Their fusion had long hair like Azazeal but black eyes like Jacob. It turned and seemed to sweep the room.

"Aqua, Snow, Lia, and myself will take one. The rest of you the other," the mixed being said.

Nobody disagreed, not even the self-entitled princesses. Suddenly there was a loud whistling sound. It was ear splitting, but the only person in the room it bothered was Sara. Probably because she wasn't exactly trained for anything like this. While I tried to discern the cause of the noise, I caught a glimpse of a bright glow down the hall. The whistling noise increased and a rushing wind seemed to blast from the dark hall. I instinctively slowed time and to my surprise the hunter's blade was at my throat. His eyes were menacing, but also sparkled like emeralds. His silver hair did a good job hiding his facial features. I positioned my hand to grab onto his wrist and moved my neck out of the way. I put my other fist to his jaw and left it there. As I un-paused time, I grabbed onto his arm. The hunter's eyes met mine and immediately he attempted to escape my grasp. For a demon tier hunter, he wasn't very strong.

"How did you see me?" he questioned while throwing punches with his free hand.

I kept batting his hand down with ease. He was even faster than Light was but didn't seem to be very strong. His attack power was pitiful.

"You're fast, that's true, but you aren't very strong. Dude, you need to hit the gym." I laughed.

He exhaled angrily, and I continued smirking. I noticed him drop his bronze-colored sword and with blinding speed, he used his free hand to catch and slash with it. He would have cut me in half if I hadn't slowed time. I stepped closer to him and positioned my free hand to grab his new sword hand. As time went back to normal, the hunter remained in my grasp. He continued to struggle, but I tightened my grip to the point I began to crack his gauntlets. The hunter whimpered in pain and his struggling decreased. I took the time to get a better look as his blade. The sword looked like it was made of clockwork machinery and bronze. I could tell, however, that it wasn't actually made of bronze. As I examined it, the hunter began to tear up.

"Man up. You shouldn't show your opponent weakness," I coached the kid.

"I'm a girl," she spat.

I looked closely at her face. The more I thought about it, the more feminine she looked. That fedora did a good job of hiding her looks. I slowed time down, smacked her hat off, then replaced my hands in position. She was actually pretty cute. I loosened my grip and wiped her teary eyes with my slow-time.

"I didn't notice how cute you were until now."

She blushed and lowered her face. At this rate I might not even have to fight her. If I continued to compliment her, I could end up taking her on a date.

"I figured you out," she suddenly said.

"How do you figure?" I asked.

"You're just slowing down time. If I speed up to reach the time state you're in, I can hit you."

Nice deduction. That was exactly what I was doing.

"I guess you should try and apply it."

As soon as I said it, she dropped her sword again. I didn't know what the hunter thought she was doing. I had both her hands pinned. I was going to simply let it hit the floor, but she caught it on her foot. I slowed down time as she balanced her sword on her foot. The sword continued toward my leg. It was slower than the average human's movement speed, but I had to release her and jump over the sword. Even though she was moving slow, with time at a crawl, she kicked her blade up into her hand. In fact, she was slowly getting faster. The whistling sound returned, but I was able to discern it this time. Steam spouted from the girl's nose and ears. She pointed her clockwork blade toward me and assumed a combat stance. I stopped slowing time because she stopped attacking. She quickly turned around and appeared to bow to the other hunter. He stood in the darkness at the edge of the room. His head was hidden, but he appeared to be wearing clergy robes. There was a cross embroidery going down the front, along with a Jesus piece on top of that. Were we about to be attacked by a catholic extremist?

"Lord Crux, I have more of a demand than a request," the girl explained to her superior.

The other hunter crept further into the room. I could see his brown skin and scarred face now. The gray handle bar mustache and chin tuft matched his long gray mane. He looked extremely old. I heard hunters live hundreds of years longer than most humans. I was happy to be part of the exception as well. The old hunter gestured for her to come nearer and she obliged. The man lowered his head, and the girl made conversation with her.

"Shouldn't we attack or something?" Virgil threw out a question.

There was an outbreak of chatter in the room. The Outcasts were kinda interested to see what she was demanding. The princess and her sister were intrigued as well. For some dumb reason, and like most stupid heroes in movies, we waited to see what the girl was planning. Eventually the girl bowed to her lord again and walked a little closer to me.

"My name is Selena. I'm ranked fourth amongst tier demon hunters. I request we do battle alone."

I was confused at first and then intrigued.

"Can you take her?" the Jacob and Azazeal fusion asked.

"Out to dinner?" I Joked.

Selena blushed. The steam blowing out of her ears and nose flared out.

"I ... you ..." Selena said, flustered.

"Got something to say, hot stuff?"

You could say whatever you want about my womanizing; it was more to get in Selena's head than to actually hit on her. That being said, she was more attractive than most. Maybe I could find a way to win without hurting her. As I weighed my options, Selena growled in anger.

"Shut up and fight me!"

She waved her sword vigorously through the air.

"Alright. Do you wanna do it here or in another room?"

"A less crowded room would be preferable. I'm hoping we can enjoy ourselves and do so alone," Selena replied falling right into my trap.

"I had no idea you were such a naughty girl." I sighed. "Trying to get a room with a man you just met."

Selena didn't bite this time. In fact, she sheathed her blade. Hopefully I could talk my way out of combat.

"So are we not fighting?" I asked.

"You interest me. I've never fought anyone who was able to detain me so easily. I'm simply going to move us," Selena explained.

The steam flared from her ears and nose, and it appeared she was charging up for something.

"I'm going now, milord," Selena said.

She moved and at blindingly fast speed, but I slowed everything down again. She, however, was still moving. She calmly walked toward me at what must be normal human speed. She tried to say something, but the speed of sound was way slower than both of us. She pointed down the hall as if to say "let's go this way." I shook my head and lifted her up bridal style. Oddly enough, Selena didn't fight back. Just because we were in a slow state of time didn't mean I couldn't still move quickly. I sped down the hall with ease until we met a wall. I skidded through the wall and jumped out the hole without stopping. I landed on a rooftop and looked around quickly. My apartment building was only a block away. I quickly moved along the rooftops while avoiding eye contact with the girl in my arms. I maneuvered through the air but as I reached peak height on one of my jumps, I noticed someone: a white-haired boy gliding from building to building. He looked a little like ... nah, it couldn't be that naive boy. He was dead. I landed on a large building which was round and had space for combat. I gently let the girl down, but she seemed a little reluctant to leave my grasp. She walked roughly twenty steps before turning to face me.

"I have no interest in killing you, just so you know," I said.

Even though that was true, I conjured an 1897 British infantry officer's sword I had in my magic storage. I was a bit of a sucker for old weaponry. Especially something the Canadian military had once used. Besides, it never hurt to have a close range weapon.

"I don't exactly want to kill you either. Let's reach a middle ground," Selena replied.

I raised an eyebrow. "Go on."

"One of us just needs to make the other surrender. The loser owes the winner a meal and their life," Selena laid out the rules.

"So you do want me to take you to dinner?" I asked, more in hopefulness than anything else.

"Yeah, you'll be taking me out alright. You'll also be paying." Selena laughed, drawing her blade.

There was a reason I lived in an apartment. All the money people made working at Outcast Corner came directly from the world government. We all either lived "on campus" or lived in apartments off of 40,000 dollars a year. I didn't exactly want to waste money here.

"My bank account begs to differ!" I replied.

Selena giggled and I realized what I'd just said. I was on the wrong end of the joke this time.

"If I lose, which I won't, please take good care of me," Selena requested.

The way she said that was kind of weird. It was like she was implying we would go on a date after this, but didn't seem to understand what taking care of her would entail. Whatever the case, Selena seemed way more innocent than most. I just smiled at her.

"Prepare yourself," I said.

I tucked my empty right hand behind my back and stood facing slightly to the right. This style of combat had been something I invented. It was a swordsman's version of drunken boxing.

"That's an odd stance," Selena observed.

"It's something I invented," I explained proudly.

Selena snickered. "Prepare your body, because I'm about to ram into you. With my sword that is," Selena threatened.

Is she so naive she has no idea what she's insinuating? That does mean my more vulgar jokes may go unnoticed.

"You have no idea what you just implied, do you?" I asked.

Selena looked blankly at me.

"Let's just fight already!" Selena complained.

I laughed while the hunter pouted. She was entertaining, that was for sure.

"Alright then. Let's do this." I said quickly, pausing time and charging Selena.

As I did, the clockwork on her bronze-colored blade began to click and move. The blade began to split into parts that were held together by some kind of wire. I jumped back cautiously and was immediately glad I did. Selena whipped the blade out like, well, a whip. It only slashed through my pant leg. She wasn't going lethal so neither would I.

"Let's have some fun," I said, grinning widely.

## *Jonathan*

As I grew nearer to the hospital, I saw someone jumping through the air. It looked like that drunk guy; I think his name was Flyx. He was carrying some girl from rooftop to rooftop. It didn't appear as if he needed me, so I continued toward the hospital. When I touched down a couple buildings away, I figured it would only take one more jump to reach the medical center. I jumped using a lot of my strength and flew higher than I had the other times.

"I suggest you use a durability multiplication and a high one at that. You may not survive this otherwise," Jeevith's voice sprang into my thoughts.

"Survive what?" I said aloud.

Even though I received no response, I used my power.

*Durability multiplication times eight*

As soon as I did, a large figure appeared and created a short darkness by eclipsing the moon. He held a long weapon, but I couldn't see what it was. I did know it was something blunt. That was because he'd just smashed me over the head with it. I came crashing to the ground like a meteorite and destroyed a fountain on impact. I sat up out of the water and put a hand to my head. When I drew it away there was a considerable amount of blood on my palm. Even with a multiplication that high, I still took damage.

"Stick our shared arm into the water," Jeevith command from inside my mind.

I did as he said and I felt the wounds on my head and back close up.

"That is one useful power," I muttered aloud.

"It only works on non-life-threatening wounds," Jeevith elaborated.

As I slowly climbed to my feet, the giant man landed in front of me. He wore a medieval cowl, which covered his face, and no shirt.

His brown skin was covered in scars and his muscles looked as if he'd taken steroids. Although, one of his arms appeared to be made of brown stone. He was holding a large war hammer that somehow fit along his broad shoulders. His eyes shone brightly through the darkness created by the cowl.

"Hey, Jeevith, do you think you can dye my hair red?" I asked.

"Yes, but why?" Jeevith's voice replied.

"When my hair becomes red, it triggers the real me."

Jeevith remained silent, but then I felt my longer hair become slick. Then I surfaced once again.

"You still live?" His voice sounded deep and menacing.

I grabbed onto my shoulder, rotated my replaced arm, and stretched a little. I didn't respond as I worked out my body. It had been a while since the version of me on the outside had given me total control. I continued to stretch, but now it was to see if he'd be annoyed with me ignoring him. The god hunter, however, just stared.

"I think I'll be okay. I might be crippled for life," I replied sarcastically after he had waited patiently for my reply.

"You dare mock me," the muscular man asked.

"Maybe."

I looked at Jeevith's arm and used some of my negative energy to turn the scaly blue appendage black. It looked a lot cooler that way.

"Be careful! He's a god tier hunter. God of the ground at that," Jeevith warned.

I should probably have picked my words sparingly. I might not be able to make any more wisecracks against a guy like this. I glared at the god hunter and he stared back. I was about to shoot first, but he was gone in a blast of dirt. It confused me because his aura also vanished momentarily. I searched above me, to my right and left, and behind me. He wasn't in any of those directions, but I neglected to check one area: below. He burst from underground and I narrowly managed to dodge his hammer swing. The debris got into my eyes, and I barely managed to miss the second swing. I retreated back toward the water. This was going to be tough without a weapon.

"We have one. Get to the water and stick your hand in," Jeevith commanded once more.

I did as he said and a halberd with a golden handle and blue blade seemed to form from the water alone. It seemed to have been summoned more than crafted from the water.

"The halberd has a name and ability," Jeevith elaborated.

I hadn't used a halberd before so I had questions, but this guy wouldn't leave me alone. It made sense for him to continue his attack. I jumped back and up, avoiding a horizontal swing. The god hunter followed me up and swung from below. I thrusted the halberd down in order to defend myself. The weapons clashed, but I was still sent shooting upward.

"It would be great to know the ability right about now," I shouted over the sound of rushing wind.

I hadn't just been sent, I had been launched. The wind was abnormally loud to the point where I couldn't hear anything at all. I managed to keep my eyes open and noticed a figure standing on a building far from me. I could only pick out dirty blond hair and a tuxedo when it came to his characteristics. It quickly became clear he was controlling the wind as his hands seemed to move frantically. One of his hands appeared to have talons instead of fingers. The wind picked up its pace and held me in midair, at least for a second. The raging winds changed and began to drive me toward the ground far below. I kept an eye open and spotted a spike of earth ascending to meet me halfway. I might not survive something like this even with my multiplication.

"Jeevith!" I shouted, searching hopelessly for help.

"Make contact with the spike using Vengeance and shout out, 'magic counter!'" Jeevith's voice sounded through my head.

The halberd was named Vengeance. Pretty cool name if you asked me. Shouting "magic counter" seemed really stupid, although it was better than getting skewered. I raised the halberd above my head and began to spin forward. I sort of began a human buzz saw as I got gradually closer to the spike.

"Magic counter!" I shouted over the wind.

As soon as the tip of the halberd collided with the rock spear, it shrank back into the ground. As I began to fall slowly, another rock spike jutted out from the ground. At the end of it sat the hunter with the giant war hammer. The rock hadn't impaled him and only carried him high into the sky. I landed and combat rolled onto the rooftop below.

"I can't believe you actually said it!" Jeevith laughed, giving me a migraine.

My head rang like a bell before settling painfully.

"What's that mean?" I asked aloud.

Jeevith only laughed more, which had begun to make me mad. I tugged at my hair, attempting to spread the pain out a little, and directed my attention to what Jeevith had said before.

"Just tell me already." I grunted, shaking my head vigorously.

"It's just like all magic," Jeevith began matter-of-factly, "You don't actually have to say any of the abilities names. You should know that."

"Don't patronize me or I'll kill you!" I threatened while massaging my temples.

The two god tier hunters had waited patiently for me. How kind. The dirty blond gently floated down from his perch on top of the tower. When he touched down, the leaves and debris on the ground were scattered by a gust of wind. As he landed the colorful feathers on his arm folded in. The wind god's true form must be a bird or something. If that was the case, then this earth god's true form must be a golem or something. I hoped back to the road and stuck the landing in front of the two god hunters—except now there were three. Another god hunter walked out from the darkness into view.

"It's quite clear you are no hunter. You do, however, have the arm of the water god hunter. So, tell me, how did you come across it?" the newest god hunter asked.

"I found it in the ocean," I replied casually.

There was a brief silence.

"Is ... that all?" the wind hunter asked.

"Were you expecting a story?"

"No, well, yes, but forget it. Let's just kill this guy, Apollonios," The wind god sighed.

"Indeed we shall uh ... what was your name again?" the giant, Apollonios, asked.

"Are you serious? the shortest of the three hunters asked.

"Yeah, how could you forget my name again!" the wind hunter angrily shouted.

"Is it Cletis?" Apollonios asked.

"No, it is not Cletis! My name is Maddox! Why are you such a blockhead?" Maddox raged.

"Don't be mad at me, Maddox. I'm sorry. Tell him I'm sorry, Thalia," Apollonios cried.

This guy was just like a big baby. How did Julian lose to a blockheaded guy like this?

"Don't underestimate him. In terms of combat and durability, he might be able to last longer in a fight than you," Jeevith warned.

I, of course, didn't buy it.

"Just drop it, Maddox. We'll just kill this guy and move on," Thalia said.

I spun the halberd between my fingers before leveling it toward my enemies. I couldn't accept Jeevith's warning. I could probably take all three of these guys. As I was planning an attack strategy, Maddox began to do something comparable to stringing a bow. As he drew back on the air bow string, I sensed something. I instinctively put up Vengeance to counter an incoming attack. As I did, Maddox relaxed his hands. When he did, I was impacted by unbelievable amount of force. I staggered back. I was sure the magical attack had been countered. When I looked back at Maddox, his hair did appear to have been forced upward and into a spiky state, but he looked unharmed. Then I surveyed the area behind and around him. The road and buildings had been destroyed by something resembling a hurricane. Maddox stared at me wide eyed. Then he began to laugh. He doubled over, holding his sides while cackling madly.

"This, well, this is just wonderful!" Maddox shouted through fits of laughter. "I can finally get serious against someone!"

I stared as the hunter began to look more insane with every passing second. Not that I was very different, though.

"No need, Maddox. This is all me." Thalia stepped in front of her allies.

She had no features to take in because a cloak covered her entire body. Maddox obliged and he, along with Apollonios, retreated. Thalia just stood there as if she was waiting for me to make a move. Then, she flipped her cloak off to reveal her glowing body. She had on a suit that only showed the necessary parts of her skin. Said parts were an assortment of long blue lines tattooed, probably magically, on her. The glowing lines seemed to change colors randomly as well. Her hair, which also changed like her weird tattoo, was cut short and her brown eyes gazed at me. She smiled calmly, and I grinned back.

"You're just like me," Thalia suddenly said.

"How so?"

"You like to fight too!" Thalia exclaimed.

She charged forward and the glowing lines stayed red. She threw a punch, which I avoided easily by craning my neck back. Except, I didn't avoid her attack. A red blast of energy almost took my head off, but I managed to raise the halberd between us. My weapon was destroyed, but Thalia kept coming. I ducked all the way underneath her attack and threw a punch of my own. Her glowing lines changed to blue. My fist was stopped by a barrier Thalia had created. Even with my, now stationary, boost of five times multiplication, everything couldn't break through.

"Only a magic attack can destroy a magic shield, hon." Thalia blew me a kiss.

Her tattoo became red again and instead of a kiss, a red blast collided into me. I crossed my arms in front of me and blocked the attack. The attack burned, but it didn't do much damage. Still, I was beginning to like this pain.

"Thank you, Ma'am, I'd like another," I hissed.

Thalia laughed and did as I asked. I sustained this hit as well and figured I'd build up the energy I needed from my pain. My favorite attack that I could only use in this form required others' fear, grief, or misery to feed off of or my own pain or malice. And I'd just gotten enough of it. The air became thick and heavy because of the large amount of negative energy I was emitting.

"Are you prepared for my attack?" I asked.

Thalia noticed the tone change immediately. Her fear spiked if only for a moment. That, however, was still enough for me. After I fed off her terror, I charged at her. As I did, the blue tattoo took shape. I stopped short, directly in front of her, and opened my palm, thrusting the heel of my hand forward. I fired a red blast that had black lightning crackling around. The negative energy may have dissipated as it contacted the shield, but Thalia's blue tattoo reacted to the attack of negative energy. It shook violently and defaulted to red. Thalia cried out in pain and doubled over.

"How?" Thalia croaked as the tattoo continued to go haywire.

"I just used all the strength I have and hit you with it."

"You didn't hit me ..." Thalia groaned.

Then I brought my knee to her side, dropping her to the ground in a heap.

"All better?" I taunted.

Thalia's tattoo suddenly became purple and her body vanished. I felt her malicious energy move behind me, and I turned to intercept her. Thalia attempted to roundhouse kick me, but I ducked underneath the attack. The red and black energy crackled to life all around me, and I blasted her back. She crashed into a nearby building, but when the beam dissipated, her body was gone.

"Think you can trick me?" I asked aloud.

I felt her malice begin to move behind me once more. She just threw a normal punch this time, but her tattoo had changed to yellow. I caught her fist and allowed my negative energy to leak out. Thalia struggled to move, but I held her in place with ease.

"I've got you," I said as I aimed another open palmed strike.

Thalia just giggled. She grabbed onto my arm holding her fist. I hesitated and that was all she needed. Yellow electricity sprung from all over her body and shocked me with more volts than I'd ever sustained. I did, however, survive the attack. As I cried out in pain, I drove my free fist into her stomach. She doubled over and stood, hanging limp on my arm. Some blood trickled into my hand so I must have cut her skin with the scaly arm. Her electric surge stopped, and I pushed her away. Her body flopped to the ground as I began to retreat. When I took a step back, I fell—more like I couldn't move like I wanted. Then I just lost my footing. Thalia began to laugh, and I stared at her from where she was lying.

"Can't walk can you?" Thalia asked as she sat up.

She was breathing heavily and wiped a steady stream of blood from the corner of her mouth. Surviving a punch with five times the power of a normal human was no easy feat. To be honest, she was taking it like a champ. Thalia gingerly climbed to her feet. I tried to get up as well, but my body wouldn't cooperate.

"What did you do to me?" I asked the hunter.

Thalia continued to breathe heavily. I was about to ask again, but she answered before I did.

"I threw your nervous system out of whack with my electrical currents. I realized I may not be able to damage you, so I changed plans."

"Well aren't you smart."

Thalia smiled at me but continued to catch her breath.

"*I'll take the hits to our nervous system. Just beat her,*" the lamer Jonathan suddenly said.

When he did what he said he would, I felt my movement begin to return. Thalia approached me with her red tattoo activated. As she did, I began to stand. Thalia stared at me in shock as I casually stood up. The red and black negative energy crackled around me menacingly.

"How can you move?" Thalia backed away in shock.

"Easy. I have another personality taking the hit from your attack. Right now he's probably in a ton of pain, but what do I care?" I cracked my knuckles.

She seemed completely lost by my convoluted and poor explanation. Thalia looked as if she wasn't sure if she should take me seriously. Then Thalia suddenly growled and lunged at me. I sidestepped her and tripped the small girl. She face planted but turned and fired an attack with insane recovery speed. I easily deflected the attack with my negative energy, though. Thalia got to her feet, but I jetted forward and delivered a hook to her side. She bent over, but her tattoo lines turned purple and she vanished.

"You can't hide from me, Thalia."

Her malice had more or less vanished, but her fear was as clear as day. I zoomed to another part of the street and grasped at the air. I managed to grab onto her arm instead of nothing.

"I can smell your fear," I whispered into her ear as I pulled Thalia close.

Thalia whimpered, but her hair changed to yellow. I used this as a warning. I released the girl as electricity surged from her body. I, however, was safely out of the attacks range. As the discharged ended, Thalia dropped to a knee and her tattoo lines faded to black. She stood up and faced me but was clearly out of energy. The tattoos blinked the other colors I'd seen before, but none of them stayed for very long. It was like the dance floor at a strip club or something.

"Is that all?" I asked.

Thalia didn't respond, but she spread her arms out as if saying, "Kill me." Even though that probably wasn't what she was saying, I obliged. I stepped close and quickly drove my blackened arm through her already damaged abdomen. She didn't even cry out in pain as her blood spattered to the ground. She amazingly continued to move. Thalia moved her hand into my hair and used my arm, which was inside of her, to look me in the eyes.

"Was it at least as fun for you as it was for me?" Thalia asked.

I looked down at the blood that had seeped into the cracks on the ground and stained my clothes.

"It was marvelous," I replied with a half smile.

Thalia smiled but her eyes looked sad. She coughed and blood splattered to the side. I didn't mind though. If you were born in such violence, it was really nothing new. Thalia suddenly moved forward and brought her lips to my ear.

"Come on, you're going to kill me without even so much as taking advantage here?" she whispered.

Before I could offer any reply, Thalia kissed me and a small amount of blood held captive by her mouth dripped into mine. I will admit with little shame that I enjoyed the taste of the hunter's blood. It tasted better than human blood by a good margin. Thalia then drew away as her body sparkled and began to vanish into the night.

"I'm a hunter so I'll regenerate in a couple days. If you ever need me, just say my name. It's an enchantment I put on your tongue."

"I'll take that to heart," I replied.

Thalia then vanished and her weight on my arm dissipated as well. I let the ring of negative energy dissipate, and I took a seat in the middle of the road.

"I'm switching back," I decided.

I closed my eyes and then I was back. I immediately went over to the fountain and washed my mouth out. I couldn't believe the real me would use our body like that!

"I feel violated!" I shouted to myself.

*"I should call her as soon as possible. Mostly because I enjoy her company, but also because she bothers you,"* the real Jonathan suggested.

"I don't want our body being used for that again!" I cried.

"That was a pretty ... vulgar scene if I do say so myself," Maddox chimed in.

I turned to Maddox, but he wasn't paying attention to me any longer. He looked off into the distance toward something I couldn't see. He then began to fly away before stopping midflight.

"I don't know how you saw the invisible wind arrow or how you defeated Thalia. I do, however, know the Fallen's king is nearby. The head of that being takes precedence over yours," Maddox said.

Who are the Fallen? More importantly, where does he think he's going?

"I don't know what you're talking about, but you're not going anywhere!" I shouted in reply.

I jumped to meet Maddox in the air, but Apollonios grabbed me by the ankle. He flung me at the road, crushing the pavement beneath me. He kept his grip on my leg and flung me down the street until I collided with a building.

"You are fighting me now." Apollonios aimed his hammer toward me.

I clawed my way out of the crater my body made in the building. Some blood trickled from my head and onto my face. Jeevith summoned the halberd for me, and I snatched it out of the air. Then, I wiped away the blood and used the halberd to force myself into a standing position.

"Keep him busy, Apollonios, I'll be right ba—" Maddox strangled out the last part.

A beam that seemed to come from the moon collided with Maddox and erased him from existence. The brilliant light slowly made Maddox's shadowy figure vanish right before my eyes. When the lustrous glow disappeared, Maddox continued to float in place. The clothing on his upper body appeared to have been dissolved and his skin was black from the burns he sustained. His hair had also been burned away, leaving the hunter bald. On the building just above Maddox stood a girl. She wasn't wearing anything but a simple white dress. Her black hair looked silver as the moonlight seemed to ooze into it. Her eyes were a sky blue that were gazing off somewhere else. Maddox growled angrily, startling the girl. Still, her attention didn't leave the stars above. The hunter slashed his talons at the girl, but they were repelled with ease. A glowing white shape, similar to that of a contact lens, blocked the attack. A white beam seemed to shoot from the lens, throwing Maddox back and through a nearby apartment complex.

"You ... you're one of them aren't you?" I heard Maddox's voice from the rubble behind Apollonios.

"Define *them*," the girl's monotone voice rang like a bell.

"The Fallen. You're the one they call Hazel right? Hazel the Energy Child?" Maddox asked for clarification.

"That is my name, yes. I am one of the Fallen."

Maddox climbed out of the rubble with his battered body. He looked like he'd been beaten until his bruises turned black, probably from the two blasts Hazel nailed him with.

"Are you alone?" Maddox asked as his charred skin seemed to molt form his body.

Feathers began to grow all over Maddox's body. His skin eventually was replaced by a rainbow feather scheme. He looked like some kind of bird-man now.

"I am not obligated to answer that question." Hazel slowly cocked her head back to its normal position.

Her unwillingness to answer didn't seem to bother Maddox. "That's unfortunate. You've cooperated so far. What changed?"

"It's against the king's rules to give away our numbers during combat," Hazel replied simply.

Instead of asking again, Maddox vanished in a gust of wind. Hazel didn't react at all but from what I'd seen of her, I wasn't surprised. Maddox reappeared behind the girl and slashed with his talons, but the white lens reappeared. As soon as Maddox made contact, he disappeared into another gust of wind. I didn't even see him strike as red sprayed into the air. Maddox had sunk his claws deep into Hazel, causing blood to spray out. Her facial expression didn't change though. The white light blasted from the palm of her hand and through Maddox's shoulder. He cried out in pain but didn't let up. He dug his free blades into Hazel's stomach, impaling her. I made a move to help, but Apollonios's hammer collided with my side, sending me crashing into the window of a shop.

"You're still fighting me so don't you dare move," Apollonios threatened.

I didn't reply, but mostly because I could barely breathe. I managed to claw my way to my feet, but cut my hand on the broken glass of the window sill. Despite his threat, I looked over to see if Hazel was still alive. When I did, something heavy crashed into me pushing me further back into the store.

"Ow, that hurts."

I checked out the object and found an unpleasant surprise. Hazel's bloody body sat motionless in my lap. Her white dress had gone from a pure white to a spotted crimson red.

"Hey, are you alright?" I asked.

Hazel's eyes seemed to flicker to life like light bulbs. She quickly got up without wincing or stumbling and began to look around. She looked back at me as if she'd remembered something.

"My condition I would define as near critical. I require your assistance in ending this quickly." Hazel lowered her hand, gesturing for me to take it.

"Alright, let's do it," I replied.

I took her hand and she yanked me to my feet. For a little girl she was actually pretty strong. Her weird contact lens shell reappeared. From the lens shot a white blast which leveled the wall in front of us. The roof somehow remained on top of the shop even with all the tremors and shakes. Hazel calmly walked back toward the street despite the blood trail left in her wake. I followed and was pleasantly surprised to not see Apollonios. Only Maddox stood on the rooftop above in his bird form.

"Where'd your friend go?" I asked.

Maddox scoffed and then laughed. "That big idiot isn't my friend. In fact, he's so stupid he left when the two of you crashed into that pharmacy. He's off toward home, but I tried to convince him to assist Lord Crux."

"That person is unidentifiable using current memory. Who is he?" Hazel asked.

She had asked a question, but it didn't sound like she would care whether or not she heard the answer.

"The strongest hunter there is," Maddox replied shortly.

# CHAPTER 25

# DEAD

## *Virgil*

This is going to be harder than we'd thought. The hospital had been reduced to ashes and rubble. This Lord Crux guy collapsed this entire wing of the long building with his words.

Shooting a beam of light was all Crux had done, but it caused this portion of the building to fold in and destroy itself.

I clawed out of the rubble and looked around. The surrounding area looked as if a bombing had occurred.

"Is everybody okay?" I managed, painfully.

My chest felt like it was collapsing on itself. I breathed heavily as I waited for an answer. No response. I trudged through the ashes with my combat boots. The gray footwear was now a deep black. When I was finally able to stand up straight, I made eye contact with the god hunter. He looked concerned, but not about me exactly. He drew a blade from a glowing gold cloud. The weapon looked like a Christian cross. The longer side was more like a needle than a rectangle. The handle was also a cylinder, but both sides were short and rectangular.

"Father, why must you force me to bring lambs to thy holy doors for judgment? You have sinned, friend, so I have come to free you. Now depart of this life and may we meet again in the eternal dance," Lord Crux spoke.

His voice flowed like silk. Not only that, but it was oddly hypnotic. I made no attempt to move because it didn't seem necessary. Lord Crux dragged the cross shaped blade through the rubble and ash. He was about to kill me, but why did I feel so at ease? He pointed the needle like blade to my throat. For some reason I just closed my eyes and waited. I felt him raise the blade, but it never fell. I opened my eyes to see Azazeal. Her wings were blood soaked and more of the red liquid dripped to the ground in front of me. She'd blocked the slash with her rapier, but Lord Crux made no motion to push through her.

"What are you doing?" Azazeal's voice slurred.

She coughed and more blood spewed from her mouth. I snapped out of my trance and stood to my feet. As soon as I did, Azazeal fell back into my chest. Her breathing was ragged and short. This much blood loss might be too much for even her. I felt bad, like I just needed to do something! I tried to support her, but she pushed me back.

"Don't pity me. Don't look down on me. And don't you dare die without my go ahead!" Azazeal commanded.

I smiled. This was just like her. Our fearless second in command.

"Yes, ma'am!" I shouted in reply.

I stood next to her even though Azazeal had already dropped to a knee. Her body was battered, but she still wanted to fight. Where was Jacob? While I looked around in confusion, Lord Crux seemed to be gazing somewhere as well. The god hunter glared at both of us before suddenly turning to his left. He had noticed it before me; someone was approaching and rapidly. Mia came jumping from a higher floor of the severed hallway. She was covered in bandages and out of breath, but she raised her fiery katana. Behind her was Marguerite, but she didn't drop down. She sat above on the ledge, and the demon twins slowly crept to her side. Azazeal noticed them and struggled to her feet. She glared angrily at Marguerite who just stared emptily.

"Why ... why did you bring them here?" Azazeal managed through scattered coughs.

Marguerite opened her mouth to say something, but closed it when Petra floated down to the ashy ground. She summoned something to her that I could only describe as a quarterstaff with a large ball on top. It looked incredibly heavy, but the small girl easily balanced it across her shoulders.

"I asked, well, forced her to bring us here. I've been itching to fight something as soon as I was born," Petra explained her presence.

Azazeal didn't reply, but she looked up at the more timid Tetra. He shrank back from his mother's gaze but seemed determined to be of assistance nonetheless. Azazeal then looked at Mia, who was more torn up than any of us. She, however, looked the most determined to fight. Her eyes literally blazed a brilliant orange.

"Still can't talk, fire girl?" Azazeal asked playfully.

Mia smiled but didn't reply. Then she vigorously pointed her sword toward Lord Crux. Her eyes translated danger, so I turned to the god hunter. He'd changed his position to a striking one: a half crouch with his cross blade in both hands. Azazeal and I instinctively jumped up high and far back. Lord Crux slashed his cross sword horizontally, nearly killing both of us. He would have severed our upper bodies from our legs without Mia's vague, but effective, warning. I stuck the landing, but Azazeal landed on her side. She cried out in pain and slid several feet back. She gingerly pulled herself to her feet but fell to a kneeling position shortly after. The blood dripping from her back made a trail from where she had landed to where she ended up sliding. Marguerite noticed her profuse bleeding and dropped to the black floor. As soon as she touched down, a voice rang through my head.

"Calling all outcasts, even if you're in combat please make your way to the largest hospital in the city. We're kind off in trouble here," Marguerite's voice sounded.

This could be risky. What if some idiot brings another god hunter here? Even worse, what if they even bring two?

## *Jonathan*

As soon as I heard the announcement, I scooped up Hazel and bolted toward the direction of the hospital. The Fallen girl didn't really react and didn't say anything for a little while. I wall-jumped until I was on top of a nearby building and scouted the hospital. It looked partially destroyed so I figured Marguerite was in trouble.

"Why are we retreating?" Hazel suddenly asked.

"What, you didn't hear that voice just now?" I answered with a question.

"I did. Although, wouldn't it be wiser to defeat our enemy first?" Hazel brought up a good point.

"Details will be saved for later," I replied dismissively.

I didn't have any time to waste.

## *Flyx*

The voice startled both of us even though the fight was over. Selena was quickly roused from her deep sleep. She had been sleeping on the couch in my apartment because she'd exhausted herself. I had planned to incapacitate her, but she hadn't been able to keep up that high a speed for very long. In fact, her body was bloody and battered because it wasn't able to take the strain. Even though I had tried to get her to leave, she told me before that she wanted to stay on our version of the earth a little while longer. I didn't exactly mind because the more time we spent together, the more attached we both became. Not only that, but she was half naked and it seemed awkward trying to get her to move.

"Shouldn't you go help your friends?" Selena asked, half asleep.

"Shouldn't you go help yours?" I countered.

Selena laughed but got quiet all too sudden. She looked toward the opposite couch which held her assortment of light gray leisurewear and her silver sword. Her silver hair seemed to hide her eyes, like it had moved itself.

"They're not my friends …" Selena muttered quietly.

"What, you guys aren't buddy-buddy?" I asked out of confusion.

"I'm sure you've noticed by now. I'm not nearly as physically strong as the other hunters or even most humans. That's because I'm really not one. I'm a half Fox Spirit and half hunter," Selena explained.

Wasn't expecting that.

"I hate to sound insensitive, but what is a Fox Spirit? Unless it's the obvious answer, of course."

Selena seemed to lighten up as she recollected her past.

"In the forest where I lived, we didn't have any technology so I only heard stories. My mother used to tell me about the two-tailed red fox. They were brave creatures that defended the forest, but they were tiny and weak. They were really fast, maybe even faster than the speed of light. The two-tailed red Fox Spirits finally found a way to merge with humans. Then the Fox Spirits race was born." Selena smiled while telling her tale.

I listened intently for the next part, but Selena's smile suddenly faded.

"Then one day some hunters showed up in our woodland village. According to my mother, they had no ill will for the two weeks they stayed. My mom spent time housing the two hunters and ended up falling in love with one of them. She had me a year later, but the other Fox Spirits were exterminated by the hunters. We threatened the survival of the planet's inhabitants because of our insane speed. When I was only ten years old, they killed my mother like everyone else but took me. I never knew exactly why, but it probably had something to with me being half hunter." Selena looked far off toward the fireplace.

I didn't know what to say. That was really the worst thing I've heard in a while. It was almost as bad as the attempted genocide of the Canadian people twenty years ago.

"Uh ... I ... uh ... I really don't know what to say," I attempted to comfort her but failed miserably.

Selena looked up at me with her emerald eyes. They seemed to glass over before becoming quite teary. Selena looked away, probably because she didn't want me to see her cry. I kneeled down and hugged the silver-haired girl. She made an odd squealing sound.

"You don't have to worry about any of that anymore because you got me," I softly whispered to her.

Selena cried just as softly into my neck. I'd never had feelings for someone other than this girl I met a couple hours ago who also tried to kill me. I smiled at the thought. Who would have guessed we'd end up like this?

## Gene

The hunters' appearance had put a damper on my plans, but the model was already complete. Soon most of the beings that opposed me will be destroyed in one swoop. More precisely, they will be exterminated by the second of the four homunculi. Ash. I turned to the sealed soul stored inside a broken body. I removed the sealing stakes in her head, heart, and stomach. The gaping holes left by the sealing blades closed up instantly. The tower then clothed the homunculus with what could only be described as a black and red school uniform. The plaid skirt wouldn't have been my first choice, but the tower did as it wished. Her black eyes snapped open, and she recognized me immediately. Ash sat up and surveyed her surroundings. Her eyes were like coal and her heart was black, just like her twin. She was the taller of the two, though. Ash grabbed her shoulder and silently rolled it a couple times. She then stared at me for a couple seconds. I looked back at her face, which had cracks as though it were a mask. The rest of her body and skin were like this as well. She'd, unfortunately, been damaged during a recovery mission.

"What is your bidding, Father?" Ash asked with a static voice.

"Kill your brothers and the filth they call allies for me," I commanded smoothly.

"A-as you commanded." Her voice had a glitch for a second.

I waved a hand, and Ash dropped through the floor. It was going to take an hour or so, but she should reappear in the catacombs. From there she could kill them all. Just as long as Jacob doesn't go back to normal before then. The probability of that happening is only two percent anyway.

## *Mia*

In a flash of light, Amy suddenly appeared with long golden locks of hair. She had Yin, who looked like she'd been through hell, on her back. Yin suddenly disappeared, but reappeared over toward Marguerite and Azazeal. Virgil stood in front of the three of them and silently swore to protect them. Amy vanished as well, but she didn't reappear anywhere I could see her. I searched quickly and noticed her standing on a missing portion of the hospital above. As her gold hair faded and she fell into the hover chair near her, I saw a small boy keep her from falling out of it. Everything that just happened were questions for later.

"M-Mia, I-I need you t-to stall. At le-least for f-five minutes," Marguerite stuttered.

I nodded and redirected my attention to the most pressing matter. I just wish I could talk right now. So much cool stuff was happening, but I couldn't even comment on the subject. It didn't help that my body felt like it was covered in invisible needles. Every little movement hurt. As I lowered my sword, I winced from the pain of just doing that. I was tasked with keeping the god hunter from moving as Marguerite tried to take care of Azazeal. I moved in front of the god hunter with slow, painful steps. I tried to look threatening, but his piercing eyes saw right through my facade.

"What is someone as broken as you doing out here?" The tan man asked.

I tried to say something, anything, but my voice still hadn't returned. At least, not completely.

"My best," I croaked painfully.

It wasn't exactly the wisest or most prideful thing to say. Although it was all I managed to churn out of my throat. The god hunter cocked his head and stood puzzled. He then smiled and changed his stance so his blade pointed at my chest.

"Duel me. It should be fun with determination like yours."

My body wasn't going to be able to handle this. I was sure willpower alone was the only reason I could stand. Still, even though I was only buying time, I wanted to fight him.

"I'm Mia Alves, and I accept your challenge," I replied between coughing fits.

"Mia what are you—" Virgil began to question my decision.

"I've ... got this." I huffed painfully.

"Alright, Ms. Alves. I am Lord Crux of the hunters' race. Now let us do battle!"

I had barely moved into a combat stance before the god hunter attacked. As soon as he moved, my vision became blurry. I wasn't at all prepared for this, but I knew one thing. It was going to take more than five minutes for anyone to kill me. Even with blurred vision, I managed to duck underneath a horizontal slash.

I slashed in a similar manner, but my battered body was hardly able to force Sunrise forward. Crux easily dodged the blow. He slashed downward, and I had no choice but to block. Even though I did so successfully, my leg gave out from the sheer force of the blow. I dropped to a knee but miraculously managed to roll out of the way of a diagonal slash. I used what little magic I had left to shoot a ball of flames, but Crux did something unexpected.

"Stop."

The ball of flames did as he said. I sat, dumbfounded, as my attack hung statically in the air.

"Return." He spoke another commanded.

I was too confused to dodge, and the ball of flames exploded when it made contact with my chest. The explosion and fire couldn't harm me, but the impact sent me careening toward the pile of rubble.

"Mia!" I heard someone's drowned-out voice call.

I expected to have my spine almost destroyed, but I collided with something fluffy and warm instead.

"What happened?" I croaked.

I looked back to see a tiger with fur as white as snow. On top sat the Blue King in all her condescending glory. She offered me her hand, but I was reluctant to take it. After she gave me a frightening look, however, I did. She easily pulled me to my feet and seemed to nudge me back toward Lord Crux.

"Screw dueling alone. We only have a chance in numbers," Aqua explained her charity.

"Can't believe I'm agreeing with her, but what she said," Virgil backed Aqua up.

"You idiots … just be careful. If you die … I'll kill you." Azazeal quietly threatened.

We all knew what she meant. That she didn't want any of us to die. I locked eyes with Yin, who moved from her seated position onto her feet. Amy reappeared with her golden hair and said something to Yin. I couldn't hear from the large distance between the three of us. My lip reading skills were pretty ishy, so I couldn't even make out what they were saying. It looked sort of like an argument. Yin tried to step around Amy, but the smaller girl stood in her way. There was more conversation, which I couldn't discern, before Marguerite pulled Yin down. Yin looked at her somewhat confused but then seemed to be content with something Marguerite said. Amy teleported to her perch, and Yin remained seated next to Azazeal. I didn't know what that was, but it wasn't really important at the moment. The child version of Azazeal was the first to step within range of Crux's sword. She swung her weapon with insane speed, smashing into Crux. He blocked it with his golden arm and pulled the small girl to him. He slashed, but she dodged. The girl somehow wrenched her weapon from the larger man's arms. She swung it once more and sent Crux flying into the destroyed hospital. Her odd staff thing looked too heavy to hold, but she swung it with apparent ease.

"You're just all talk!" the girl taunted.

As she did, a pack of wolves made out of golden light charged her. Even though there were six or seven of the golden beasts, they were all stuck with what appeared to be arrows. It was also completely simultaneous. The purple arrows dissolved along with the wolves bodies. Everyone looked up toward the ledge where Amy and that boy were sitting. The boy's wrist appeared to have some kind of peg driven through it. The upper and lower limbs of a bow jutted out from the peg. He didn't appear to have any arrows, but the string was glowing purple along with the other parts of the bow. He seemed to be huffing like just firing the weapon was tiring. The fingers he'd used to fire the bow appeared to be cut and bleeding. The closer I looked at both kids, the more they looked like twins. And even more like Azazeal and Jacob.

"Did ... did I do a good job, Petra?" the boy asked timidly.

Petra seemed confused by his question before realizing what he'd meant.

"Uh, yeah. Well done, Tetra," Petra halfheartedly congratulated her twin.

Even though the compliment seemed fake, Tetra's face glowed. Just that much kindness made him so happy. To each their own I guess. Suddenly there was an unbelievable gust of wind. It even began to pick me up off my feet, but Aqua grabbed onto my leg. She didn't seem to be having any problem with the powerful winds. As soon as the tornado wind died down, I dropped to the ground like a rock. Maybe Aqua enjoyed my pain because she'd made no motion to catch me.

"Why didn't you catch me?" I groaned in pain.

"I thought you would be able to land by yourself."

I turned to her, and she was smirking. God, I still hated her. As I glared angrily at Aqua, something akin to a meteor crashed into another corner of the ashy wasteland. Out of the smoke stood a figure along with a young girl. I instantly recognized the white hair and was about to shout to him, but that arm was new. It looked like something reptilian, all scaly and blue. Next to him stood a young girl in a white dress, though her dress was more blood red than white. That was odd because the dress itself didn't appear to have cuts on it.

"You okay?" the familiar voice asked the young girl.

"Define okay," the girl more stated than asked.

"Just forget it."

The girl suddenly seemed to become alert to something and started searching in every direction. She then desperately rushed over toward an untouched pile of rubble. Some lens shape appeared in front of her and she began to blast the rubble, destroying it on impact.

"What's wrong?" the white-haired boy asked.

"I can sense the fading life forces of two of my sisters. I can also feel the aura of the earth god hunter, Apollonios, underneath this wreckage," the small girl frantically, but emotionlessly explained.

She fired another powerful blast to clear the remaining rubble and revealed a deep, dark hole. She then dropped down before anyone could say anything.

"Hazel, wait!"

When there was no reply, the boy stood and combed the area. He locked eyes with me and those bright golden eyes were unmistakable. We stared at one another for what felt like an eternity but was probably just a couple seconds.

"You coming or what?" Jonathan asked with his stupid but lovable grin.

Jonathan then turned and stepped off the ledge into the pit. Instead of shouting my reply, I rushed to him and dropped down into the deep abyss.

## *Jacob*

Maybe I should help them out. Lord Crux wouldn't go down easy, but I would. The buildings collapse had only done a little damage to mine Azazeal's and fusion. Still, the damage we receive in fusion form doubles if we don't kill our opponent. Definitely the worst double-edged sword I've encountered. I stood on a building a couple hundred feet away from the battle ground. I could see it with perfect clarity. These eyes really were the best part of my Holy Grail powers.

Suddenly, I got the urge to search the sky. When I adjusted my gaze slightly to the left, I caught a bird-like man in the distance. He was flying this way, and I quickly recognized him as a god hunter. I raised Brimstone with my left arm since the right wasn't responding. I fired once, just above his head, then another just below. He seemed to notice the shot from above but ended up ducking into the shot from below. He cried out in pain, but the shot somehow didn't kill him. He glared at me with his talon-hand covering his right eye. He slashed his wing arm through the air, and a blade of wind came flying toward me. I easily sidestepped it because it wasn't invisible to my eyes.

"How did you see that?" the bird-man asked.

I didn't say anything.

"The silent type, huh?"

"I didn't reply simply because there is no reason to. For one, it is bad to give away one's battle abilities and two, because you'll be dead soon anyway," I said.

The hunter stood with a look on his face that I couldn't describe. Then he bent over, clutching his stomach, and made audible contractions using the diaphragm along with other parts of the respiratory system. Azazeal had made me research laughter once, but that was all I got out of it.

"You really do know how to tell *a joke,* right?" the hunter's vocal pattern changed when he referenced jokes.

Still, I ignored his unimportant questions. I fired another shot, but he quickly dodged it. I fired three simultaneous shots in all of his cardinal directions and halfway in between those. I didn't fire a shot at his chest, assuming he'd dodge, but he saw right through the plan. He remained in place and the red blasts dissipated in the night sky.

"Thought you could out smart me, huh? Too bad!" the hunter shouted as a sea of wind began to form in the sky.

A raging storm rolled in, but without the thunder and lightning. It formed a cyclone-like shape before attempting to lift me off the ground. I offered no resistance to the winds, knowing it was futile, and let them lift me into the sky. Despite the raging tornado, I attempted to fire a shot at the god hunter. The blast collided with the wall of air and was swallowed by it.

"Your efforts are being wasted, half-demon!"

The hunter began to laugh. First normally, but it slowly became louder with more ragged. I had read this was the mark of one's descent into insanity. I had also read that insanity was when one could not distinguish fantasy from reality, could not conduct her/his affairs due to psychosis, or was subject to uncontrollable, impulsive behavior. By the looks of this bird-man, he was probably already there. The cyclone kept me in the air, but wasn't damaging me. I fired six staggered shots into the same part of the raging wind cave. Briefly, the cyclone opened up to reveal the god hunter, but only for a second. Six shots was enough to destroy one small part of the barrier.

"You'll have to do better to get through this barrier!" the hunter mocked.

"Alright then, I'll do better," I replied loudly over the wind.

I fired twenty-four shots in a square like pattern, simultaneously opening up a hole. I could only see the hunter's upper body, and I only had time for one pot shot, so I took it. The hunter wasn't expecting it at all, but the singular blast only destroyed part of his leg. He cried out in pain and the winds began to dissipate. As I started to fall, I bent my knees and hoped for a survivable landing. I landed and fell through the skylight on the building below. It hurt, but it wasn't as bad as landing on the dining table. My feet hit first, but I bounced and fell through a small glass table. There was a sharp object jabbing into my side when I sat up. I felt around my side and grasped onto what must have been a table leg. I tugged at it, but it hurt to move. Blood sprayed across the marble floor I sat on.

"This is ... unsavory ..." I said, looking at the growing crimson puddle.

I managed to stand even with the foreign object protruding from my side. I holstered Brimstone so my only arm would be free. I quickly scoured the room, looking for a way back up. There was a chandelier that was maybe a small jump away from the skylight. Although, I certainly couldn't climb it with one arm and an injured abdomen. I noticed a stainless-steel plate cover with a couple shards of glass scattered around it. I looked at my reflection in the broken glass then I gazed up at the broken skylight. I then began to scoop up the glass with the plate cover. If he stayed in the same area I wouldn't miss with this. After I gathered the glass, I hopped up on the dining table. I positioned myself to fling the shards of broken glass into the night sky.

"This should work …"

I flung the glass into the moonlit darkness and quickly unholstered Brimstone all with the same hand. I waited a couple seconds for the mirror glass to reach high into the night sky. Then, when a shard tilted at the perfect angle, I held down on Brimstone's trigger. The red blasts bounced off the broken glass and toward where the god hunter had been before. I heard a short cry of pain and then silence. At least until a car below was crushed by something. The car's alarm rang suddenly, eclipsing the silence. My hit had killed him. I trudged over toward the balcony and shot the glass door open. At least, I tried. The blast bounced off the mirror, and I barely threw myself out of the way. Why was everything here made out of mirror glass? It didn't matter nearly as much to me as that hunter's death. I pistol whipped the glass, breaking it, and stepped through into the cold air. I looked over the railing and was pleasantly surprised. The god hunter's body had already begun to fade away. As it did, I noticed something, someone, far off and just out of my clear eyesight. Still, I could feel their gaze lock with mine. All I knew was that they weren't on my side.

"One down, *three* to go," I whispered into the night breeze.

Now to find a way out of here.

## Lia

"Really, Sara? At a time like this?" I shouted over the explosions and flying rocks.

She didn't reply, simply because she'd been knocked out in one hit. I was carrying her on my back, but I was fading fast. My leg was not in the best shape, but I was somehow running off pure adrenaline.

"Ish, frak, darn it!" I shouted to myself.

Just then something exploded from the ground and blocked my path. The giant god hunter raised his enormous hammer and swung. I stopped it with my telekinesis and managed to dodge out of the way. I fired a purple fireball and it exploded on impact. The giant man wasn't bothered by my attempt at slowing him down. I dropped Sara and gently floated her across the room.

"I'll show you to ignore me!"

While I focused on that, the giant man swatted at me like a bug. I heard something crack but didn't feel a thing. I flew back until I crashed into, and became imbedded in, the wall. My body wasn't responsive, but my mind still worked. I must have looked dead because the hunter began to move toward Sara.

"No, stop!" I shouted, but it was like I wasn't there.

My mouth didn't move. Nothing happened. He just continued toward my sister. To … to kill her …

"I said stop it!" I tried again, but nothing.

Wait, my mind still worked. What if my powers did too? I didn't have to do much in terms of concentration. All my senses were gone except for sight. With that much focus I could … well … I could tear his heart out from here. And so I attempted just that. I focused on where the god hunter's heart should be. I thought, *Give me your heart*, over and over in my head. Still, nothing. The hunter raised his hammer, ready to turn my little sister into a freaking pancake! And here I was, powerless to stop him …

"Darn it all …" I began to cry, defeated.

My body didn't easily give anything away, however. My eyes did have tears streaming from them. I hadn't been defeated before, not even once.

"You haven't lost yet," a voice cut into my despair.

I couldn't move my eyes to look, but someone stepped in front of me. I immediately recognized them as Hazel. Behind her came Mia and … Jonathan? I was sure it was him, but he looked so different. Not just the blue reptilian arm, but he looked older. Darker too. I noticed Hazel put up her energy shell, so I figured she was going to put me out of my misery. She didn't hesitate to shoot, but she didn't hit me. I fell out of the wall and into my sister's arms. I wasn't really surprised she'd caught me, but I didn't understand why she bothered freeing me. I stared up at the ceiling, unable to move. Hazel bent my neck so I could see her. She looked at my face for a second before leaning me against the wall in a position where I could see the whole room.

"You should really be more careful," Hazel lectured.

I couldn't reply or give any sign of recognition. So I did nothing. Hazel left me alone before forming her energy shell in front of her body. She fired a blast of moon energy toward the giant god hunter. He turned and thrust his hand out to defend himself. The blast collided with his hand, but the god hunter collapsed his palm and caught the beam. Hazel looked surprised and the moon blast was tossed back at her. Hazel took the blast head-on and was sent flying further into the dark cavern.

"Hazel!" Jonathan called, worried.

Hazel didn't respond, but I thought she was okay. Mia moved in front of me and held her sword out as if to intimidate the god hunter.

"Apollonios, I have a proposal," Jonathan shouted across the room.

The god hunter seemed to perk up. He stood tall from his hunched position. As he did, the rock above collided with his head but the earth was the thing that got destroyed.

"What is it, puny human?"

Jonathan, surprisingly, dropped his halberd. The magic weapon turned to water as it splashed onto the ground.

"You and me, one on one. No weapons, no magic, just our fists," Jonathan proposed.

It wasn't the worst plan ever. He stood a better chance in a one-on-one fight. I just hoped he could win.

## *Jonathan*

*"You should let me do this. We both know you stand no chance,"* the real me said.

That was where he was wrong. Little did Apollonios know, I would be using magic.

*Strength, durability, and speed times ten*

*"Wow. I'm impressed. You actually stooped as low as cheating."*

I ignored the inner me. His physical abilities should, hopefully, be outmatched by that. Apollonios seemed to ponder my proposal.

"I accept."

He then tossed his hammer which created a crater to his right. He cracked his knuckles and neck, and I raised an eyebrow.

"That sounded like it felt good, let me do mine," I mocked.

I cracked my knuckles and neck as well. To be honest, it really didn't feel that great. At least the crick in my neck was gone. Apollonios advanced toward me, and I dashed behind a stone pillar. He charged it and destroyed the rock structure. I danced underneath his flying fist and delivered a jumping uppercut. Just like that one in the street fighter video game. Apollonios, however, barely reeled back. He then backhanded me out of the air. I was sent flying and crashed into a stone pillar, but it hardly hurt. I started to stand, but Apollonios came over and punted me like a football. I shot up into the ceiling and became stuck in the rock. I managed to power my way out, but as I fell, Apollonios grabbed my head and slammed me into the ground. I immediately went limp, but on purpose.

"Jonathan!?" Mia shouted.

I held my finger up to my mouth in a shushing motion as Apollonios turned his attention toward her. Apollonios raised his bare foot to stomp me, but I rolled out of the way. The god hunter, however, didn't seem to notice. I snuck behind him as he lifted his foot to stomp once more. I hopped onto his back and wrapped my arms around his neck. I wasn't just trying to choke him out, I was trying to collapse his windpipe. Apollonios clawed at me, but his own muscles prevented him from reaching me on his back.

"You—" Apollonios choked.

He wildly swung his body trying to throw me off. I wasn't budging, and I heard the bones in his neck begin to crack. Apollonios slammed his back, with me on it, against the wall over and over again. It slowly began to hurt as my magic faded and blood began to trickle from the back of my head, but I didn't let go. My grip began to slacken as Apollonios continuously throw his elbow into my side. His struggling, however, lessened and my grip only grew stronger.

"Sorry for this ..." I muttered under my breath.

I then swiftly snapped my opponent's neck. There was a sickening snap and Apollonios fell forward. I fell with him as well. I bounced when I hit his back and rolled to the dirt floor. I ended up gasping for the air that had been pounded out of my lungs. I heard someone rush toward me, and I forced myself to sit up. It hurt so bad I was sure all my ribs were broken. I turned to Mia, who dropped to her knees at my side.

"That was all kinds of reckless." Mia laughed.

"I'm still here, aren't I?" I replied with a smile.

She leaned in and, to my surprise, wrapped her arms around me. I lifted the arm I wasn't using to support myself and hugged her back. She then suddenly pulled back. I was confused for a second, but then she leaned in and kissed me. Even though she was probably moving a little too fast, I enjoyed it.

*"You cheat, win, and get the girl. Well done,"* the real Jonathan rang in my head.

I continued to ignore his comments, but after a few seconds a cough interrupted us. We both turned to see Lia being supported by Hazel. Both girls were in one piece and leaning on one another. Sara also approached from behind and walked over toward her sisters.

"Now ... really isn't the time," Lia said, sounding strained.

"I ... uh ... sorry, let's go," Mia said, standing up.

"Yeah," I agreed quickly.

Sara and Hazel had been the only ones conversing for a while now. Although, it was mostly just Sara asking questions about Hazel and her other siblings. Hazel responded quickly, seeming happy to answer even though she kept her monotone voice. We started to make our way back to where we'd jumped in. I took a glance back at Apollonios's body. It had almost completely dissolved into the golden particles that dispersed throughout the room. There was something beautiful about it. I looked at Mia, who was messing with Sunrise's sheath. If only momentarily, her body seemed to glow gold. I blinked and the glow was gone. It was just my imagination, right? Mia noticed my staring and smiled brightly at me. I draped my arm over her shoulder, and she leaned into my chest. I winced slightly from my injured ribs, but I didn't mind. This moment was something I wanted.

"Let's hurry the frak up here! They'll need us up top," Lia called from her staggering lead on us.

She'd already almost fully recovered. She was right, though. We needed to get up there soon.

✳ ✳ ✳

## Virgil

Petra brought down her weapon from above. Crux sidestepped, and she destroyed the spot he'd moved from.

"Quit running away," Petra gasped.

She was exhausted but kept going anyway. She swung again, but Crux backed just out of range. Petra lunged forward, but Crux ducked under the attack and moved in close. He held up his hand and a golden light sent Petra flying back. She would've crashed into the ground if Marguerite hadn't jumped down and caught her. Marguerite immediately checked her vitals and looked relieved.

"She's just unconscious," Marguerite called to me.

While that was good, backup would still be much appreciated. Especially since Petra was in need of recovery. Her god tier strength was very helpful and had let us land a few hits, but now she was down. And that meant we were in trouble. It wasn't like Aqua wasn't equal to Lord Crux, but she wasn't able to damage him. She was taking damage after every clash of their light and water. I fired a bolt of lightning, but one of Lord Crux's light hounds took the blow for him.

"This guy's defense is incredible!" I shouted.

Aqua finally managed to graze Crux with her water cutter attack. She, unfortunately, barely drew blood. Crux made up the distance between us and slashed my chest. I'd managed to move back and the kevlar suit took most of the hit. Still, my skin was exposed the open air. Crux's onslaught continued, with me barely escaping his attacks. He sweep-kicked my legs out from underneath me and I collapsed into the ashy ground. He brought down a slash to execute me, but I discharged electricity from all over my body. Even though I was sure the volts hit him, Crux barely hesitated. He continued his swing, but a blue arrow redirected the attack. His sword hit the dirt instead of cleaving through my neck. I glanced at Tetra, who managed to get a shot off even though his fingers were raw and bloody from all his shooting. He looked exhausted, but he nodded to me. I understood what he meant and I grabbed onto Crux's cross sword. I discharged as much electricity as I could from my hand, up the sword, and into Crux's body. He cried out in pain and dropped to a knee. I half stood and was about to deliver an electricity-charged haymaker, but suddenly everything seemed to slow down. I watched in horror as Crux slowly moved his body and turned his blade toward me. I brought my arms into my body and instinctively defended myself. His blade pierced through both of my arms but stopped just short of my chest. At least, it did for a moment. The blade of the cross sword was suddenly extended by a golden light. I managed to force its direction upward and the sword protruded into my shoulder.

"You can't escape me," Crux's deep voice rang, but his mouth didn't move.

He pulled his cross sword back and as I fell forward, he slashed again. I was in no position to block or dodge so I waited for the inevitable. Instead, I heard the clash of metal and a cry of pain. In between Crux and myself was someone I didn't recognize. At least, not from the back. I stumbled to Crux's side and saw a short green blade deep inside of Crux's side. The blade seemed to hum slightly and its glow highlighted a face I recognized as Theo's. His head didn't appear to be put on his body as well as I'd seen it previously, though. Crux drove his sword into Theo's back, but the blade didn't get very far into the metal. Crux seemed surprised, and Theo just looked annoyed.

"What are you waiting for? Hit him!" Theo commanded.

I obliged and delivered a straight punch into Crux's jaw. He flew back and rolled a couple meters. Theo's body looked like brand-new chrome, like it was built by Ando. After all, Shojiro was the only person who knew how to put Theo back together perfectly. He was in Japan, so there was little chance of him being responsible for Theo's new body. Crux stood, even with my electricity still shocking his body. He thrust his cross sword out and the blade extended toward me. Its speed was faster than I could react to, and I would have been impaled, however, Theo smacked the blade into the air. It went just over my shoulder and seemed to extend infinitely. The blade suddenly thrust down, and I dodged out of the way. I turned to see where the extended cross sword was headed. Aqua was standing in its path, but she was facing the other way.

"Aqua, watch out!" I called to her.

But it was too little too late. Aqua turned, but the blade had already reached her side. I expected the worst, but a silver figure pushed itself into Aqua's previous position. Aqua gasped in surprise as the white tiger I'd seen before was impaled by the cross sword. After going straight through the tiger, the blade zipped back to Crux.

"Snow!" Aqua cried, going to the tiger's side.

Except, it wasn't a white tiger anymore. A girl, who stood a striking resemblance to Aqua, had replaced it. Her stomach looked like a tank round had blown it open. She was losing way too much blood to recover from that wound. Snow moved her hand to Aqua's face. She said something in what I believed was Russian. Aqua replied in Russian, and then Snow's body went limp. Her hand began to fall, but Aqua caught it within her own. She wept into Snow's chest. Her cries echoed, cutting into the dark night. She wept, but Theo and I turned our attention from it.

"We'll get you for that," I said while cracking my knuckles.

Crux didn't reply. Instead, he knelt to the ground and lowered his head until it was buried in ashes.

"Forgive me, Father, for I have sinned. But, Father, pardon me for the sins I will commit next," Crux prayed.

He kissed his Jesus piece and rose to his feet.

"Don't think your god can save you from me!" Aqua threatened.

It began to rain, lightly at first but soon it poured. It was almost like the sky was crying.

"Roman, make sure she is buried," Aqua commanded.

A large man I hadn't noticed before picked up Snow's body. Roman made a sad and worried expression. He and Snow vanished and were replaced by a glowing white feather. It was odd because I hadn't met him before. It looked kind of like he was worried about me. Moving swiftly from that, Crux seemed unfazed by Aqua's threat.

"It is unfortunate. I must kill all of you," Crux stated more than threatened.

Still, those words made my skin crawl. I backed away in fear and collided with Yin. I wasn't bothered by our collision, but Yin was knocked off her feet. What was she even doing there? I thought she was too weak to fight.

"What do you think you're doing?" Theo began. "Your body is as broken as the human body can be while still functioning."

His eyes were green and displayed some wall of code. He appeared to be scanning her, and I knew his results were at least 95% accurate. The five percent being something we'd rather not talk about. In any case, Yin used her long broad sword to force herself to stand.

"I'm … helping …" Yin mustered.

She stumbled and began to fall, but Amy supported her. They traded words, but my attention had been redirected toward Aqua. She'd stepped in front of Theo and me. Her eyes seemed to ripple like a pool of raging waters.

"If you want to live, move back," Aqua warned.

Without argument, we began to slowly retreat backward. Then, suddenly, we were standing on top of the hospital. I looked around and spotted Amy falling, being caught by Yin. Her yellow hair reverted to its natural brown. I also noticed that the people who'd gone down the hole were also on the hospital with us.

"Do you bring us up here?" I asked Amy.

"She did," Yin replied instead.

Everyone went silent, and I looked down at the battle below. Aqua didn't take any particular stance. In fact, she just seemed to stare emptily at Crux. Crux charged and Aqua made no motion to dodge or defend herself. The blade easily slid into her stomach and out the other end. Except, it didn't. Aqua's body exploded into a burst of water. I then noticed her standing ten paces, give or take, behind Crux. She drew a symbol that looked close to a harpoon and said something I couldn't hear. The water that had made Aqua's clone transformed into harpoons. The blades fell into Crux, impaling him in several places, but as the water dissipated the wounds closed up. Now that I thought about it, all of his magic-induced wounds had healed. I had confidence in that assessment because Theo's attack had left a bloody gash on his side.

"Magic isn't going to work on him. She'll be dead in five more minutes," a familiar voice said.

Everyone was startled and turned to see who it was. A man wearing a *takuhatsugasa*, a traditional Japanese hat, stood in the center position of how we were scattered about the rooftop. He wore a pair of geta, essentially wooden sandals, on his feet and a black red rose-patterned ronin samurai gi. His voice was one I could mistake as no other.

"Shojiro Ando?" I asked.

I said his full name so there would be no mistaken identity. The man, who I was convinced was Shojiro, didn't acknowledge me at first. He turned to Yin and just kinda seemed to stare. Yin quickly stood and said something in Japanese. I'd picked up a little Japanese from Shojiro, but the only words I caught was brother.

"It is a surprise to see you, Yin. I was up on Julian's ship when it appeared you all needed help," Shojiro explained.

"I haven't seen you in years and that's all you say!" Yin pouted.

She embraced her brother, but Shojiro only received the hug. He made no attempt to hug her back. Instead he turned toward me.

"You should go help the Blue King. She'll be dead soon if you don't."

I nodded and dropped down to the soggy earth. He had been right about Aqua not lasting long. She'd already worn herself out with magic attacks that had had no effect. I moved to her side as Crux charged. Aqua traced a square in the air and a wall of water moved between us. I considered he stopped, but a golden hound burst through the water wall. A blue arrow was fired, but it missed the mark by a hair. Another arrow caught the light beast's leg, but it continued its charge. I tried to fire lightning at it, but the powerful shower of water made me shock myself as soon as the energy reached my fingertips. I cried out in pain and stumbled back. As I fell, I watched in horror as the light hound collided with Aqua. It exploded on impact and sent the Blue King flying high and back. She crashed to the ground, making a sickening thud.

"Aqua?!" I called, hoping for a response.

I didn't get one. The only sounds I could hear were the pitter-patter of rain and Crux's footsteps. I realized he was after me and jumped to my feet. I backed away, but my attack power was gone and my body was still recovering.

"No escape now," Crux stated as he fast-walked toward me.

He thrust his cross sword forward, but it clashed with a black blade. The rose pattern on the blade confirmed it as Shojiro's. He deflected Crux's attack, but Crux thrust out his hand as if to fire a beam. Shojiro reacted quickly and caught him by the wrist.

"Too slow," Crux said with a sad frown.

I didn't know what he meant until I heard a sort of hissing sound. I turned to see a large wolf made out of the same golden light as the other hounds. It didn't try to bite me, however. It instead, it sped forward and easily cut through my chest. I felt the pain of being impaled, but not of falling. I knew I'd hit the ground, but I didn't feel that either.

"Virgil!" I heard Shojiro's voice call but it sounded distant.

Then I realized I was dying. I made no sound and I had no worries. To be honest, death in my line of work was like retirement. I smiled and everything went white. Then I saw—

# CHAPTER 26

# $\mathcal{V}$ICTORY

## Mia

I hardly knew the guy. Yet, as everyone safe on top of the roofs stared down at the scene, there was something akin to a silent mourning.

"No … Virgil." Lia gasped, holding her hand over her mouth.

Her eyes welled with tears and she slid down onto her knees. The personal grief must have been immense and painful for her. Sara bent down and hugged her older sister, but Hazel just stared.

"For this you die," Shojiro muttered.

Shojiro lashed out at Crux. Their blades clashed, but Crux was sent skidding back. Shojiro pressed on and slashed again. Even though their swords clashed at the same time, Crux was sent flying once more. Shojiro attacked with what could only be described as gentle force. His sword swings were calm and gentle, but the impact had more force than a tank round. Crux rolled and returned to his feet.

"Yin," Shojiro's voice calmly rang over the pouring rain.

Yin didn't seem to hear him. At least, not at first. She seemed kind of far away, like she was wandering through her thoughts.

"Yes?" Yin asked, startled.

Shojiro vanished in a flash of rose petals. Those petals dispersed and evaporated into the air. Suddenly the sound of wind, when there was none, echoed from on the roof top. I turned and saw Shojiro reappear in a storm of rose petals. He tossed his hat and it, too, disappeared like the roses. Without it I could see his scarred face and black hair, which was gelled so much that it stuck straight up. One of his eyes had a patch on it, but the scar covered more area than the eye patch could hide. It was stitched up, but the stitches made the scar look as though it were attempting to tear Shojiro's face open. The large scar moved down to the five-o'clock shadow on his face before stopping abruptly. Shojiro held his hand toward Yin, who looked at it, confused.

"This will be easier with your help."

Yin said something in Japanese, and Shojiro quickly snapped back. They weren't arguing—at least, they didn't appear to be, though it did seem kind of heated. Yin looked away, and Shojiro tapped her hand, causing her katana to appear in it. Shojiro then calmly said something in Japanese, and Yin seemed taken off guard.

"So it's okay to use it?" Yin asked in English.

"Absolutely," Shojiro replied.

Yin paused before nodding. With that, they were back down below.

"What was that? Arguing about using a sword? I want to kill these guys as soon as possible and you're not doing it fast enough!" Lia raged suddenly.

"That's not fair, Lia," Sara spoke up. "I know you're hurting, but being rude isn't going to help anything."

Lia seemed amazed Sara stood up to her. She got to her feet, as if to be intimidating, but both girls were the same build and height. Lia glared at Sara, but her younger sister held her ground. Hazel seemed to notice their staring contest.

"Fighting Fallen number seven, Sara, will solve nothing," Hazel pointed out in her own weird way.

Lia seemed to growl and made a motion toward Hazel. I finally got fed up with her.

"Just let it go!" I tried to just say, but a distorted voice loudly rang out instead.

Everyone on the rooftop stared at me in surprise. Surprise and ... fear.

"What?" I tried to play dumb.

I didn't seem to fool anyone. They continued to stare as I searched for an explanation.

"Fine, you Goody Two-shoes win." Lia suddenly exhaled, throwing her hands up in the air.

Lia took a seat and Sara bent down as well. She wrapped her arms around her older sister again.

"Glad you're not angry anymore!" Sara laughed.

"Don't push your luck," Lia muttered.

While they half argued, I moved a little closer to the ledge so I could watch the battle below. When I looked down, I suddenly wasn't looking down anymore. Rose petals flew into my field of view. Then I was suddenly standing on the battlefield. I stood, momentarily confused.

"What just happened?"

Yin seemed surprised I was there, but Shojiro laughed.

"You wanted a better view, so I gave you the best one there is: in the fight!"

I wasn't exactly mentally prepared for that. I looked at Crux, who was still patiently awaiting an attack.

"Just do your best and don't use magic." Yin tried to motivate me.

Except there was more than one problem. I was a below average swordsman and magic was the only thing I was good at. Then I remembered something. I opened my magic storage and pulled out my Galil. It had been a while since I'd used it but now seemed like the perfect time.

"Alright. Just don't get mad if I screw up."

Shojiro nodded and Yin giggled. Then both of them got serious. Shojiro tapped Yin on the shoulder and her casual clothing was exchanged for an outfit similar to his. Except Yin had a porcelain mask that resembled a lion. Shojiro slipped one on as well, but his looked like a rose.

"Do I get one?" I asked jokingly.

"Do you want one?" Shojiro asked.

"Wait, really?"

Shojiro nodded. I pondered the idea for a moment. "Yeah, let's do it!"

Shojiro tossed me the mask which formed from nothing. It looked white as it flew through the air, but as soon as it touched my hands it changed. It was like a swirling vortex of black, red, and orange. It was slightly mesmerizing.

"So cool. How does it work?" I questioned.

"It represents your soul, and I have to say, yours must be a tormented one," Shojiro replied.

I didn't understand what he meant, but it didn't bother me. I was more concerned with whatever Yin was doing. She was trying to summon something, but as the weapon formed it seemed to become distorted and the summoning failed. Shojiro noticed as well and watched his sister struggle for only a moment.

"Think of that sword as untamable. Reach a consensus instead of trying to force it to submit to your will. The blade is just like you, a caged lion," Shojiro metaphorically explained to Yin.

She didn't reply, but the summoning worked this time. A katana with a golden blade and green handle glowed brightly in Yin's hand. I didn't think I'd ever seen it before. On the handle a there was a black insignia that looked like a living lion. Shojiro nodded in acknowledgement of Yin's achievement.

"Let's get him," Shojiro said.

He positioned himself with the black rose sword being held by both hands. Yin did the same, but her stance had the sword leveled at Crux instead of by her shoulder. And I just kind of stood there. I wasn't a swordsman and my free hand was being used to hold my Galil. Crux seemed to look us over before raising his hand. When he lowered it, two other hunters appeared in a flash of smoke. I could tell because of their bowler hats. Had they been waiting to attack this whole time? The one on the left didn't appear to have a weapon, but the other had a saber and a submachine gun that looked like it was from World War Two. They both wore long gray robes. I realized that I could fight the one on the left because it would—

"I call the one on the left!" Yin suddenly shouted out.

Darn it, Yin beat me to the punch. I walked toward her and she toward me. We were now standing across from our opponents. Shojiro was the first to move as he disappeared in a flash of roses. Crux jumped back, and Shojiro gave chase with a trail of roses left in his wake. I wanted to watch the epic battle, but my opponent charged me. The hunter slashed with their saber, but I blocked with Sunrise. Their strength, however, was far superior to mine and I was sent rolling back. I fired a short burst of bullets, but the hunter ducked underneath most of them. The wall of ammunition did manage to destroy the hood and bottom half of the gray robe. I didn't have time to take in their features, but my opponent was definitely a girl. She fired her submachine gun, and I rolled out of the way. When I regained my balance, I fired back, but she deflected the bullets with her saber. She then moved in close, but not before I shot her submachine gun out of her hand. She was faster than me, however, and as I tried to retreat, she cut my Galil in half. The two pieces of the gun clattered to the ground.

"Hey, you're paying for that!" I said angrily.

She didn't reply and moved both her hands onto the saber. She stepped forward to attack, but I blocked her using my flames. At least, I thought I had. She jumped through the air and over my wall of fire. She slashed downward, but I deflected her blade with my own. She landed just in front of me and thrust her blade out. I just barely sidestepped it and decked the taller girl with my left. She seemed surprised I punched her but recovered by sweeping my legs out from under me. I fell and banged my head on the floor. I managed to roll out of the way as she swung her saber down. I fired a blast of fire and the girl took it head-on. I kept shooting flames so I could be done with her, but suddenly a shield forced its way through the flames. She bashed me with it, and Sunrise flew out of my hands. I was completely stunned as she walked over. Where'd that shield even come from? Her saber kicked up sparks on the floor as her shield seemed to glow. It was white with a golden cross on it, similar to the cross on Crux's sword. Was she part of his personal guard? I struggled to my feet and fired a blazing ball, but the hunter casually blocked it with her shield. I ran toward Sunrise, but when I bent down to grab it, I was met with a boot to the jaw. The mask cracked and half of it fell off as the hit sent me flying back until I was stopped by what was left of the hospital building.

"You have no chance against the members of Lord Crux's honor guard," the girl taunted in an African accent.

I was face-first in the muddy floor, pondering my options. It looked like I either die facedown or standing up. I dragged myself out of the mud and onto my feet. I tugged at the remaining half of the mask, but it wouldn't come off. Then, it suddenly began to reform itself. When I looked up, the hunter was standing within sword slashing distance of me. She brought down her saber, but I caught it with my robot arm. I then used it to pull her toward me. I tried to punch the hunter, but her shield was the only thing I made contact with. She brought her knee to my side, and I collapsed. I coughed, painfully, but the hunter didn't let up. She placed her shield on her back and grabbed a clump of my hair.

"Ow, ow, ow, that hurts!" I complained, but she didn't care.

She tried to run me through with her saber, but I caught the blade again. And this time, she had her shield put away. I threw a flaming punch and the hunter took the full force of it to the jaw. She flew back further than I thought I could possibly send her. When she hit the ground she rolled back onto her feet immediately. She touched a hand to her now burned face as she stared at me angrily.

"I'll get you for that!" she threatened, and I believed her.

I ran toward her as if to attack, but halfway there I scooped up Sunrise. I hadn't expected her to, but the hunter met me halfway. She slashed, but I blocked. Even though her strength and sword skill were superior to mine, I was still surviving. I rolled under an especially lethal swing and slashed the hunter's thigh. Blood jetted out from the wound, and the hunter collapsed with a cry of pain. I raised my sword high above my head for a quick execution, but something poked into my stomach. I looked down and froze in surprise. I had walked directly into the hunter's saber. The pain and realization hit at the same time. Sunrise slipped out of my hands and stabbed the ground behind me. I coughed and blood shot out onto the hunter's face. She looked disgusted, but I found it funny. I might have even laughed if there wasn't a sword in my stomach. The girl stood and viciously dislodged the saber. I dropped to my knees as she did and watched my blood pour out of the gash.

"Good bye and good riddance, unworthy adversary. I suggest you pray to your pagan god, if you have one," the hunter said as she lined up her saber.

"Define pagan, because I'm a catholic," I replied jokingly.

The girl didn't look happy or upset. In fact, I don't think anything I could have said would have changed her facial expression.

She brought the blade down, but a figure got between us. A warm jet of liquid splashed all over me, but my face was protected by the porcelain mask. The figure began to fall back and I caught them. The body was somehow already getting cold, but I recognized the person as Aqua. Even though I thought I hated her I instantly began to cry.

"What were you thinking!?" I shouted.

Aqua laid in my lap and blood began to drip from the corner of her mouth. She reached her hand up to my neck and pulled me down to her mouth. She undid the porcelain mask with one hand and it clattered to the ground. My ear was almost touching her lips as she spoke to me.

"I'm sorry for everything. Don't make the same mistake I did. Care about people … unlike me," Aqua choked out with her dying breath.

I didn't respond. I cried until my throat started to become raw. In a cruel twist of fate, Aqua remained alive longer than I had thought she would.

"Shut up. I hate to see people like you cry over people like me …" Aqua's words trailed off as her breathing stopped.

"Aqua? Aqua?" I shook her even though I knew she was gone.

I took a half glance at the hunter who was minding her own business. She seemed like she wanted to give me this moment. I grabbed the mask and tried to put it back on but it wouldn't cooperate. Then, suddenly, the mask suck itself to my face and I felt the all emotion drain from me. I calmly laid Aqua on the ground and grabbed Sunrise. The bright blade dimmed and its shine faded when I grabbed it. It then began to glow a menacing black and red instead of gold.

"Kill … you … you … kill …" I heard myself began to chant, but I wasn't saying anything.

The girl looked alarmed at my sudden shift in behavior. She distanced herself from me and re-equipped her shield.

"Stay away from me, Satan!" the girl commanded in fear.

Satan? Is that what the berserker's magic did to me? It was like I was trapped in my own body so all I could do was watch the scene unfold. I watched myself charge forward and slash. The hunter blocked the attack, or so I thought. Half her shield splashed into the muddy ground. I slashed again, but her saber deflected the attack. Still, I kept attacking and the hunter could only survive the onslaught. That, however, she failed at. I cut off her free arm first. She cried out in pain, but I felt nothing from her agony. I grabbed her saber and jabbed the blade into her leg, forcing her to the ground. I then watched myself decapitate her in a quick slash. Warm blood splattered onto my skin, but it didn't make me feel anything. I watched myself scour the battlefield for another opponent. Yin had already defeated the other hunter and was making her way toward Crux. Except I moved to intercept her, for some reason.

"No, don't!" I tried to cry, but my mouth was not my own.

"Mia what are you—" Yin began to ask, but I attacked without warning.

Yin reacted fast and blocked the quick strike. I continued to bombard her with strong but formless strikes. Her sword skill nullified my immense strength and, to my relief, it looked like she would easily defeat me. Yin planted her fist squarely into my jaw and the mask broke off. Whatever she saw below it froze her in place. If she was terrified, the lion mask hid it well, but I could *feel* her terror. When I felt my own mask reform, my body began to move again. Even though I didn't want to, I attacked while she was stunned. I brought Sunrise down, but Yin snapped out of her fear and barely managed to dodge. I did, however, manage to cut Yin's mask in two. Her eyes were gold and looked as though there was a black slash cutting them in half. It kind of creeped me out, but my body kept on attacking. I slashed high and low, but Yin easily danced around my attacks. Then I thought about something, how come her mask didn't reform? I couldn't think of an explanation as Yin continued to evade my body's attempt at murder. I slashed at Yin, and she ducked underneath the attack. Behind her, however, I locked eyes with Jacob. He looked wounded, but was holding up Brimstone with one hand. To my surprise, he fired the magic pistol. It hit me square in the face and the mask was destroyed once more. Except, this time it hurt. It felt as if something was trying to escape my head by tearing it open. I regained control of my body but could only curl up in the fetal position. I screamed louder and louder as I could almost feel my head actually being cut open.

"Mia? Mia are you alright!" I heard Yin as she rushed to my side.

I felt her grab onto me, but when she did the pain only got worse. I pushed her off and curled up once more. Then I felt another hand being laid on my head. Except it made the pain fade. I blinked the tears out of my eyes and saw black hair with a streak of pink.

"Marguerite," I managed to say.

I heard her tell me to be still. Except, it was inside of my head. I did as I was told and soon I felt my consciousness begin to fade.

## *Yin*

I didn't know what had happened to Mia. She had lost her mind. It must have been the effect of the berserker's magic. Marguerite had calmed her down at least. I grabbed Lion'el, my sword, and sheathed it at my side.

"Yin, get up. I still need you," Shojiro cut into my thoughts.

I nodded and rose to my feet. I glanced back at the porcelain mask that hid my eyes from my friends. These tormented eyes marked me as nothing more than a lion. Shojiro noticed my strife and yanked me over to him.

"They don't know what it means to be a lion, Yin. To them it just makes you seem cooler," Shojiro reassured me.

He was right, but it still ate at me. No matter how strong I was, everyone back at home knew me only as a simple lion. Nothing more, nothing less. While the idea itself seemed stupid, the effects were very real. My father had deemed me an animal that only hunted or protected what it was told. Shojiro took his stance and I assumed mine. Crux looked back and forth between us before charging forward. Shojiro blocked his straight thrust, and I lunged at his side. The blade would have made contact if it wasn't for Crux's pesky light hounds. I slashed the dog in half, but it exploded sending me flying back. Despite my injuries, I stuck the landing and charged again. Shojiro had just deflected Crux's sword, and he was wide open once more. I slashed him across the chest and this time I made contact. Blood shot out from his open wound, but he used his free hand to smack me across the face. Even though it was a simple slap, his strength sent me to the ground. I slashed at his ankles from my position, but he jumped over Lion'el. Still, Crux was caught in midair by Shojiro. Even though he blocked the slash, Crux was sent flying into the hospital building because of Shojiro's superior strength.

"Did you get him?" I asked, but Shojiro didn't reply.

Then, out of the dust and smoke, the cross sword stretched at breakneck pace toward us. Shojiro easily sidestepped the attack, but we both realized who the real target was.

"Jacob, dodge!" Shojiro warned.

Jacob already appeared to be on it, but his legs failed him. His knees buckled and the blade made its way to his throat. It would have killed him, but another body stopped the blade just short of Jacob. Marguerite took the cross sword through the chest and as the blade retracted, she fell forward. Jacob caught her and prevented her from hitting the ground.

"What were you thinking? Throwing your own life away for someone with one foot in the grave?" Jacob didn't seem upset, but he wanted an answer to his question.

"It wa-was because I ca-cared about you. You we-were like a bro-brother to m-me," Marguerite stuttered while she choked on her own blood.

She touched her hand to Jacob's head, and he was blanketed by a pink glow. Suddenly his eyes began to show color and emotion. Tears escaped from his eyes for probably the first time. Marguerite, however, was already gone before she could see her handy work. Jacob had noticed her passing and let out a howl akin to a wounded wolf. Jacob seemed broken for the very first time, like every emotion he'd ever had was catching up to him. Maybe coincidentally, but probably not, Brimstone began to glow brighter than I'd ever seen it. Jacob buried his head into his dead friend's chest. In the same moment, white wings cut their way out of Jacob's back. It was quite disgusting as blood splattered to the ground from the holes created by the brilliant angel-like appendages. The ground around Jacob began to become distorted and a pentagram formed around both of them. Marguerite's body floated outside of the shape. As soon as it did, Jacob's shirt was torn off and his pants seemed to meld to his lower body. A pointed tail grew out his tailbone, and he began to scream. It looked painful.

"Everyone clear out! We don't want to be around for this!" Shojiro suddenly commanded.

I began to move, but suddenly I was standing on a building a good distance from the scene that was now below me. I felt someone press themselves to my back, and I looked over my shoulder to see Amy's smiling face.

"We're all taken care of," Amy said.

Lia, however, wasn't so sure.

"Did you get Marguerite? I want to make sure she's ok."

Amy looked annoyed that Lia even asked. Then her eyes widened as she realized Lia still thought Marguerite had survived.

"*Her body* is over here," Amy insensitively pointed out.

She was right though. Azazeal held the girl's corpse in her arms. She looked sad but had easily come to terms with the fact that her friend didn't survive. Azazeal stroked Marguerite's short hair as if to comfort the dead girl. Lia walked over and began to bawl as she saw how cold Marguerite had already become. She seemed so sad for a reason I hadn't thought of previously. The people who lived and worked at Outcast Corner were the only family she'd ever known. Besides her seven sisters, of course. Another primal cry took me away from the depressing scene around me. I looked down as Jacob began to exit the fading pentagram. He grabbed Brimstone and as soon as it made contact with him, it changed. The gun morphed into what could only be described as a double-barrel shotgun with a sword jammed between the two barrels.

"I guess this is what happens if a demon shares too much of their blood with a human," Azazeal suddenly pointed out.

Everyone on the roof stared at her in shock.

"Did you think that was a good idea?" Sara asked.

"He was going to bleed out on a mission once, so I shared my blood with him," Azazeal calmly replied. "Although, the side effects are pretty bad."

"Can we do anything about it?" I asked.

Azazeal seemed to think.

"Nope. We just wait until he runs out of steam. I would subdue him if I wasn't as injured as I am."

"I guess we just hope he takes his time tearing that bastard to shreds," Lia muttered.

As we sat and waited for Jacob to make a move, I heard something. It was like a long whistling sound.

"Does anybody else hear that?" I asked.

Instead of a response, Shojiro stepped in front of me and deflected something out of the air. The tiny object flew straight up and exploded like a grenade. I heard the sound again, and Shojiro reflected the attack again.

"What's going on?" Jonathan asked.

"About two miles that way there is a sniper. She has a rifle that shoots exploding bullets. The rifle is bolt action, however, so it's taking time for her to fire," Shojiro explained.

He had pulled up his eye patch momentarily in order to zoom in on the attacker. The rose emblem embedded into his eye had all sorts of perks, but he says having one in both could easily kill him. Using it constantly would also be terrible for his health.

I was thinking about it when Shojiro suddenly shouted, "Watch out!"

One of the bullets got by him and it collided square into Jonathan's chest. He was sent flying from the impact and explosion but immediately started coughing afterward. He was barely hanging on the ledge, though. Still, he was fine and that meant we needed to get this girl.

"Amy, teleport me over," I demanded.

Amy shook her head.

"I won't willingly force you into danger," she explained.

"Then come with me," I extended the offer.

Amy frowned and suddenly we were in another building. Amy's golden hair faded as soon as we arrived, but her eyes remained gold. I expected to have to catch her when she staggered, but she didn't fall.

"I've worked out a way to steadily use magic and still be able to walk," Amy proudly explained.

I didn't know she was so good with magic.

"That's great but what now?" I asked, looking around.

I heard the rifle being fired, but I didn't see the shooter. Amy shushed me before pointing down and I realized what she'd meant.

The person shooting was just below us. I dug through my magic storage until I found a plasma blade. I was surprised I even had it; Amy wasn't strong enough to use my other weapons so I gave it to her. She took it a pulled a plasma pistol out of her own storage. I nodded to her and I kicked through the floor. I dropped down onto the sniper's back and drove Lion'el into her back. She cried out in pain, but used her sniper to bat me off of her. Even with the sword wound, she stood looking undamaged. When I looked at her face I realized just how much she looked like Jacob. Like they were twins or something.

"You are a target. Under the order of Father I will eliminate you," the girl's robotic voice echoed through the empty room.

"Who are you and who's this father person?" I asked.

"Father has named me Ash. I cannot give you information on Father, however."

Well, she gave me half the information I wanted. I glanced at her giant sniper rifle that had now transformed into a part of her body. The mechanical pieces made a sort of headgear and chest piece. Her fingers all had claws on the ends as well. The red robotic pieces made up for her schoolgirl outfit that offered no protection. She charged me, but Amy dropped down and slashed her back open. She didn't cry out or anything of the sort. She turned to stab Amy with her claws, but the brunette teleported back to where she'd dropped form.

"Come back here," Ash commanded.

Her finger blades turned into tentacles and shot through into the room above. Amy was dragged down and slammed face-first onto the floor. The finger tentacle things then began to shock Amy, making her cry out in pain. I ran over and cut the tentacles off of her.

"You okay?" I asked.

"I've been impaled before. This is nothing," Amy joked.

Yeah, she was fine. Amy lifted her plasma pistol and blasted Ash in the face. The shot destroyed her helmet, but her attack continued.

She slashed her finger claws at Amy, but I blocked the attack by chopping her arm off. Ash's severed limb tweaked on the ground like a fish out of water. Then it crumbled into dust.

"That actually hurt ..." Ash trailed off.

Then her chest piece moved to her missing arm's previous location and replaced it. Now it looked like a red and black version of Mia's mechanical arm. Ash charged again, but her whole arm was dangerous. I quickly equipped an average suit of armor and was instantly glad I did. I blocked her new arm's attack, but it took both of my hands on Lion'el. Her finger claws jabbed into the side of my armor and the entire suit crumbled apart. I tried to jump out of range, but her claws extended and managed to nick my side. I expected to crumble to dust or something, but the claws only made me bleed. Ash attacked again, but Amy slashed her mechanical arm off with the plasma blade. Ash redirected her attack at Amy, who wasn't prepared to defend herself. Luckily, Ash didn't stab Amy, but she did kick her back into, and through, a pillar.

"Amy!" I shouted.

She coughed in reply as Ash went around the pillar to finish her of. Her robot arm had reattached, and she used it to hoist Amy up by her throat. Ash moved her hand to disembowel Amy, but I stepped between them and took the blow for Amy. I fought through the pain and used Lion'el to chop Ash's remaining arm off. She shrieked and staggered back as I fell into Amy. Amy caught me and shrank against another pillar.

"Why'd you waste that chance to kill her?" Amy coughed, still catching her breath.

She wasn't really angry about that, she just didn't want me taking hits for her.

"I don't expect you to understand what this means, but I'm just a Lion. Defend what I love despite me and hunt what I'm told despite me. That's all I knew growing up."

I pressed my hand to my side to stop the blood, and Amy pressed her hand over mine.

"You're right, I don't know what that means. All I know is you're my Lion," Amy replied.

I blushed when I heard those words. Then I forced myself to my feet as Ash began to move again. Amy climbed to her feet as well. Ash's robotic machine didn't replace her missing arm this time. Instead it turned her machine arm into a scythe.

"Kill ... I will kill you ..." Ash's voice seemed to short out.

I looked at Amy, and she looked back at me.

"No, no you won't," Amy replied.

Ash charged forward and slashed recklessly. I deflected her blade and she was left unguarded. Amy ran her though with the plasma blade. She wasn't done there, however. She fired a plasma shot that made Ash's head pop like a balloon. Somehow, there was less blood than I'd expected. Ash's body disintegrated into a pile of ... well, ash.

"I guess Ash just turned into a pile of herself." Amy stole the joke out of my head.

"You're awful, that joke sucked." I said with a smile.

## Gene

To think that Ash would be defeated so easily! And by two girls no less! Still, I couldn't exactly be angry. I knew if Jacob had used his demonic powers, the demonic energy in the area would all be used up by him. I slammed my fist on the electronic table, cracking it. I even spilled some of my wine.

"No matter. I'll use *him* the next time I try to erase my creations. And I'll rebuild Ash as well," I spoke to myself.

I began to burst into a fit of laughter. Something about murder just tickled me nicely.

✳ ✳ ✳

## *Shojiro*

You go, little sis. I was able to see Yin and her friend triumph from this distance thanks to Rose's eye. I flipped the eyepatch back on, however, as things started to get a little hot and heavy over there.

"Did they get her?" one of the Fallen asked.

I hadn't met this one before, and I didn't recall anyone ever saying her name. I just knew she was younger than Lia and Hazel.

"They took care of our attacker, yes," I replied.

I then turned my attention back to Jacob manhandling Crux. He was smashing the god hunter into the ground over and over. When Jacob got tired of that, he would attempt to shoot or stab Crux, but he seemed to slip away during those attacks. Behind me, the youngest Cain brother began to rouse. He sat up and clawed at his chest. His shirt had been burned off, but the exploding bullet had only done impact damage to the boy.

"Ow, my chest." The boy groaned as he struggled to his feet.

"Are you unharmed?" Theo asked the boy.

"I don't think unharmed is the word I would use. More like I'm ok."

Then, I noticed the battle below had quieted down. I looked below to see what had happened. Jacob stood, but he looked as though he'd returned to normal. His wings, however, still remained. Crux made his way toward Jacob, but out of the two, Jacob looked more damaged. Crux's clergy robes, however, were destroyed. He was just wearing a black wife-beater with a golden cross on it. Even though the others couldn't, I could hear their chatter below.

"Run out of steam, have we? You seem to have slowed down considerably," Crux pointed out.

"A great philosopher once said, 'It does not matter how slowly you go as long as you do not stop,'" Jacob cryptically replied.

Crux looked confused but then realized what Jacob had meant. The wild attacks had all been a ruse to clear any debris that could obstruct his attack. Crux tried to retreat, but he was already trapped. Jacob fired a blanket of shots from his new gun so they would be completely unavoidable. More bullets than I cared to count made contact with Crux. His blood splattered onto the ground as he fell forward. Jacob, however, wouldn't let him fall. He grabbed Crux by the hair and yanked him up.

"Now, you die like she did," Jacob coldly stated.

He drove the blade at the end of his gun through Crux's chest. Crux gasped for air and clawed at Jacob's weapon. Jacob just watched the man struggle. As Crux's life began to wane, Jacob savagely ripped the weapon from his chest. He then began to stab Crux over and over without rest. Even though Crux was past dead, Jacob continued to make the god hunter's blood spray into the air. I let him continue like this even though I knew it was unhealthy because who was I to stop him? Jacob continued, without fail, until Crux's body faded into the night sky. Jacob watched the sparkling lights vanish and as soon as the last one was gone, he dropped his weapon. When it hit the ground it morphed back into Brimstone. The wings on Jacob's back seemed to fold back underneath his skin and bones. A gruesome crushing and cracking sounded, but Jacob only winced at the apparent pain. As his wings retracted, Jacob pulled the metal vapor tube out of his pocket. I took a look at Jacob's eyes so I could note the change. As of that moment, they looked like a solar eclipse was occurring within them. As he took a long drag from the nicotine vapor, his eyes returned to their previous state. Dead and black like coal.

"Whoa, look up!" one of the demon twins pointed out.

Just then, the sky above began to return to normal. It was actually night in real time but less dark. As we all watched the change, suddenly we were no longer standing on the rooftop. I immediately recognized the area as part of Julian's airship. I quickly scanned the room to find everyone, that still lived, present.

"What did you do?" the youngest Cain brother asked.

"Young Jonathan, I've only brought you here to protect you from the public. You'll be war heroes in a couple days," Julian explained.

He waved his hand toward a giant wall of holo-screens. Each screen showed some part of the battle with the hunters.

"I recorded the entire thing and sent a tape to CNN. Now the whole world will know of your good deeds," Julian explained.

"What could you possibly gain from this? Also, where are our allies' bodies?" Jacob immediately began to question.

Julian waved his hand once more and the holo-screens disappeared to reveal something like a docking bay, except instead of ships there were hundreds of caskets with the Outcast Corner logo on them. Yin gasped in surprise. She knew there were fallen comrades, but she hadn't taken into account the average mages that worked under Jacob.

"All will be buried with hero's honors, and I'm paying," Julian explained.

"Who put you up to this?" I asked.

Julian raised an eyebrow.

"The Red King. He said, and I quote, 'Burry the Black King's dead men and record the entire battle.'" Julian began to make everything clear.

"How did you get all the bodies here? Also, how can we be seen as heroes with all the property damage we caused?" Yin asked.

Suddenly, Chloe appeared at Julian's side.

"The bodies being moved to caskets and you being teleported here was my doing. I had to draw pentagrams and chant spells, unlike Amy, but I got it done," Chloe cheerfully boasted.

"What about the damage?" Yin asked again.

Julian opened his mouth to say something, but I decided to make it short and sweet.

"There is none. After a hunt occurs, all damage caused within that area is restored," I explained.

Julian crossed his arms and vigorously nodded in agreement.

"How did you record all of the battles at once?" Jonathan asked.

Julian walked over to the nearest of his control panels. He pushed a button and a black ball the size of a fly flew dropped from the ceiling. A holo-screen was pulled up in order to show the footage it was recording. We could see ourselves staring at the tiny camera on the screen.

"Out of questions yet?" Julian more mocked.

It was quiet for a little too long. I had nothing to say to break the suffocating air.

"What now?" Azazeal asked, cutting through the silence.

"What do you mean, my dear?" Julian answered the question with a question.

"What *do we do* now?" Azazeal rephrased her question.

Julian seemed to ponder the question. He thought long, but he also appeared to be stalling.

"You wait," Julian said.

"For what?" Jonathan asked.

"For your father's next move," Julian quickly replied.

I just hoped it would be soon. The only reason I was here was to bring Yin and her lover back with me, though she didn't seem to have one at the moment. Let's hope that didn't need to happen—and not for a reason resulting from death.

# End

www.ingramcontent.com/pod-product-compliance
Lightning Source LLC
Chambersburg PA
CBHW020332120726
47904CB00002B/384